KISS THE BRIDE

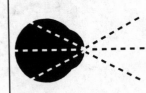

This Large Print Book carries the
Seal of Approval of N.A.V.H.

KISS THE BRIDE

THREE SUMMER LOVE STORIES

MELISSA MCCLONE,
ROBIN LEE HATCHER,
KATHRYN SPRINGER

THORNDIKE PRESS
A part of Gale, Cengage Learning

GALE
CENGAGE Learning·

Farmington Hills, Mich • San Francisco • New York • Waterville, Maine
Meriden, Conn • Mason, Ohio • Chicago

GALE
CENGAGE Learning®

Thorndike Press® Large Print Christian Fiction.
The text of this Large Print edition is unabridged.
Other aspects of the book may vary from the original edition.
Set in 16 pt. Plantin.

LIBRARY OF CONGRESS CATALOGING-IN-PUBLICATION DATA

Names: McClone, Melissa. Picture perfect love. | Hatcher, Robin Lee. I hope you dance. | Springer, Kathryn. Love on a deadline.
Title: Kiss the bride : three summer love stories / Melissa McClone, Robin Lee Hatcher, Kathryn Springer.
Description: Waterville, Maine : Thorndike Press, 2016. | Series: Thorndike Press large print Christian fiction
Identifiers: LCCN 2016018335 | ISBN 9781410491947 (hardback) | ISBN 1410491943 (hardcover)
Subjects: LCSH: Christian fiction, American. | Romance fiction, American. | Weddings—Fiction. | Large type books. | BISAC: FICTION / Christian / Romance.
Classification: LCC PS648.C43 K578 2016b | DDC 813/.01083823—dc23
LC record available at https://lccn.loc.gov/2016018335

Published in 2016 by arrangement with The Zondervan Corporation, a subsidiary of HarperCollins Christian Publishing, Inc.

Printed in Mexico
1 2 3 4 5 6 7 20 19 18 17 16

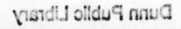

CONTENTS

■ ■ ■ ■

PICTURE PERFECT
LOVE

MELISSA McCLONE

■ ■ ■ ■

To my husband and three children for their patience, prayers, and making sure at deadline time my iced tea glass is full, there's a bag of M&Ms in the house, and Peanut Buster Parfaits show up at just the right time.

CHAPTER ONE

Oh, no. Jenna Harrison stared at the clock hanging on the wall of her photography studio — aka a converted bedroom. Only fifteen minutes until her clients arrived for their engagement photo session.

The *tick-tock* of the second hand pounded in her brain like a marching band bass drum. She tightened her grip on the sparkly tiara cutout attached to a long stick.

With a flurry of June weddings to shoot, her business, Picture Perfect Photography of Sweetwater, Washington, had been crazy busy since the month began. She hadn't planned on a new save-the-date photo idea striking her at lunch today. But she recognized the potential, so she'd been making new signs to go with the photo booth props — mustaches, lips, glasses, hats, and dialogue bubbles.

She placed the tiara with the other items on a nearby table, then printed out the couple's photo requests, including shots with the new puppy they'd rescued from a local animal shelter. They wanted fun and fabulous engagement pictures. As if Jenna took any other kind. And her calendar stayed full with proposals, weddings, and engagement sessions.

Her cell phone rang. The generic ring tone didn't belong to her parents or her brother, Colton. With no time to talk, she glanced at caller ID. Kerri Williams, a friend from church and one half of the couple Jenna was expecting for the photo shoot. Better take this call.

"Picture Perfect Photography. This is Jenna."

"Hey, it's Kerri." The October bride's breath sounded ragged and uneven, as if she'd been exercising. "We're running late."

"No problem. We've got all afternoon." A half-howl, half-whimper filled Jenna's ear. More animal than human. "Is everything okay?"

"Now, yes. Ten minutes ago, no. When Michael arrived at my house, we realized Peaches had escaped from the backyard. The shelter told us she was a digger, but we hadn't seen her do that yet. We found her splashing in a puddle a block away. I'd taken her to the dog groomer this morning, and she looked so pretty. Michael has her in the bathtub and is washing off the dirt."

Michael was Kerri's high school sweetheart and fiancé. A nice guy who cracked jokes and treated his bride-to-be like a princess.

"I'm sorry. We can reschedule the session if that would be easier."

"Today is fine," Kerri said. "Peaches would rather be dirty than clean, so this might happen again if we reschedule. Who am I kidding? I'm sure she would get herself into some kind of mess or trouble."

Kerri's exasperation brought a smile to Jenna's lips. "Don't worry. There's no rush." By the time Kerri and Michael arrived with Peaches, Jenna would be ready. She added two veil cutouts and three different bow tie selections to the other props on the table. Now to select frames. "You're my only appointment today."

Having a few extra minutes to prepare for the session meant no more rushing around. Not that Jenna's clients would know she was behind schedule. She'd built her reputation being calm and cool under pressure, especially on wedding days when stress levels could skyrocket into the stratosphere over a loose thread or scuffed shoes.

"Oh, thank you." Kerri's relief was palpa-

13

ble. "We shouldn't be long. I never realized a puppy could be such hard work. Or how fast those little paws could dig or run."

"Yes, but they're so cute!" Jenna searched through her frame assortment for ones to match the couple's outgoing personality. Maybe the black one. "Plus you get amazing welcome-home greetings and unconditional love."

"Sounds like you want a puppy."

"I thought about getting a dog two years ago after my wedding was canceled, but decided against one." A pet was more than she could afford then. Maybe when she was out of debt . . .

"Speaking of canceled weddings, I saw Claire Conway this morning at the bakery." Kerri sounded worried, the way all of them had been about the physical therapist. "Maybe she should get a dog so she won't be so lonely."

Jenna's chest tightened, a mix of sadness and empathy for her former client whose groom had called off their upcoming wedding because he'd fallen in love with someone else. "How is she doing?"

"Hard to tell. She looks tired. Not at all like her normal bubbly self."

"She needs time to deal with what happened and sleep." Jenna hadn't slept through the night for months after being jilted at the altar during her wedding rehearsal. Tears had flowed like Sweetwater Creek after a rainstorm. Smiling hurt, as if her facial muscles were attached to her aching heart. "It'll be tough for a while."

She let go of the black frame. Too thick. Fanciful design, but a lighter color would suit Kerri and Michael better.

"Claire said you returned her nonrefundable deposit."

"Least I could do." Jenna had been destroyed emotionally and financially by her breakup. She was still paying off the wedding-that-didn't-happen debt. "When I went through this, more than one person told me that God had a plan. I didn't believe them. Turned my back on everything, on Him. But thankfully had a change of heart."

"And found Sweetwater Community Church."

"That's right." The church felt like a second home now, and Jenna's friends had become family with hers so far away. "My faith grew stronger after the breakup. My life changed for the better. I'm grateful for that. Something I never imagined happening at the beginning. I pray the same thing happens to Claire."

15

"There's always a plan." Kerri's voice lightened. Her puppy frustration disappeared. She sounded like she was smiling. "Not yours or mine, but His."

"Couldn't agree more." That was why a never-worn wedding dress hung in the back of Jenna's closet, a reminder that relationships weren't always as wonderful as they looked through her viewfinder. "If I fall in love and want to get married again, I'm eloping. That was my parents' advice the last time since plane tickets weren't in their budget and my brother was deployed. Should have listened."

Kerri laughed. "That's funny coming from a wedding photographer."

"Maybe." Jenna pulled out a scalloped white frame. This would work better than the darker one. She placed it against the table, then grabbed a brown frame. "Though I'd better find a date before I start talking about another wedding."

"Does that mean you're ready to be set up?"

"No." The word flew from Jenna's mouth faster than a moth dive-bombing a lit candle. She nearly dropped the frame on the floor. Her heart was still on sabbatical. "Thanks, but I'm not ready for blind dates."

Jenna had faith that God would bring her

the right guy. One who believed in her and loved her unconditionally. Until then, she had to be patient and trust in God's plan for her. The last thing she wanted was a repeat performance of what happened with her ex-fiancé. No more rushing into a commitment.

"Maybe not, but I've never heard you mention the d-word," Kerri teased.

D-word. Date.

Jenna's skin prickled. Her stomach spun like she'd ridden the Tilt-a-Whirl at the fair. Nope. Not ready yet. And that was okay. No matter what anyone else said.

"Uh-oh." Worry returned to Kerri's voice. "What's wrong?"

"The blow dryer stopped. Better find out what's going on."

"Okay. See you soon."

The call ended. Jenna placed the brown frame next to the white one she'd selected, then double-checked the list of shots. Formal portraits and fun ones without Peaches would come first. Then puppy madness photography would ensue.

Most ideas would come to Jenna during the session, but she planned ahead to make sure she didn't miss anything. One time, early in her career, failing to get a picture of the bride with her parents had taught Jenna the importance of lists.

A knock sounded.

Kerri and Michael couldn't have arrived that quickly. A client must be here to pick up prints. Sometimes they didn't call ahead of time if they knew their package was ready.

Jenna crossed the studio, stepped into the small foyer, and opened the door.

Her heart slammed into her ribcage like a battering ram against a fortress gate. Her world tilted sideward. She clutched the door handle, as if it were a lifeline.

What in the world was *he* doing here?

CHAPTER TWO

Her ex-fiancé, Ashton Vance, was the last person Jenna expected to see. Wanted to see. Ever.

He looked . . . good. His classically handsome features seemed more chiseled than two years ago. Maybe that was due to his shorter, corporate haircut. So different from the longer, curly-at-the-ends style he'd worn before. His tailored suit screamed successful attorney. No sign of the beard stubble she'd found so appealing.

She blinked, thinking she must be hallucinating, then refocused. He was still standing on her front step, an unreadable expression on his face.

"Hello, Jenna."

His voice washed over her like chocolate fondue. Deep, rich, warm. Exactly how she remembered. But hearing him say her name no longer gave her the good, shoot-to-her-toes chills. More like a shiver down her spine.

Please, God, give me strength. A little grace wouldn't hurt.

She forced herself to breathe. "Why are you here?"

Her voice sounded shaky, the way her insides felt. Ashton had been the man she'd dreamed of being with for the rest of her life. The man who hadn't believed his own fiancée was telling the truth. The man who'd broken her heart.

"A fair question."

Nothing had been fair. Not the weeks of crying. Not the months trying to get over him. Not the nearly two years putting herself and her life back together. Jenna's muscles bunched, one after another, into a mass of triple knots.

She raised her chin, not about to make this easy on him. She was no longer a pushover and had found strength, not in herself, but in God. "Then answer my question."

Ashton flinched.

Jenna didn't care. Ashton Vance . . . Ash had been her world. She would have done anything for the man, but she had zero patience now. She wanted him gone.

He glanced around. "May I come in?"

"No." Turning the cheek was one thing.

Acting like an idiot was another. She wasn't being rude, but practical. "Clients will be arriving soon."

"Fine."

A vein throbbed at his jaw. His blue eyes resembled the color of the Columbia River during a storm. She probably shouldn't take so much pleasure in his unease.

He cleared his throat. "I just found out you didn't post that photo. I'm sorry for blaming you and calling you a liar."

Finally.

She waited for relief to hit. It didn't. Nor did any other emotion now that he'd accepted the truth. She felt disconnected, more observer than participant. Strange, given the times she'd imagined this moment, but his showing up seemed anticlimactic. Maybe because she'd realized their relationship hadn't been based on unconditional love, but on being the perfect couple, attending the most popular church in town, and having a big wedding so voters would think he was a happily married family man, rather than a bachelor who lived in a downtown condo.

"Amber came clean," Jenna said.

His lips parted, matching the surprise in his eyes. "You knew my sister sent the photo?"

"Having me Photoshop the picture was her idea. She was the only other person who knew it existed."

Ash's gaze narrowed. "Why didn't you tell me?"

"I did, but you'd made up your mind I had to be the one who posted the picture to the newspaper's Facebook page."

"I had. That's why I want to apologize." He rubbed the back of his neck. "I'm sorry. I feel horrible for everything that happened."

"Welcome to my world."

"Jenna . . ."

"What?" Okay, maybe her words hadn't been polite, but she'd been honest. The one thing she'd been through the ordeal. Though few had believed her. Everyone — from their friends to those who attended Westside Christian Church — had sided with him. "I'm not sure what you want me to say."

"Accepting my apology would be nice."

"Nice." The word tasted like dirt in her mouth. "There's nothing nice about this."

"I thought you'd be happy I don't blame you any longer."

"I am, but I would be happier if you'd believed before this."

"I thought about calling you. Several times."

"But you didn't. You're only here because you have proof."

His mouth twitched. "Don't make this more difficult on me than it already is."

"Difficult on you?"

He couldn't be serious, except he wasn't smiling. His chin jutted forward.

Unbelievable. He meant it.

Her blood pressure rocketed into the danger zone. "You canceled our wedding and broke up with me over something I didn't do. You called me a liar in front of your family, friends, and church. My business suffered because no one would hire a distrustful, lying wedding photographer."

"Jenna —"

She held up her hand, needing to say more. "I'm not finished."

He nodded once.

"You're the one who didn't want to get married, but I had to call the guests, return gifts, and deal with the finances."

"You planned everything and knew who to talk to."

She glared at him. "Because you were too busy with work and your campaign. Your last-minute cancellation meant deposits weren't returned. Most I'd charged on

23

credit cards, thinking we'd pay them off together after we married. A few places were still owed money so I had to cover those bills, even though you were the one who wanted the huge, expensive wedding that cost two times what I make a year."

Her tone was hard like granite, the way her heart felt, but she kept her voice low and steady. Yelling wouldn't accomplish anything.

Jenna ignored the look of shock on his face. She wanted him to know how difficult the past two years had been because of his actions. "My name was on the contracts, but legally you were the one responsible since you broke our engagement. That's considered a contract, which you ignored. Unfortunately I couldn't afford an attorney to sue you."

"I had no idea." He sounded genuinely surprised.

His not knowing didn't absolve him of what he'd done. "Weddings cost money. Did you think they would return the deposits when we were supposed to get married the next day?"

"I didn't think about that part."

"Well, I had to. I took on two part-time jobs, and my brother paid the mortgage while he was deployed so I wouldn't lose this house. I thought about taking you to small claims court, but had no spare time and no transportation after my car was repossessed."

Ash raised his hand as if reaching out to her, then lowered his arm to his side and blew out a breath. "I . . . Sounds bad."

"I hit rock bottom. I was on the verge of losing everything. Then, one afternoon, I got caught in a downpour. I ran into the Sweetwater Community Church and met the pastor. I don't know where I'd be today if I hadn't wanted to get out of the rain."

Pastor Dan and his wife, Trish, had worked with Jenna to make a debt repayment plan and given her two part-time jobs at the church — one on the cleaning crew and another with the espresso cart. The couple was a true blessing in her life, a gift from Heaven to help Jenna find her way back, and continued to be so now.

"The pastor and his wife helped me straighten myself out. I'm down to one extra job as a part-time barista and less than a year from having the credit card debt paid off from the wedding you canceled. So excuse me if I'm not sympathetic that your having to apologize for being wrong is difficult."

Ash stared at Jenna as if seeing her for the

first time. He shifted his weight between his feet. "You should have contacted me."

"I tried." A thousand-pound weight of broken promises and crushed dreams pressed down on her chest. She took a breath, then another, trying to remain calm.

This wasn't the time to lose it. Pastor Dan had counseled her on the importance of forgiveness and putting the failed relationship behind her, but she needed to get everything out, once and for all. "You never responded to any texts, e-mails, voice messages, or registered letters. When I went to your office, your personal assistant threatened me with a restraining order."

"That was my father's idea. He . . . I thought you wanted to get back together."

Another chill traveled the length of her spine. She met Ash's gaze straight on. "I can honestly say getting back together has never once crossed my mind."

Hurt flashed across his face.

Oh, no. The last time he'd looked that way had been when his photo went viral.

"I shouldn't have said that." Jenna had been broken and bent over this for too long. No more. She straightened. "I appreciate your coming here. Apology accepted. Let's put this behind us."

Relief filled his gaze, but his facial expression remained cautious. "Thank you."

"You're welcome." See, she could be civil. Polite, even.

"If you tell me the amount, I'll pay back the wedding expenses."

Jenna drew in a sharp breath, exhaled slowly. She didn't know if he was serious or not, but she told him the amount. One number she wouldn't forget. Ever.

He didn't grimace or flinch or frown. "Check okay?"

She nodded, not trusting her voice. Any money he sent would help her get out of debt that much sooner. She wiggled her toes.

"Okay," he said.

Jenna waited for him to say good-bye. He didn't. "You've apologized and offered to send me a check. Anything else you need?"

He rubbed his lips together, rocked back on his heels.

Uh-oh. Only one person made him react like that. "Amber?"

"Yes, she's the other reason I'm here."

His younger sister had claimed to like Jenna, went so far as to say she was good for her too-serious older brother, yet Amber had allowed Ash to not only blame Jenna for something she hadn't done, but stood silently at Jenna's side when he stopped the

27

rehearsal and asked for his grandmother's ring back.

That had been the worst day of Jenna's life. Her fingers squeezed tighter around the doorknob. "Amber must have picked today to tell the truth for a reason."

"She's getting married this month."

A June bride, like Jenna would have been. Claire too. "Amber's what? Twenty-two now?"

"Yes."

"Young."

"She's convinced our father this is what she wants. Her fiancé clerked for my dad. He introduced them, so the guy has the judge's seal of approval."

Unlike Jenna when she'd been engaged to Ash. But an upcoming wedding didn't explain why Amber told the truth today of all days. "Is your sister in a twelve-step wedding prep program and addressing past wrongs?"

Ashton's mouth twisted. "I wish."

"That bad?"

"Afraid so."

Jenna didn't care about his sister's wedding. She wanted nothing to do with either one of them. Especially him.

He stood with one foot on the welcome mat. Too attractive for her to remain neutral.

Not even picturing a color swatch of beige helped. The least he could have done was gain fifty pounds or have a receding hairline — not look better than he did before.

What patience remained evaporated like mist on a hot day. "Just say it."

"Amber and Toby's photographer was placed on bed rest and can't do their wedding. A replacement was offered, but Amber wants to hire you. She said you'd never agree to the job if she didn't tell the truth."

Amber's motivation didn't surprise Jenna. The young woman had been pampered and spoiled like a precious pet her entire life. She always got her way, but not this time. "Tell your sister I appreciate her admitting what she did, but I can't photograph her wedding."

A beat passed. And another.

"If it's any consolation, Amber's sorry." His tone contrite, he looked as if he'd rather be anywhere but here. "She would have come with me to apologize, but she had an important appointment."

Jenna considered his words, then rejected them.

"If Amber was sorry, she wouldn't have waited until she wanted something from me to tell the truth. She would have come herself, not sent you to do her dirty work."

Jenna kept her voice steady and calm. He wasn't responsible for his sister's actions even if his doting had enabled her. She had no doubt that nothing had changed in the sibling relationship or Ash wouldn't have brought this up himself. "I understand if my decision means you don't want to pay —"

"You'll get your check." The muscle at his jaw continued to throb. His facial expression grew serious, his lawyer face. "If I double your fee, would you reconsider photographing Amber's wedding?"

Oh, wow. Jenna inhaled sharply. She could use the extra money. But she didn't want to negotiate a contract with him. "Ash —"

"Let's talk about this. I'm positive we can come to an agreement."

Tempting. She wouldn't deny she found the offer appealing. Her business was doing well, but the additional money would allow her to repay Colton for the months of mortgage payments he'd covered. He'd never asked for the money back, but he'd mentioned looking at new pickups. "An apology was more than I expected. You've offered to cover the wedding expenses."

"This money will be for you. For your business or whatever you want."

Jenna weighed the pros and the cons.

"I don't blame you for saying no. That would be most people's instinct." Understanding filled Ash's voice, and the clock seemed to rewind, reminding her why she'd fallen for him. "But we can work this out. Your fee is only a starting point in the negotiation."

A silver hatchback pulled to the curb and parked behind a shiny, new, blue sports car. Paying extra wouldn't be a hardship for Ash. Money had never been an issue for any Vance, unlike her family, who'd lived paycheck to paycheck, sometimes on food stamps or other assistance. She and Colton had received free breakfasts and hot lunches until they graduated. School supplies and weekend food packs too. But having money didn't equate to being happy.

Yes, the money would help her brother, but Jenna couldn't get past what Amber had done, then and now. Playing into the young woman's hands would show her she could get whatever she wanted no matter how she acted.

"June wedding, right?" Jenna asked, not really wanting to know the date in case she was free.

"Yes, on the twenty —"

"I don't think so." The words came out of her mouth so quickly she could have been

31

written a speeding ticket.

"You don't have to make a decision now."

Ash reminded Jenna of a younger version of his father, the respectable and intimidating Judge Douglas Vance, not the eager young lawyer who did pro bono legal work at the community center. Had Ash sold out completely?

The thought made her sad. She didn't know why, given what he'd done to her. Memories rushed back. Arguments over the photo. Her denials. His disbelief. The breakup standing at the altar. A living nightmare she wanted to forget but couldn't.

Her throat tightened. She thought she'd put this behind her. Ash too. Maybe not, given the way she kept staring at his face and noticing little things like the lines at the corner of his eyes. She swallowed. One more reason to turn down his offer. "I've made my decision. It's no."

On the street, Michael walked around the front of his car to the passenger side where Kerri sat. Perfect timing. "My clients are here. I have to go."

Jenna hoped her words sounded calm when her insides trembled like a 6.0-magnitude earthquake. She wanted to grab a bottle of chocolate sauce, bypass the spoon, and squeeze the liquid straight into her mouth. Maybe that would stop the emotions — anger, sadness, relief — threatening to overwhelm her. She forced a wasn't-this-nice smile instead.

Ash glanced toward the couple getting the puppy out of her crate. "If you reconsider . . ."

"That probably won't happen." She knew she'd left wiggle room with the *probably.* Maybe he wouldn't notice. "I appreciate your stopping by and apologizing."

"Jenna . . ."

An elephant stomped on her chest. Okay, not really, but the imaginary weight made her take shorter breaths. Or maybe Ash was the problem. Either way, she couldn't do this any longer. She'd thrown away the pictures of them together. Time to close the door for good. "Hope life treats you well. Good-bye."

CHAPTER THREE

Ash stepped from Jenna's porch onto the brick walkway that split the neatly mowed lawn in half. He passed a smiling couple. The woman held a pink dog leash attached to a small tan puppy who wanted to sniff the grass. Ash's feet dragged as if he'd walked across quick-dry cement and was carrying ten extra pounds on each shoe. He and Jenna had been happy like her clients, gazing into each other's eyes, laughing, and picturing a future together.

He'd messed up. Big time.

The sun beat down from a clear, blue sky, a taste of summer on this early June afternoon. The warm temperature had nothing to do with the sweat dampening his hairline and dripping down his neck.

Jenna.

Over the past two years, he'd thought of her — a flash of a memory during a deposition or an image of her pretty face, warm green eyes, and long blonde hair sitting in church. He had thought about calling her. More times than he wanted to admit. But he hadn't. Couldn't. Not after what she'd —

She hadn't done anything.

That realization troubled him, as did the last words she'd spoken.

His shoes clicked against the brick, an echo of her good-bye, the sound of finality, the end. If only he'd listened to her, but he'd thought he knew best and put his belief behind his family instead of his fiancée.

Ash's cell phone vibrated, the third time since he'd arrived at Jenna's house. Amber's name and number were on the screen.

His heart ached, a combination of regret and frustration, over what had happened, what he hadn't done two years ago.

He should have believed Jenna. He should have stood by her. He should have done things — everything — differently.

But he would make amends. Pay her back with interest. Repair the damage to her reputation and business. Making things right for Jenna might make him feel normal again. Nothing — work, friends, church — satisfied him lately, but he had no idea why.

The phone vibrated again. He wanted to ignore the call. Talking to Amber would upset him more, but knowing his sister, she wouldn't stop until he answered.

Might as well get this over with. He tapped the screen. "Hello."

"I've been calling for the last ten minutes." Amber sounded annoyed. She should join the club. "Why haven't you answered?"

"I was speaking with Jenna."

"Oh, good. When does she want to talk about the wedding?" Amber's words ran into each other. "Did you tell her about the reception location? And I'd like her to take photos of me in my gown after the final fitting? I need one for the *Sweetwater Post*'s bridal page."

His sister didn't pause to take a breath. She kept on talking.

"Ash?" Amber's voice rose. "Are you there? What did Jenna say?"

He loved Amber, but his sister had ruined everything two years ago. All because she thought he was too serious about his run for the state legislature and needed to loosen up and laugh.

Going to a comedy club would have accomplished the same goal better than leaking the photo of him walking out of the courthouse in a bunny suit with a trail of rabbits following him. That picture, courtesy of Jenna's Photoshop skills, hadn't made him laugh, but turned him into a laughing-stock.

The Pied Piper of the County Court-house.

The Bunny Guy.

The Rabbit Representative.

The nicknames were as bad as the photo.

Ash crossed the sidewalk and unlocked his car. "Jenna said no."

"What?"

Amber's high-pitched, eardrum-bursting screech made his ears ring. He winced, lowered the phone.

"I can't believe this. Why would she say no? That's so rude. We were practically family."

"Think about what you did before you start going off on Jenna."

"I made a mistake. Two years ago. That's, like, forever." Amber was probably shrugging, her favorite gesture, and one that rarely meant confusion or indifference. "Does she want more money?"

"I offered more. She still said no."

"That makes no sense."

"An in-person apology from you might have helped your cause."

"Not possible. I couldn't be late to my spa pedicure."

Unbelievable. A headache threatened to

erupt. He rubbed his temples and decided against sitting in the car to continue this discussion. He wouldn't be tempted to raise his voice out here. "That's the important appointment you couldn't miss?"

"Don't go all cross-examining incredulous on me. Foot care is important."

Ash gritted his teeth. "Finding a photographer for your wedding should be more important than your toenails."

But he wasn't surprised by Amber's actions or her words. Their parents had divorced when she was three. Ash had been thirteen, not old enough to understand why his mother had left or why she hadn't wanted visitation rights, but his younger sister had been traumatized by their mother's absence. Nightmares, hunger strikes, tantrums. The behavior issues kept compounding instead of improving. He'd done what he could to make things better for Amber. So had their father. Maybe they'd gone too far indulging her all these years.

"Puh-lease talk to Jenna again." Amber used her little-girl voice. "Offer her more money. I know. Ask her out on a date. You guys were a cute couple."

"We were." He remembered more good times with Jenna than bad ones. "But those days are over."

"Second chances, bro."

Not going there. At least not with Amber.

He should get in his car and drive away, but he didn't want to leave yet. "Jenna accepted my apology. If you want to change her mind about photographing your wedding, your first step is apologizing in person."

Silence filled the line. Not surprising. Amber never liked being told she was wrong.

Something moved in his peripheral vision. He looked, but saw nothing.

"I made a mistake and didn't own up to it," Amber said finally. "But you're the one who overreacted because of a joke."

"I didn't overreact. My opponent used the photo in an ad. My campaign manager resigned. I had no choice but to drop out of the race."

Or face the biggest loss in the district's history.

"You aren't cut out for politics. If Jenna had been the right woman for you, Dad said you would have stuck by her, not blamed her the minute something went wrong."

Ash stiffened. "What are you talking about? Dad led the case against Jenna."

Motive.

Means.

Opportunity.

The last two had been slam-dunks where Jenna was concerned. Only her motive seemed inconclusive. His father, who had sat at both prosecutor and defense tables, thought she might not want to share Ash with constituents and be thrust into the spotlight, given her upbringing, but the odds had been against Jenna from the start.

"Dad never liked her," Ash continued. "Wrong family. Wrong part of town. Wrong schools. Wrong type of wife for a lawyer with political aspirations."

"You must have agreed or you wouldn't have called her a liar and broken up with her."

Maybe he hadn't loved Jenna enough to trust her or forgive her.

I would be happier if you'd believed before this.

Maybe she deserved a man who would have done both those things.

"I was wrong." Praying for guidance would be the smart thing to do, but not even prayer brought him comfort these days. Nothing did. "I hurt Jenna, and I've apologized for my mistakes. It's your turn."

A loud sigh sounded in his ear. "O-kay. But I want you with me."

Amber sounded nervous — like the time

when she was eight and didn't want to ride the roller coaster at an amusement park near Tacoma. "When?"

"I'll be finished in an hour."

Not enough time to go back to his office. "I'll grab a cup of coffee, then meet you at Jenna's house."

Another sigh. "Fine. But if I'm going to this much trouble, she'd better change her mind about photographing my wedding."

"Don't you mean your and Toby's wedding?"

Amber harrumphed. The line disconnected.

Ash opened the car door. Something flashed by again. He looked over the top of his car. Focused. Not a blur, a puppy, the one he'd seen a few minutes ago. She chased her tail.

He assumed *her* given the pink collar. The couple she'd been with wasn't around. Her leash was missing.

Coffee could wait. The pup shouldn't be out on her own. She could wander into the street or get lost.

Holding onto the handle to cushion the noise, he closed the car door. His old dog, a German shepherd named Jefferson, hadn't liked loud noises. Car doors slamming spooked him. Ash didn't want to scare the puppy and send her running. Chasing a dog didn't appeal to him, but neither did the alternative.

The puppy glanced his way, then returned her attention to her tail.

He came closer, trying to be quiet and move slowly. He kneeled at the edge of the sidewalk, reached into his pocket, and jiggled his keys.

Keeping his fingers cupped, he pulled out his hand. "Hungry, pup?"

The dog scurried forward. The rounded belly and short, uncoordinated legs looked out of proportion to the rest of her.

"Sorry." He scooped the dog into his arms. A lick on the cheek was his reward. "No treat this time. We need to get you back where you belong."

Ash walked toward Jenna's house, his steps lighter than they'd been minutes ago. He would get to see her sooner than he expected. He hadn't wanted to leave, but he had no reason to stay. Until now. He looked at the squirming puppy in his arms. "I have no idea what you're doing out here, but thank you."

CHAPTER FOUR

"Perfect." Jenna took two steps back, checked the lighting in her studio, then adjusted her camera lens while Kerri and Michael made silly faces and played with the props. "Ready?"

The couple nodded.

Jenna hoped working would push thoughts of Ash from her mind. She forced a smile. "Let's see those pearly whites."

Two toothpaste commercial–worthy smiles appeared.

She readied her camera. "Now show me your crazy personalities."

Michael brought the empty frame closer. He and Kerri stuck their heads through the opening as if they were coming out of the picture.

"That's great." Jenna hopped on a chair to look down on the couple and get another angle. "You two are naturals."

Kerri kissed her fiancé. "That's because

he's so photogenic."

"You're the gorgeous one," Michael replied.

"Happy couples make for happy photos." Jenna kept taking pictures. Kerri and Michael weren't just happy to be together; they were deliriously happy and very much in love. The way Jenna thought she and Ash had been.

She swallowed around the lump in her throat. Water under the bridge and all the way out to the Pacific Ocean by now.

"I want our portrait on your wall like the other couples," Kerri said.

"One will be there," Jenna assured. "But I have a feeling choosing what photo to use will be difficult."

A knock sounded.

She ignored it. "Now I want you —"

The doorbell rang.

Strange. She wasn't expecting anyone.

Another knock.

Kerri glanced at the doorway. "Sounds like they aren't going away."

"I'm sorry." The only people who stopped by were clients. Well, except for Ash. "Someone must want to pick up their prints. Excuse me for a moment."

"Take your time." Grinning, Michael held a top hat prop over his head. "We've got plenty to keep us busy."

Jenna hurried to the entryway and opened the door. Gasped.

Ash stood with Peaches cradled in his arms.

She shuffled back a step. Her skin tingled as if brushed by a feather.

Two little paws wrapped around his right arm as if holding a beloved toy. Adorable. Puppy drool left dots and drips on Ash's tie. The tender way he stared at the dog brought a sigh to her lips. Appealing and attractive.

"Look who I found in the front yard," Ash said. "I assumed that wasn't the place for her."

His words shook Jenna out of her daze. She motioned him inside. "Peaches must have escaped from the backyard. Thank you for catching her."

Ash entered the house, then closed the door. "Least I could do."

His six-foot frame filled the entryway in a way she didn't remember. He'd always been fit, a runner and cyclist, but his shoulders and chest seemed wider, as if he'd been weightlifting. The scent of his aftershave brought a rush of memories, including when they'd met in a church parking lot. "Ash to the rescue."

He rubbed Peaches' head. "Right place, right time."

That had been what he said about their meeting. Her battery had died while she'd been trying out a young adult group at a church on the other side of town, and he'd offered to help. She hadn't noticed Ash during the gathering, but she'd been swept off her feet with a pair of jumper cables and his stunning blue eyes.

Ash stopped rubbing the puppy.

Peaches whimpered.

He grinned. "Her owners are going to have their hands full."

"They already do. She escaped earlier today." Jenna remembered her clients waiting for her. "I need to get back to Kerri and her fiancé in the studio."

"I'll carry the puppy." Ash hadn't been inside the studio since she took photographs for his primary run over two years ago.

Kerri screeched. "Peaches!"

The dog wiggled, squirmed, and barked. Of course, she wanted her mommy.

Ash handed over the puppy. "I found her running and chasing her tail in the front yard."

"Oh, thank you so much. I can't believe she got out again." Kerri cuddled the dog close, cooing and kissing at the puppy as if she were a child. "What am I going to do with you, Peaches?"

"Her paws are getting more efficient." Michael gave the pup a pat. "I'll repair any damage she did to the yard or fence."

"No problem," Jenna said. "I'm just grateful Ash found her."

Kerri nodded. "You saved us a lot of heartache. Thanks."

Ash gave a lopsided smile. "Happy to be of service. I love dogs."

"I'm Michael Dewar." He shook Ash's hand. "This is my fiancée, Kerri Williams."

"Ashton Vance."

Kerri cradled the puppy like a baby. Her gaze traveled between Ash and Jenna. "We passed you coming up to the house."

Jenna recognized the curious tone. She didn't want Kerri to think Ash was a potential date. "Ash and I have known each other for a while."

"Almost three years," he said.

Two-thirds of that time, they'd been out of contact. A part of her wished they still were. Well, except for Ash finding Peaches and offering to cover some of the wedding expenses.

"I want to take more pictures of you in here, but I'm afraid Peaches will escape if we put her in the backyard again."

"Give me Peaches's leash, and I'll watch her," Ash offered.

Jenna drew back, surprised. "You?"

"I don't have any plans this afternoon," he said. "Playing with a puppy will be fun."

Kerri removed the pink leash from her purse, then clipped the end to Peaches's collar. "She loves to play."

"So do I," Ash said.

Jenna's breathing hitched. His words did funny things to her tummy. She focused on her camera, adjusting settings that were fine, but she wanted to distract herself from . . . him.

"Is that okay?" Michael asked her.

She leveled her gaze at Ash. But her breath remained caught in her throat, as if she'd wound a scarf around her neck three too many times. Not trusting her voice, Jenna nodded.

What was happening? Her reactions didn't make sense. She didn't like the guy. He'd broken her heart and nearly sent her into bankruptcy. She shouldn't care what he did or how he looked at her. Even if a cute puppy was involved.

"Finish up in here." Ash took the dog from Kerri. "Peaches and I will be in the backyard. Maybe she'll show me how she escaped."

Jenna wished the puppy would show her how to get out of here with no one noticing. She pasted on yet another smile. "Thanks. A couple more shots, then we'll join you."

"Have fun," Kerri called out.

"Oh, we will," he said.

Maybe Ash hadn't sold out completely. Jenna watched him leave.

Not that she cared. Not much anyway.

Thirty minutes later, Ash sat on an Adirondack chair in Jenna's backyard, shaded by the covered patio. He held onto Peaches's leash, though the tired pup wasn't going anywhere except Dreamland.

A welcome breeze rustled tree leaves and toyed with the ends of Jenna's blonde ponytail. She moved effortlessly around her subjects, drawing his attention wherever she went. She could have been taking pictures of a lion on the loose, and he wouldn't have noticed anything except her.

Beautiful.

More so than he remembered. But she looked thinner — not I've-been-working-out slim, more like worn out and eating less.

Too many June weddings on her calendar, or something else?

None of his business. Yet he felt responsible.

Who was he kidding? He was responsible. *His fault.*

Ash had a feeling those words would be echoing in his mind for a long time.

He looked down. Peaches, worn out from playing and posing for photos, slept with her head on his left shoe. Her paws moved back and forth, running in her dreams.

Cute, but he'd rather watch Jenna.

She stood near a colorful garden complete with bright blossoms, a charming birdhouse hanging from a weathered post, and a quaint, slat-back bench. The last time he'd been here, the yard consisted of a cement patio, dying grass, and trees needing TLC. Now the lawn and plants thrived, creating an outdoor oasis.

"I'm going to take candid shots using the garden as the backdrop," she instructed Kerri and Michael. Their smiles hadn't wavered once this afternoon. "Don't worry about posing. Talk. Hold hands. Wander around. Do whatever feels right. You can't get this wrong. Okay?"

Kerri and Michael nodded.

Ash found himself doing the same, captivated by Jenna. Writers used a journal; she recorded memories with photos. She'd always been comfortable behind a camera, but her new confidence impressed him.

"Can we smooch?" Michael asked.

She smiled, a mischievous gleam in her gaze. "Up to you."

Michael winked at Kerri. Her blush, a charming shade of pink, matched her short-sleeved dress.

Jenna lowered her camera. "You two are total pros. Great job."

Her bright-as-the-midday-sun grin lit up her face. How could Ash have believed she'd lied? Talk about stupid. Stupid for breaking up with her. Stupid for not calling her these past two years. Stupid for pretending he'd been fine since asking for his ring back. He wasn't fine and only had himself to blame.

He'd been so quick to judge her. Strange, given she'd been a ray of sunshine in his life. Even after he'd called off their wedding, she'd changed his life when the viral photo led to a job offer at the top law firm in town. His now-boss had wanted to hire someone who didn't fit the typical lawyer mold to work with out-of-the-box clients — creative types as well as eccentric ones. Jenna's embarrassing picture had earned Ash an interview.

"We'll have plenty of photos to choose from for your engagement portrait and save-the-date card." Jenna continued snapping photos. "I'll upload the proofs, then send you a link to your online album tomorrow."

"This was more fun than I thought it would be." Michael's words earned him a slight elbow from Kerri. He laughed. "Just being honest, babe."

"So am I." Kerri shimmied her shoulders. "This was great, Jenna. Thank you. I can't wait until you're photographing me in my wedding dress."

"Did you find one?" Michael asked.

"Not yet," Kerri said with a smile. "But I will."

Finding a dress wasn't hard, Ash thought. Amber had found hers the first day she looked.

Jenna's forehead creased. "Are you planning to buy off-the-rack?"

Ash had no idea what that meant.

Michael scratched his chin. "Is off-the-rack like buying illegal Fourth of July fireworks out of the back of a white van?"

Kerri shook her head. "No. And I hope that's not how you're planning to buy fireworks this year."

Michael pleaded innocent with a who-me look that suggested he'd already placed his order.

Jenna looked like she was trying not to

smile. "Off-the-rack means buying a dress that's in stock rather than ordering one from a designer, which can take months."

"And is more expensive." Kerri's serious tone contradicted the grin on her face. "The bargain shopper in me cannot fathom paying full price for a dress I'll wear only once. I've been checking bridal store clearance racks and scouring thrift stores and consignment shops."

"October isn't that far away," Jenna said.

"I'm not worried." Kerri sounded confident. "I'll find what I want. I always do."

"Yes, you do." Michael touched her shoulder. "She did the same thing when we went to our senior prom in high school. Found a beautiful dress."

Kerri beamed. "For less than twenty dollars."

"Sounds like you know what you're doing," Ash said, impressed.

Nodding, she picked up Peaches. "Thanks for taking such good care of my baby. She's worn out from playing. That'll make the car ride back to my place quieter."

On the way to the front door, they exchanged good-byes. Kerri, Michael, and Peaches left. Ash hung back.

Jenna kept the door open, her hand on

the knob. "I appreciate your help with the puppy."

"Peaches and I had fun."

"Well, thanks." Opening the door farther, she looked at Ash expectantly.

He remained in place. Michael had joked about being honest. Honesty here would serve Ash best with Jenna. "Amber is on her way."

Something flashed in Jenna's eyes so fast he didn't have time to figure out the emotion. She gripped the knob so tight her fingers looked frozen.

"That's not necessary." She spoke slowly, as if considering each word.

"Maybe not for you, but Amber needs to apologize in person. She believes the world is Amber-centric. She needs to learn the universe doesn't revolve around her."

"Amber might not want to learn that lesson."

"It's time and for her own good."

Jenna started to say something, then stopped herself. "You can wait in the living room. I'm going to clean up the studio."

"Want help?"

She eyed him, warily, cautiously, as if she hadn't decided if he was friend or foe. "No, thanks. It won't take me long."

At least she hadn't told him to leave or

54

asked him to wait outside. Progress? Ash hoped so.

Inviting sunlight shone through the wood paned windows in Jenna's living room. So homey and quiet compared to Ash's condo in Sweetwater's downtown district, where the train station and fire department made silence a rarity, not the norm.

He recognized the braided rug and the white coffee table in front of the couch. Many nights he'd kicked his feet up, shared a bowl of buttered popcorn with Jenna, and watched a movie.

The bookcase sat against the opposite wall. He remembered when they put the pieces together. Lots of laughter and debate over whether reading the directions was necessary.

The new blue and white plaid slipcovered couch was more welcoming than the solid yellow one. A red blanket lay on an old rocking chair along with a pillow.

Pictures of him and Jenna used to fill the shelves, mantel, and walls. Not any more. He rubbed his chin and stared at the unfamiliar faces with her. A weight — two tons of regret — pressed on Ash's chest, making each breath a struggle.

What had he expected? That she'd kept

the photographs of him on her walls? Or stopped going out and having fun?

He hated that his answer to both questions was yes.

A family portrait hung on the cream-colored wall next to images of rock climbing, hiking, horseback riding in a collage frame. He had no idea she liked those activities, but the smile on her face suggested she was enjoying herself.

The pictures showed all he'd missed these past two years. His stomach churned so badly not even a bottle of antacids would help. Jenna had created a life without him. A career. A home. New friends. Knowing she'd moved on unsettled Ash.

"Would you like a glass of lemonade or iced tea? I can mix the two into an Arnold Palmer if you'd rather."

Jenna's voice startled him. He stepped back from the wall of photos, feeling like a visual eavesdropper on her life. "Lemonade would be great. Thanks."

"Be right back."

As soon as she left, his gaze refocused on the pictures.

One thing in the images jumped out. Fun. She'd been having fun, something missing from his life, not to mention his vocabulary. Work had become his priority. He took

Sundays off, but the extra hours during the week and on Saturday would help him reach his goal of partner sooner. He'd be the youngest at the firm. Maybe a promotion would bring the same satisfaction he'd felt when he first started working there.

"Here you go." Jenna handed him a tall glass full of lemonade. "Just made this morning."

He took a sip. Sweet and tangy, a combination that reminded him of Jenna's kiss. "Delicious."

"My mom's recipe."

Homemade. Not surprising. Mrs. Harrison had been a good cook, specializing in comfort foods like meat loaf, cabbage rolls, and macaroni and cheese. Entrees their health-conscious housekeeper Mrs. Beatty had never made. "How are your parents?"

"Doing well in Connecticut."

"What about Colton?" Ash asked.

"Still in the marines. Stationed at Camp Pendleton. He came home on leave last spring. Brought a couple friends. They redid the backyard for me."

Again, not a surprise. Ash had met her brother once. Colton Harris was an in-shape, hard-as-nails guy who loved America and his sister, not in that particular order.

"Fishing, river rafting, paddleboarding."

Ash raised his glass toward the framed photos on the mantel, curious about the other people and her new hobbies. "You've been staying active."

"Yes."

He waited for her to say more. She didn't. "Looks like fun."

"Yes. I love being outdoors."

More words this time. Maybe he'd get an entire paragraph from her next.

"Me too." Except he spent his time at work with occasional trips to the gym. He tried to remember the last time he'd gone for a run outside and not on a treadmill. His mind went blank. "When I have time."

"Still working long hours?"

"I'm going for partner." His defensive tone made him want to grimace. Was his work schedule what she remembered of him? He sipped the lemonade, which tasted less sweet.

Ash stood only four feet away from Jenna, but the quiet pushed them further apart. Unease knotted his muscles. He wanted to mend the rift between them, but that wasn't going to happen. Things were never going to be the same. The realization made him sad.

She glanced at the clock on the end table. "I don't mean to be rude, but are you sure

Amber's coming? I have plans tonight."

Plans? A date? Ash's collar tightened. A million questions sprung to mind. None of which he could ask without appearing to be a stalker-ex. "I'll see where she is."

He pulled out his cell phone. No message from Amber about running late. He typed, *Jenna doesn't have much time. Now or never.*

A reply came quickly: *Be there in 5.*

Ash put away his phone. "She's almost here."

"Okay." Jenna didn't sound okay, more like nervous.

Nothing was working as he . . . he hadn't planned any of this, but he'd expected her to be happier to see him. Upsetting her more was the last thing he wanted. "This will be quick. I promise."

She nodded.

If this were a contest for saying the fewest words, Jenna would win. No, that wasn't fair after what he'd done to her. He should be happy she'd moved on. Not be disappointed she was doing fine without him.

Ash was. Sort of. But he didn't like how their time together had been wiped away like the mascara-stained tears streaming down her cheeks when he'd asked for his grandmother's ring back. Sure, things had ended badly, but they'd shared good times, cared about each other. He still had the wedding gift he'd bought for her. That had to count for something.

He wanted to try. "Is there any way we could be friends again?"

"Friends," she repeated, as if testing out the word. "We bypassed that step when we met and went straight to dating."

"That doesn't mean we can't be friends now."

Her eyes darkened. She rubbed her lips together. "I —"

The doorbell rang.

Relief filled her face. "That must be Amber."

Leave it to his sister to arrive at the wrong time. Ash followed Jenna into the foyer.

The discussion might have been interrupted, but he wasn't giving up. He wouldn't walk away from her again. Being friends was better than nothing. He hoped Jenna agreed.

CHAPTER FIVE

Amber Vance was the last person Jenna wanted to see, but the doorbell had saved her from answering Ash.

Be his friend?

Uh, no.

As soon as he and Amber left, Jenna never wanted to see either again.

You've gotten me through so much, Lord. I thank you for that. A little more patience this afternoon would be greatly appreciated.

She opened the door. Amber stood next to a familiar-looking man wearing a suit.

"Jenna!" Amber's expertly applied makeup made her look older than twenty-two. Her long brown hair swayed as she sashayed on four-inch heels into the house without an invitation. She kissed the air next to Jenna's cheek. "It's been way too long. You look amazing. You've dropped, what, ten or twenty pounds?"

Twelve, after gaining back a couple. "A few."

"What's your secret?" Amber asked.

"Getting dumped the day before your wedding does weird things to your appetite." The words were out of Jenna's mouth before she could stop them.

Amber's laugh sounded forced. Neither Ash nor the man standing on the welcome mat said anything. Jenna didn't blame them.

Amber shrugged. "Well, at least something good came of it."

It?

Did she mean the photo going viral? Or the cancellation of the wedding? Or maybe Ash breaking Jenna's heart. Probably best not to ask.

The man on the porch cleared his throat.

Amber glanced over her shoulder, as if in an afterthought. "Oh, I'd like you to meet my fiancé, Toby Matthews."

Toby entered the house, then closed the door behind him. His worried expression contradicted his loosened tie and casually styled blond hair. He seemed uncomfortable like Jenna, and she felt a surprising kinship. He was attractive in a smart, nerdy-guy kind of way, a one-eighty from the fraternity pretty-boy type Amber dated two years ago.

"Hi," he said. "Thanks for seeing us on such short notice."

Polite. Jenna tried to place him. Not church or school, but she knew him somehow. "We've met before."

A hesitant smile formed on Toby's face. "You photographed my cousin Ben's wedding last summer. That's why I suggested you for our wedding."

"*You* wanted to hire Jenna?" Ash asked Toby.

"She did a great job. Put everyone at ease, especially me. I don't think I've ever smiled so much having my picture taken."

Toby wanting to hire her made more sense than Amber wanting to do so.

"Ben and Julia Garrett." The pictures from that day flashed through Jenna's mind like a slideshow. "The reception was held at Fallen Leaf Park. You were a groomsman."

Toby nodded. "One of five."

Jenna felt bad for saying no. She remembered Toby Matthews. He defined the term *nice guy.* He'd danced with the single women, young and old, at the reception, stepped out of the way so the best man could catch the garter, and given the last piece of chocolate cake to the flower girl.

"Orange tie," she said.

"And socks." Toby's grin widened. "That

was Julia's idea. Orange is her favorite color."

Jenna remembered. Not peach like some brides might have chosen, but bright orange, nearly neon. "You rolled up your pants to show off the socks in one of the pictures."

"Good memory, considering the number of weddings you must work," Ash said.

Her gaze collided with his. Unexpected warmth spurted through her veins, heating her from the inside out. Not good. "Memorable wedding."

Amber flipped her hair behind her shoulder, a practiced move that put the glam in glamour. "That was before Toby and I were seriously dating, or I would have attended with him."

"You would have had fun." Additional memories of the wedding returned. Jenna couldn't help but smile. "I loved the dance you groomsmen did. I wanted the photographs to capture that fun feeling."

"They did." Toby's features relaxed. His posture looked less stiff. "I'm not big on having my picture taken, but you made the process painless. I didn't feel like a robot or a puppet on strings."

Jenna wiggled her toes. "Those are words every photographer loves to hear."

Amber leaned against Toby like a possessive cat. "You were his choice of photographers, but I knew you'd say no so we went with someone else."

"You understand why my answer is no now, right?" Jenna asked.

"Yes." Amber stared at the tiled entryway, then raised her gaze to meet Jenna's. "What I did. It was . . . wrong. I'm sorry. I should have spoken up right away, but I didn't think Ash was going to cancel the wedding and ask for Grandma's ring back. I felt horrible, but I was too afraid of getting into trouble to say anything. Thinking only of myself was selfish. If I could do it over again, I would."

The words sounded sincere, more grown-up than Jenna expected. No doubt Toby was a good influence on Amber. "I appreciate you coming here and apologizing. Thanks."

"I know you'd rather not photograph our wedding, but you were Toby's first choice," Amber added. "That's the only say he wanted with the wedding planning."

"The photographer and wedding cake," Toby clarified.

"Oh, yeah," Amber agreed. "And you didn't get a say in that, either. But now that the other photographer is on bed rest, I thought maybe you could forget I'm the bride or pretend I'm someone else so Toby could have the photographer he wanted."

Toby took a step forward. "No pressure, Jenna. This is an awkward situation, and we understand if you don't feel comfortable."

Amber opened her mouth as if to speak.

Toby shot her a sideward glance. "Don't we, honey?"

"Of course," Amber said.

A battle waged inside Jenna. She wanted to help Toby, but the idea of spending time with the Vance family made her stomach hurt. "My June is pretty booked with people adding Friday night and Sunday afternoon weddings to the mix."

"Understood." Ash held the empty lemonade glass. "Amber and Toby are getting married on Saturday, the twenty-seventh."

Available. The word swirled through Jenna's head, becoming louder and louder. She fought the urge to cover her ears to quiet the noise.

The twenty-seventh was supposed to have been Claire's wedding day. But that didn't mean . . .

Torn, Jenna prayed. "That date's open, but —"

"Score!" Amber jumped up and down.

Toby's grin spread across the width of his face. "Tell us what it'll take."

Ash nodded. "I'll double your fee."

Saying yes appealed to Jenna as much as eating liver and onions, her dad's favorite dinner. Her mother had made the meal once a year. Jenna and Colton had gagged their way through miniscule servings to be rewarded with hot fudge sundaes for dessert. Maybe she could treat this wedding the same way. Sending extra money to Colton would be the cherry on top.

Except she still wanted Ash and Amber to leave. But they'd apologized. Jenna couldn't shove them out the door. Pastor Dan had counseled her on the importance of forgiveness for her faith and so she wouldn't be consumed by bitterness.

"If there's anything else you want . . ." Ash added.

Wait a minute. She straightened, an idea forming in her mind. There was something she needed. Not her exactly, but the church's youth group. They were short chaperones. If the three agreed to help . . .

She drew in a breath to calm her nerves. "My church needs adult volunteers for our youth group outing on Saturday or they'll have to cancel. It's all day at a ropes course, so if you're busy —"

"I'm in," Ash said without any hesitation.

Toby nodded. "Me too."

Amber received a nudge from her fiancé. "Uh, sure. I can do that. But what's a rope course?"

"Never mind what it is, you'll have fun." Ash looked at Jenna. "We're happy to help out. But the decision to photograph Amber and Toby's wedding is yours."

Jenna had three yeses. What had Kerri said earlier?

There's always a plan. Not yours or mine, but His.

Jenna took a deep breath and another to try to calm her nerves reaching near panic mode. Not for her. She repeated the three words in her mind. This was for Colton, her friend Sam the youth pastor, and the teens at her church. "If Ash doubles my fee and the three of you volunteer with the youth group on Saturday, I'll photograph the wedding."

CHAPTER SIX

Saturday morning, Jenna stood in the parking lot outside the Sweetwater Community Church with Sam Carson, the youth pastor in charge of today's outing. Birds chirped from nearby trees. The sun shone bright. Soon heat would reflect off the asphalt. Only two cars — hers and Sam's — and the church's bus were in the parking lot. She'd arrived early to help him prepare.

Placing water bottles into a large ice chest, she yawned, tired from working a wedding last night. A restless sleep hadn't helped. Thoughts of seeing Ash had kept her awake long after her body wanted rest.

Sam removed the plastic wrap from a case of water bottles. "You're exhausted. You should have slept in this morning. Go take a nap in my office."

"You're as bad as Colton."

"He asked me to look out for you when he was here on leave."

"No wonder I feel like I have two brothers." She stifled another yawn.

Sam gave her a look.

"I'm fine." She was. Just a little wigged out about seeing Ash this morning.

He'd sent a check, as promised, for the full amount plus interest. She'd expected a portion, half at most, and had been surprised. Stunned, really. Once the check cleared, she would be free from credit card payments and able to repay Colton. Out of debt with money in a savings account. An exciting, new place to be, but that didn't stop another yawn. A nap on the hour-long bus ride to the ropes course might be in order, if the teens let her sleep.

Sam dumped the water bottles into an ice chest. "You work too hard."

"Do you want to be the pot or the kettle? The choice is yours." She didn't expect him to answer. "It's going to be hot today."

"The trees will keep us shaded, but I brought extra sunscreen and grabbed a few more cases of water last night, just in case."

"We should be good then."

"Especially with your extra volunteers coming along." Sam's grin took ten years off his face. The twenty-six-year-old looked more like a teen than the group's leader. "Thanks for finding more chaperones. The kids have been looking forward to this outing. I'm relieved we didn't have to cancel."

"Me too." Except the thought of spending the entire day with Ash jangled her nerves. She poured half a bag of crushed ice over the water bottles. "Everything worked out."

"Easy-peasy, smooth as French silk pie, as Trish would say."

A smile tugged at the corners of Jenna's mouth. "I can hear her say those words. And Pastor Dan laugh."

"Yep. Only I'm not kidding." Sam closed the lid on the ice chest as if accentuating his point. "Your three volunteers showed up at my office the day after you texted me and filled out the background check form. That's usually the stumbling block to getting help."

"I knew we needed more adults."

Sam carried the ice chest he'd filled to the bus. "So what's it like having your ex-fiancé back in your life?"

Her past wasn't a secret. Pastor Dan had asked her to give a testimonial after joining the church. Sam was one of her closer friends, so he knew a few extra details. "I wouldn't say Ash is back. I've only seen him the day he apologized."

"Gutsy."

"Ash realized he was wrong."

"Takes courage to admit that."

"Yes. He's contacted people who took his side and explained what really happened. I've booked photography shoots with a couple of them. He's gone above and beyond to make things up to me."

"But you wish he hadn't needed proof."

She straightened. "I didn't say that."

"Still true."

"Maybe."

Sam shot her a curious glance. "Thinking about getting back together?"

The water bottle in her hand slipped, crashed into the ice chest. "No."

"Sure about that?"

"Yes. Definitely." Though Jenna wished she wouldn't think about Ash so much. "I'm not the same person who dated him. Working here, attending services, making new friends . . . I don't want to go backwards to who I was with him."

"Sounds like you're trying to convince yourself."

"No. It's the truth." She wanted to do the right thing and not get hurt again. "I'm photographing his sister's wedding. That's all."

"Nice of you, under the circumstances."

"An act of forgiveness." That was how she'd explained her decision to shoot Amber's wedding to Colton. He wanted Jenna far, far away from Ash. She assured her brother that her heart was immune. Come June twenty-eighth, the day after Amber and Toby's wedding, she would never see Ash again.

"But I'll be honest." Jenna knew Sam would never judge her actions. "Agreeing to photograph the wedding isn't completely altruistic. I knew the youth group needed volunteers, so I made that part of the deal, and Ash offered to double my normal rate."

"That's a win-win-win. If you're going to have an ex, sounds like Ashton Vance is one to have."

Jenna half-laughed. "I suppose you're right."

"Glad you agree, because he's here."

Butterflies went bonkers in her stomach. No biggie. One day with him was nothing. Two days if she counted Amber's wedding. Two and a half if she included the rehearsal dinner. Every muscle tensed. She looked over her shoulder.

Ash walked across the parking lot dressed in khaki shorts, a T-shirt, and tennis shoes. He wore a backpack and carried three pink rectangular boxes.

Her mouth watered. The reaction had nothing to do with what might be in the boxes and everything to do with him. He looked as good dressed casually as in a suit.

Sam blew out a breath. "Oh boy. If Ashton brought donuts, you're going to have to start dating him or convince him to volunteer more."

"Because of donuts?"

"Three boxes' worth? You bet."

She shook her head. At least she knew what to get Sam for his next birthday.

"Good morning." Ash raised the pink boxes. "Stopped by the Donut Hole. Figured we might need some sugar to jumpstart us this morning."

Sam kept his hands at his side, but he looked like he wanted to grab the boxes and get first choice. "Thanks. The kids will love them."

"There's plenty for everybody." Ash handed over the donuts. "Help yourself now."

Sam set the boxes on his car's trunk. He practically drooled opening the first lid, then removed a maple bar. "Happy you're onboard, dude. We haven't had donuts since one of our volunteers moved to Seattle last year."

Jenna understood Sam's excitement. Youth ministers didn't earn a big salary, and donuts weren't considered a necessity. When she'd been working three jobs, a stick of chewing gum could make her day. "Generous of you."

Ash's smile crinkled the corners of his eyes. The additional lines appealed to her. Not that she should be noticing how he looked. Or find him attractive. Jenna stared at the asphalt in the parking lot.

"I got your favorite," Ash said. "Old-fashioned chocolate."

Jenna raised her head. "You remembered?"

"Don't sound so surprised. Two years isn't that long."

"I guess not." Still, she was . . . touched. Part of her wondered what they'd had together those two years — love, like, convenience. She'd tried to purge everything about Ash from her memory. "You like sugar donuts, right?"

"That's right." He sounded pleased.

Funny he liked that type, because he preferred things neat. Maybe the messiness appealed to him on a subconscious level.

Sam's maple bar disappeared in a final bite. He wiped his mouth with the back of his hand. "I'm not surprised Ash remembered your favorite donut. You're an old-fashioned girl."

"You think?" Ash asked.

"Homemade lemonade, baking pies for mission suppers, sewing her own slipcovers, singing along to beach movies from the sixties." Sam's words flowed without hesitation. "I'd call that old-fashioned."

Ash studied Sam with a hard gaze. "You know Jenna well."

Uh, oh. Ash's tone sounded almost jealous. But that made no sense. And Sam was her surrogate brother. "I think I'll have a donut."

Sam handed Jenna her favorite kind, but his posture changed. He stood taller, his shoulders square to Ash. "I do know Jenna well. She's worked at the church for over a year and a half. I see her almost every day, including Sundays during the youth service. But I didn't know her favorite kind of donut until now."

"That's because you're too busy during fellowship time to notice what I'm eating," she told Sam.

Ash held his donut midair. "You work here at the church?"

She nodded. "I used to be on the cleaning crew, but now I just work the espresso cart. I also fill in if the office is short staffed."

Ash looked at her with an odd expression. "I wondered why you no longer attended Westside Christian."

"This is closer." Jenna could have said that she felt more comfortable here after folks at Westside took Ash's side, but chose not to. She'd accepted his apology — saying more would solve nothing. "Pastor Dan and Trish help people who find themselves lost or in difficult positions."

Sam raised his hand. "Like me a few years ago. I'm another stray they took in. They helped me turn my life around."

"They're like the animal shelter, except we have a forever home here." A warm and fuzzy feeling enveloped Jenna. "I can't see myself going to church anywhere else."

"We're happy you found us." Sam picked up the ice chest she'd filled and loaded it into the bus.

"Sounds like a good place. Maybe I'll attend a service here," Ash said to her surprise. "Westside's been a little . . ."

"Lukewarm," Sam offered.

Ash rubbed his chin. "Yeah."

"You need heat. Fire. Give us a try. Join us tomorrow." Sam eyed the box of donuts again but didn't take one. "I'm going to grab a few things from my office. The kids won't be here for another half hour or so."

With that, he walked into the church.

"Seems like a nice guy," Ash said.

"The best. Understands the teens. Listens

to them and hears what they're saying." She ate the rest of her donut. "I received your check. Thanks. Including interest was generous of you."

"It's fair."

Fair wasn't a word she would have used, but she wasn't going to argue semantics.

Ash motioned to the church's bus, an old school bus donated a few years ago. Trish said the kids' paint job with multicolored shapes reminded her of *The Partridge Family*, an old show she watched as a kid.

"Is the youth group responsible for the adventure photos on your walls?" he asked.

"No. The church's singles group is."

He took a step toward her. "Singles group?"

She raised her chin. "Yes."

"Good for you."

He didn't sound upset, more . . . supportive. Maybe he hadn't been jealous of Sam.

"I forgot to bring napkins. You have some chocolate here." His fingertip brushed the corner of her mouth, sending a burst of sensation from the point of contact. "Now it's gone."

He'd touched her lips before with both his fingers and his mouth, but this gesture felt more intimate. Heat singed her insides.

Chills tingled on the outside. All she needed was a kiss . . .

What was she thinking?

So what if she hadn't felt this way in two years? They weren't a couple. Wouldn't be one. She crossed her arms over her chest and rubbed her bare arms.

"Cold?" he asked.

"I'm fine." Or would be as soon as she stopped thinking crazy thoughts about Ash.

He removed a sugar donut from the box. "Have you ever done a ropes course before?"

"No, but Sam said the activities build trust and camaraderie. Have you been to one?"

"No, but I'm looking forward to this. Building trust is something I need to work on."

The anticipation in his gaze made her mouth go dry. She cleared her throat. "Sounds like something we all need."

"You're very trusting."

"I used to be."

"What happened?" he asked.

She moistened her lips. "You."

CHAPTER SEVEN

You.

During the drive and now on the high ropes course, Jenna's word echoed through Ash's head. What she said bugged him. He sat with eight teens and their guide thirty feet above the ground.

The midday sun blazed down from a cloudless blue sky. He tried focusing on what the guide, an army vet named Rob, was saying about the challenging exercise they'd just finished, but Ash's thoughts were on Jenna.

Yes, he deserved the blame for what happened, but she'd accepted his apology. He'd paid her back and was restoring her reputation with mutual friends and acquaintances. He didn't know what else he could do to prove he was sorry. Couldn't she meet him halfway? Or was that asking too much?

"An interesting task." Rob, a friendly, in-shape guy, emphasized the learning process while sprinkling in character and common sense and a little scripture. Like Sam, Rob had a way that drew the teens in. "So what else did we learn?"

"To communicate," someone mumbled from the back.

Rob nodded. "Knowing how to communicate in different circumstances is key, no matter if you're on a ropes course, in a classroom, on a field, or down on your knees praying. Did you communicate?"

Heads hung low. A few shook back and forth.

The teens owning up to what they hadn't done pleased Ash. As frustration levels rose during the last task, so had voices, until the volume got stuck at yelling. They'd completed the exercise through brute force, not teamwork. But Rob's question was directed at the teens, so Ash remained quiet.

"Screaming at each other isn't communicating," another teen added.

"If we don't work as a team, we won't get far," a boy with wavy red hair and wearing a Seattle Seahawks T-shirt and board shorts answered.

A girl, her wrist covered in friendship bracelets, sighed. "Too bad we didn't figure that out sooner."

Two kids who'd started off strong, then

gave up in the middle of the task, laughed, the sound full of nerves, not humor.

"You need one leader." The boy's serious voice matched his facial expression. "Someone who doesn't act like a dictator and will listen to feedback."

"You have to follow who's in charge even if you might not agree with them," said a girl, the self-appointed leader no one wanted to follow.

"Excellent observations." Rob looked at each teen, waiting until he'd made eye contact before going to the next person. "Could any of you have completed this challenge alone?"

"No," they said in unison.

"That's right." A satisfied smile graced Rob's lips. "It's one reason you struggled more with this task than others. You had to rely on each other to succeed."

The redheaded kid snickered. "You set us up to fail."

"Nope." Rob leaned back on his hands. "Following a leader who does a task differently is a lesson we must learn."

"Impossible," one mumbled.

Another nodded. "What does it matter? We won't be on a ropes course again for a long time. If ever."

Other kids agreed.

"True, but you have teachers and coaches. One day you'll have a boss, unless you start your own company or win the lottery. Trust me, they'll tell you what they want you to do. You might get married and have a spouse who wants things done a certain way."

Several boys groaned.

Ash bit back his smile. He remembered the marriage preparation class he and Jenna had been required to take at church. The ropes course would be good for a couple to do together before planning their big wedding day and setting up their gift registry.

Rob stood, brushed his hands against each other. "Pick a new leader for the next element and show me what you've learned."

Ash took the rear to keep stragglers from falling behind.

"Come on." Jenna's voice carried from the lower ropes course, where she and her group worked with their guide. Lack of elevation didn't make a task easier. She clapped, the sound carrying on the warm air. "You've got this."

Her enthusiasm and cheerleader attitude didn't surprise Ash. But her chaperoning the more difficult group did. None of her teens acted like they wanted to be here.

Two boys dressed in black, with bangs hanging over their faces and shoulders hunched like they'd escaped from a nineties MTV show, had been looking for a place to hide since stepping off the bus. One girl's eyes gleamed as if she might burst into tears with a wrong word or glance. Another girl complained about the lack of a cellular phone signal.

Had Jenna purposely chosen the more difficult path today? Ash didn't know, but she hadn't been that way before.

She clapped again. Whistled. "I know you can do it."

On the ground, the noise level rose. The guide shouted directions. Jenna offered encouraging words.

Rob stopped to watch. "I don't believe it."

The I'd-rather-be-anywhere-but-here teens were killing the most difficult task on the course. Succeeding where the other groups had failed. At the end, the group of misfits and addicted texters high-fived, hugged, and shouted woot woots.

Rob pointed toward Jenna's group. "That's teamwork in action. The most efficient groups don't always have the strongest individuals, but everyone working together and doing their part makes up for skills they lack."

Jenna also knew how to encourage people to move beyond themselves and their comfort levels. When they were dating, she'd encouraged Ash to offer pro bono legal services through a community group. As soon as they broke up, he'd stopped. Lack of time due to his new job and too many memories of her, even though he'd found the volunteering fulfilling. Maybe he should start again.

Rob led the group to the next element. He grabbed hold of a safety tether. "This final challenge is called On the Edge. Working together and pushing yourself is key to completing the task. Who's ready?"

Everyone, including Ash, raised hands. As soon as they took a break, he wanted to ask Rob to do a trust-building exercise with Jenna. One that might help Ash's cause.

He liked the changes in her. The Jenna he'd known went along with whatever he'd said. The new Jenna was stronger, more confident, and not afraid to put herself out there or say what was on her mind.

Friends helped each other. He was going to do whatever he could for her.

During a break from the ropes course, Jenna stood leaning against a tree trunk. The teens lounged on the grass and ate Popsicles. She glanced at Rob, the guide who'd worked with Ash's group. "You want me to do what?"

"The Trust Fall. You climb up on the platform and fall backwards." He motioned to the adults. "They'll catch you."

Sam would catch her. She had no doubt about him. Toby and the guides too. But Amber would be worried about breaking a fingernail. And Ash . . .

No way.

Jenna forced a lighthearted smile. That was better than a save-me-now-Jesus gasp she held back. She knew He was with her, but she didn't feel up to this. "Let someone else have a go. I'll catch them."

"You were picked." Rob's gaze narrowed. "Tell me what's holding you back."

They would be here all day. "I've never done something like this."

That much was true, as were her reservations about Ash and Amber.

"The kids will be doing the exercise next." Rob lowered his voice. "Seeing you do this will help them overcome any fears or doubts they might have."

Why me? Why now? Jenna wasn't sure she wanted to know the answer.

"You haven't backed down from any challenge." Toby sat five feet away. Amber was at his side. The two had only been apart when they were with their respective groups.

"Come on. Where's your sense of adventure?" Amber asked.

Could everyone hear this discussion?

Ash gave Jenna an encouraging smile. "We're not going to drop you."

If only she could believe him. But she didn't. Uncertainty kept her from stepping forward. "Maybe not on purpose."

"Eight people are required to catch you. The chaperones, then guides will fill in."

Rob's casual tone made this sound like no big deal. Maybe to him, but not to her. What he asked was huge.

Teens and adults stared at Jenna like she was performing center stage at worship service. That was the last place anyone would find her. But backing down would have repercussions. Teens might say no when their turn came, and she didn't want that to happen. She was, in a word, stuck.

Her stomach sunk to her feet. Splat, how she would hit the ground if someone didn't catch her.

Jenna recognized the benefit of the Trust Fall. Her hesitation told her she needed to do this even if she didn't want to.

Slowing her breathing didn't help calm her nerves. "You've done this before, right?"

"Many times." Rob's smile didn't waver.

"This is a mental challenge, not a physical one. Walk by faith."

Jenna understood. She'd been living that way since she stumbled into Pastor Dan's church that rainy afternoon. She trusted her group, aka the detention crew, to catch her more than Ash and Amber. Not that either would let something happen to Jenna on purpose, but subconsciously . . .

Guilt coated her dry mouth. She shouldn't think that.

"Do it, do it," the teens chanted.

She looked at Sam. He winked, then grinned. Some friend he was.

"I'll be there to catch you." Sam's tongue was bright orange from eating a Popsicle. "No worries."

Easy for him to say. Her heart pounded like a timpani while her pulse resembled a snare roll.

Ash walked toward her, his steps purposeful. "You can do this."

A lump formed in her throat. "Not sure I can."

He stopped next to her, placed his mouth by her ear. His warm breath blew against her skin, soft like a caress. If she turned her face to the right, his mouth would be nearly touching her lips.

Bad idea.

"I won't let you fall," he whispered. "I promise."

Oh, how she wanted to believe him. She'd believed him before, only to be dropped by him in the worst possible way. In public, for all to witness. She'd survived that. She didn't know if she could survive again.

Jenna trembled, but she had to keep the youth group kids in mind. She'd worked with the teens and Sam for over a year. The program grew from the kids' word of mouth. She couldn't allow her fear to jeopardize Sam's hard work.

Ash's gaze remained on her, a connection she wasn't sure how to define. "Climb up there."

Praying for courage, she made her way to the four-foot-high platform and climbed the ladder. Her legs trembled with each rung. The kids applauded. On top, she gave a bow, but her insides twisted like curling ribbon on a gift.

Logically the chances of being dropped were slim. The course elements they'd finished had been more challenging, yet doing the Trust Fall was taking every ounce of strength and courage she could muster.

Ash took his place, crossed his arms with Sam's. Toby did the same across from Amber. Pairs of guides stood on either side of the four.

Rob hopped onto the platform. "See how they've made a canopy to catch you."

She nodded. Her voice would sound too shaky if she spoke.

"Turn around," Rob said.

Her gaze lingered on Ash, then she turned.

Rob gave her an I-know-you-can-do-this smile. "Now fall backwards."

Jenna tried to relax her tense muscles. She shook her hands, as if that would make any difference about being caught. And then she realized she had no reason to worry or be afraid.

Knowing who had their arms crossed waiting for her to fall didn't matter. She had nothing to fear. She trusted He would be there to catch her the way He had been so far.

She closed her eyes, leaned back, and fell into the air.

CHAPTER EIGHT

Later that afternoon, Ash sat in a booth at a café in downtown Sweetwater. Empty plates once full of appetizers covered the table. He and Jenna sat on a bench seat opposite Toby and Amber. Sam had a date so he'd headed home, even though he, too, had been starving after the ropes course.

Toby set his glass of iced tea on the table. "I'm never going to forget the look on Amber's face when she realized she had to catch Jenna. Pure panic."

"Well, I honestly didn't think you'd do it." Amber studied her fingernails. "I was sure you'd back out at the last minute."

"That's okay. I had doubts myself." Jenna's eyes shone brightly. "But I'm glad I went through with it."

The Trust Fall had been a struggle for her, but Ash couldn't have been prouder of Jenna. He picked up his huckleberry lemonade, the café's specialty. The condensation from the glass felt good against his palm after a hot day outside, working and playing.

"Not as glad as Rob." Ash laughed. "The guy was sweating bullets until you got on that platform."

Toby nodded. "Thought Rob might offer to do the fall himself, but Jenna's group never had any doubt."

"Neither did I." Ash hadn't, even if she'd hesitated. Nothing wrong with taking her time. Made sense, given he and Amber had broken her trust and would be catching her. He understood her reservations.

"Next time someone else can take the fall," Jenna teased.

Next time.

The thought appealed to Ash. Getting outside, surrounded by trees and fresh air, was good for him. The course had challenged his muscles and his mind. Spending time with Jenna had been the best part, filling him with contentment and making him want more.

"I'd do this again. Today has to be one of my most fun days in . . ." Ash did a quick calculation. The date was over two years ago, back when he was engaged to Jenna. "A while."

"Sam always needs volunteers." She

leaned back against the booth. Her eyelids looked heavy, as if she needed a nap. "If you have time to help out, give him a call."

"Is that what you do?" Toby asked.

Jenna nodded. "There aren't many Saturday events. We've had the ropes course planned for months, so I kept the date open. But the group meets every Tuesday and has an optional Bible study on Thursday."

"Sam keeps the kids busy," Toby said.

"That's the best way to keep them out of trouble." Jenna rubbed the back of her neck, making Ash wish he could do that for her — then she could return the favor. "Life is rougher on the east side of town. Many kids are from single-parent homes. Most need someone who'll listen. Sam hopes to start a mentoring program."

"I'll touch base with him." If Ash happened to see Jenna while volunteering, that would be a bonus. Like dinner tonight.

"This was fun. But I prefer an activity where I don't break any fingernails." Amber held up her right hand. "Good thing I'm having a gel manicure done for the wedding."

Toby kissed Amber's hand. "Broken nails or not, I appreciate the way you stepped out of your comfort zone for those kids. You were great."

Amber beamed. "I guess a couple broken nails was a small price to pay."

Toby stared into her eyes and nodded.

Ash realized this was likely his sister's first service opportunity beyond buying gifts off giving trees at Christmastime or donating money and canned food. He would talk to Amber about getting involved in the youth group too.

"A good day all around," Jenna said.

"I know who to thank." Ash raised his glass. "Here's to Jenna for inviting us, trusting us to catch her when she fell, and not screaming once gravity took over."

She tapped her glass against his, then Amber and Toby's. "I was too busy praying to scream."

Ash believed that. The urge to put his arm around her the way he'd always done was strong, but he didn't want to ruin dinner. Controlling his growing attraction wasn't easy.

Jenna glowed with her newfound confidence, contentment, and faith. Not only visible, but appealing. Getting involved at Sweetwater Community Church had been good for her. He wanted to attend a service and see what she'd found there. Maybe that would help him.

Amber shivered. "I'm glad they didn't

pick me."

Toby gave her a one-arm hug. "You would have fallen off backwards."

"Maybe." Amber sounded doubtful. "But I wouldn't have wanted to go first."

"The kids did well." Jenna toyed with her cloth napkin. She didn't look nervous, but her fingers hadn't stopped moving for the past five minutes.

"They were successful because they saw you do the Trust Fall even though you weren't sure." Ash smiled, easy to do when he was around her. If only things could be different between them. He didn't want to go back to where they'd been two years ago. He wanted to start fresh. Maybe today would be a new beginning. His gaze locked on hers. "Excellent job."

She smiled at him.

He smiled back.

Ash could sit with her the rest of the night and be happy. A strand of hair fell forward across her face. He tucked the piece behind her ear. So beautiful.

"Oh, no!" Amber's voice resembled a shriek. She tugged on Toby's arm. "I forgot we had plans tonight. This has been great, but we have to go. Now."

Toby's brow drew together. "I don't have anything in my calendar."

"I must have forgotten to tell you." She placed the strap of her purse over her shoulder. "Come on, sweetie."

Two twenty-dollar bills dropped onto the table, courtesy of Toby. "This will cover our portion. See you later."

"I'll be in touch about your wedding," Jenna said.

"Sounds good." Amber scooted out of the booth. She practically sprinted to the door with Toby at her heels.

Jenna stared after them. "Must be important plans."

"With Amber you never know."

The waiter removed the empty plates. "Tonight for dessert we have a three-layer chocolate cake with fudge filling and icing, crème brûlée, cherry cheesecake, or a marionberry cobbler with a scoop of French vanilla ice cream."

"Marionberry cobbler," the two said at the same time.

Jenna's cheeks turned a charming shade of pink.

"Would that be one cobbler or two?" the waiter asked.

"I don't think I can eat one myself," she said.

"Me, either." Ash looked at the waiter. "One, please. With two spoons."

"Coming right up." The waiter carried the dishes away.

"We both still like berries," she said. "Marionberry cobbler."

"Huckleberry lemonade."

"Raspberry vinaigrette."

They used to play this game when they shared food. He was out of practice coming up with another food item. "Strawberry smoothie."

"Blackberry jam."

He wasn't about to be outdone. "Blueberry muffins."

"Boysenberry syrup."

"Cranberry jelly."

Jenna's shoulders slumped. "You win."

Ash had won the moment she sat next to him. He nudged his arm against hers. "Not bad for being out of practice."

She nodded. "You get first and last bite."

Being with her today felt familiar, but differences stuck out. Jenna left room between them rather than sitting close so their thighs touched. The distance — inches — made him want to invade her space with not-so-accidental brushes of his hand, arm, and leg. If only . . .

"One marionberry cobbler and two spoons." The waiter placed the dessert and silverware between them. "Enjoy."

Jenna picked up her spoon but didn't take a bite. "You first."

He ate a spoonful. The warm cobbler softened the cold ice cream into a heavenly mix of flavors.

"Delicious." Though he'd rather have a taste of Jenna. She tasted better than any — Stop. Those thoughts would get him into trouble. This wasn't a date. Not even close. "Your turn."

Jenna broke off a piece, then raised her spoon to her mouth. Her lips closed around the bite of cobbler and ice cream. She closed her eyes, chewed, swallowed. A soft sigh escaped.

The memories of her kisses hit like a left jab to his jaw. Talk about pure torture. Her kiss would be sweet, warm, completely filling. The best dessert on the menu. Ash shifted in his seat.

Opening her eyes, she lowered the spoon. Her mouth curved upward. "Yum. This is really good."

Customers filled other tables, but the conversations and laughter didn't distract Ash. He was all about Jenna. She was his focus, his world tonight. An alarm blared. A danger ahead sign flashed. If he wasn't careful, he was going to do something he regretted . . . like kiss her. "We can order another."

She raised the spoon to her mouth. "This is enough. The calories are going straight to my waist and hips."

He didn't see that as a problem, but knew better than to say the words aloud.

Jenna looked at him. "Can I ask you a question?"

He scooped up another bite. "Shoot."

"I don't mean to be nosy. Okay, maybe I do, but why are you paying for Amber's wedding photographer instead of your father?"

Ash choked on the cobbler in his mouth, coughed, drank a sip of lemonade. That helped. Sort of. He drank more.

A concerned look on her face, Jenna touched his shoulder. "You okay?"

He nodded. Her moving closer and touching him felt good, comfortable, right. Pathetic, yes, but he was only human.

"Sorry, must have swallowed wrong." His throat burned and so did his brain. He couldn't tell her the truth about his dad not liking her. The only thing that mattered was Ash liked her. "You'd asked about my father."

"I wondered why you're paying for Amber's photography and not him."

His father refused to pay Jenna. Ash didn't want to lie about the reason, but he would not hurt her again. "My father paid for the original photographer. Her assistants can shoot Amber's wedding, so he refused to pay for a different one."

Namely Jenna.

Ash watched the melting ice cream pool on the plate. He hoped by the time of the wedding his father would be cordial to Jenna. "My dad shocked Amber by giving her a budget for the wedding. She's gone over, so she is paying for her dress, veil, and shoes."

Jenna scooped up a spoonful of marionberries. "What else are you paying for?"

"The cake and DJ."

"Amber's fortunate to have such a generous brother."

"Her wedding day should be special."

Jenna's fingers went knuckle-white-tight around the spoon. "Every bride dreams of the perfect wedding."

"Did you?"

She nodded once.

He hadn't listened to what she wanted. "You wouldn't have had your dream wedding if we'd married."

"You would have had yours." She ate more cobbler.

Would that have been his ideal wedding? He didn't know. Jenna had suggested eloping, but Ash's campaign manager and his father believed the publicity surrounding a big wedding would be a boost for the campaign. He'd convinced her that was for the best. She hadn't put up much of an argument.

His fault. Again. He set his spoon on the cobbler plate. "I owe you another apology."

"Let's call it good." She didn't sound upset, but she fiddled with the napkin again. "There's no reason to look back. We can't change what happened."

"True, but I don't want to make the same mistakes again."

God, you've given me so much. But please, could I have a do-over with Jenna?

Ash nearly laughed. A misguided prayer, but he had no one else to help him.

"I'll be your cashier tonight." The waiter set a black leather bill folder on the table, then walked away. Ash reached for the check only to find his hand on top of hers. "I've got this."

"I do."

Her skin was soft and warm. He fought the urge to rub her hand with his thumb. "Please. Let me cover dinner."

Eyes dark, she kept hold of the folder. "How about we split the check?"

Jenna didn't look like she would surrender

without a fight. That would mess up whatever limited chance he had with her.

He let go of the bill. "That works. I'll subtract what Toby left, and we can each pay half."

A satisfied smile graced her lips. "Wonderful."

Ash missed her hand on his. "You look happy."

Her grin spread to her eyes, where a twinkle returned. "I am. Thanks to you."

"I seem to be missing something."

"This is the first time you've let me pay."

"Ever?"

She nodded. "I never thought the whole man-always-pays thing seemed fair in an equal relationship, but you were always so adamant."

"Adamant?"

"Very much so." Her smile didn't falter. "I didn't make as much as you. Still don't. And I appreciated you wanting to pay, but contributing, even a little, makes a person feel like they're in a partnership, not just being taken care of."

He hadn't known she felt that way. "I'll remember that."

"A warning. Not all women feel this way."

But the one who counted did. "Still good

to know."

Especially if he got a do-over.

Chapter Nine

On Sunday after the youth service, Jenna entered the church hall. Two teens acknowledged her with nods. She gave them a thumbs-up.

After the ropes course and Pastor Dan's sermon, she couldn't stop smiling. She kept thinking about the future. Something she hadn't done in two years. It felt good, normal.

Jenna followed the smell of fresh-brewed coffee to a large pot. She filled a cup, then added a dash of milk. The caffeine would keep her going with another wedding to shoot this afternoon.

"Hey." Sam wore a white button-down and khaki pants — dressy attire for him. The clothes made him look more his age than his normal shorts and T-shirts. "Guess who's here?"

"Pretty much everyone we know."

"True, but that's not who I meant."

She sipped her coffee. The scent of something baking in the hall's kitchen tickled her nose. "Is Mrs. Phillips making scones?"

"Yes."

Jenna's stomach grumbled in anticipation. "Just what I need this morning."

"That's what Ash said."

She nearly dropped her coffee. "My Ash?"

"Yours?" Sam's eyes narrowed. "Didn't think you wanted to date the guy."

"I don't. Figure of speech."

"Yeah, right. And I'm the tooth fairy."

She ignored him, searched the crowded hall, but didn't see Ash. "Where is he?"

"At one of the tables by the back door." Sam's mouth slanted. "You'd better hurry. I think a few women are calling dibs."

Jenna made a beeline toward the other side of the room. Laughter drew her attention. Michael, Kerri, Claire, and two women from the singles group sat with Ash. No empty seats remained at the table. The least Jenna could do was say hi.

She walked up. "Good morning. I'm surprised to see you here, Ash."

He rose, looking handsome in his blue shirt and slacks. An almost finished scone sat on the plate in front of him. "I decided to attend the service this morning."

"Enjoy it?"

"Very much." He sounded relaxed for being in a brand-new place. "Pastor Dan is great. I liked the music. Everyone is so friendly. I'll be back next Sunday."

A thrill shot through her. Not that what Ash did should matter. "This is a great place."

The others at the table agreed. She sipped her coffee.

"You should go to the singles group meeting," Kerri suggested. "Unless you're in a relationship."

"I'm not dating anyone."

His words squeezed Jenna's heart like a vise and left her feeling . . . weird.

"The next meeting is on Wednesday," Claire said.

Ash looked at Jenna. "Will you be there?"

She shook her head. "Photo session."

"I'll check my calendar," he said to the others.

The three single women at the table sat taller, with big smiles. Jenna understood. But the thought of Ash dating one of them — or anyone — made her stomach churn. She didn't know why. He was no longer her fiancé. They weren't dating. They weren't even friends.

"We're going to brunch," Kerri said to Jenna. "Ash suggested a place downtown.

Join us."

She'd eaten dinner with him last night. Brunch today wouldn't be the smartest move if she wanted to keep her distance. But a part of her wanted to spend time with him.

The other women stared at Ash like a new pair of shoes they wanted to try on. Which would he fit? Probably better that she wouldn't be around to watch Sweetwater Community Church's G-rated version of *The Bachelor*. "Thanks for the invite, but I have a wedding to shoot."

"You had one on Friday," Ash said to her.

"Busy month."

Jenna shouldn't have said the word *wedding* in front of Claire, but considering what she'd been going through, Claire didn't seem to mind. She looked good. She'd chopped off inches of hair and added coppery highlights. Her eyes were bright, not a hint of red or swelling.

The alarm on Jenna's cell phone beeped — a reminder to head home and pack her photography gear. "Have fun at brunch."

Ash smiled at her. "Good to see you."

Her heart bumped, not much, like she was driving over a cattle guard at the O'Donnell ranch west of town. Of course, she knew not having a reaction to Ash involving that particular organ would be better. Safer.

She should reply. "You too."

Seeing him was good.

Except she had no idea what that meant or how she wished she could go to brunch or why she felt . . . jealous.

Tuesday at eleven, Jenna parked her car in downtown Sweetwater. Camera bag bumping against her hip, she headed to Bridal Sweets. The high-end wedding shop catered to wealthy clientele or brides wanting to splurge on a gown. She'd never been inside.

Her dress hadn't been expensive, but it was perfect. Too bad no one except Amber and two friends had seen Jenna wearing it. Would Ash have liked the gown she'd chosen?

Ack. She was losing her mind thinking about Ash. She wasn't the only woman, based on the chatter at the espresso cart and texts wanting to know more about the handsome man who'd attended service and gone out to brunch. Even Sam had been asking questions.

That didn't make pushing Ash out of her mind any easier. He'd taken up permanent residence in her brain. No matter the time of day, he was there, a mishmash of a relationship-gone-wrong memories and new feelings developing.

Not that they were. At least not on his part, or he would have contacted her, texted or called, right?

She didn't want to know the answer. She needed to get him out of her head. This wasn't middle school or the youth group. She was too old for drama.

Jenna entered the bridal salon. Luxurious gold, pink, and white décor greeted her. Crystal chandeliers hung from the ceiling. Her feet sank half an inch in the plush carpet. The scents of vanilla and lavender filled the cool air — not to mention the smell of money.

Out of her price range, out of her league.

"Welcome to Bridal Sweets." A thirty-something sales clerk dressed in a cerulean-green fitted jacket and matching skirt smiled warmly. She looked like she'd stepped out of a wedding reality TV show. Chunky, stylish silver chains hung around her neck. Her high heels seemed to have been dyed the same color as her suit. "May I help you?"

"I'm Jenna with Picture Perfect Photography. I received a call from Amber Vance to meet her here."

"Oh, yes, Amber. Such a delightful, glamorous bride." The woman motioned to a gold velvet curtain. "She's in one of the dressing areas. Follow me, please."

Jenna did, and had to keep herself from staring at the couture dresses on display. The kind of gowns seen in bridal magazines.

Behind the curtain, an exotic scent — a mix of jasmine and sandalwood — wafted in the air. Perfume or potpourri? Classical music played, a quartet doing their version of the quintessential wedding music, Pachelbel's Canon in D. She expected to hear a cork pop and the clink of crystal champagne flutes.

So not her world, and that was okay. She enjoyed this glimpse into how others lived.

The woman knocked once on a door. "Your photographer has arrived."

"Make sure Jenna has her camera ready." Amber sounded as if she'd forgotten how to breathe.

"Putting the lens on now." Jenna stood at the door. "I'm ready."

"Come in," Amber called.

Camera in hand, Jenna opened the door and stepped into a large room with two loveseats. Heavy gold curtains cut the room in half. The elaborate dressing room decor fit Amber's personality perfectly. "I'm inside."

The curtains opened.

Amber stood on a carpeted platform in front of three floor-to-ceiling mirrors. Her sleeveless wedding gown was Westminster Abbey-worthy. Intricate beading and lace covered the dress. The skirt's cathedral train cascaded down two steps.

Jenna's breath caught. "You look like a princess bride."

Amber spun with her arms out. The action made her look like a little girl, not a woman about to say I do. "I feel like royalty in this dress."

"It's perfect for you." Jenna raised her camera and clicked off shots.

Amber worked hard to present a rich-girl image. She traveled across the Cascades to shop at the top Seattle department stores and boutiques. This dress was stunning, not as high fashion as Jenna would have imagined, but the whimsical, fairy-tale design truly suited the bride-to-be. The elaborate lace veil topped by a rhinestone tiara was a perfect match. "I love it."

"Thank you!" Strands of hair artfully fell from Amber's updo, softening her face. Just beautiful.

"Let's get some shots using your reflection in the mirrors."

Amber struck a pose. "I hope they turn out."

"They will."

A knock sounded at the door. "May I

come in?"

"Ash!" Amber squealed. "He was in a meeting so I left a message. I didn't think he'd make it."

The door opened. He looked at his sister and froze. "Wow. Just wow."

The expression on his face was half stunned, half amazed. Jenna took his picture, liking the contrast between his tailored gray suit, white dress shirt and red tie, and his look of awe.

Amber swished the skirt of her dress. "You like?"

"I love. You're beautiful. Stunning." Walking farther into the room, he wiped his eyes. "I can't believe my little sister is going to be a bride. Seeing you in the dress makes it real."

The raw emotion in his voice brought a softball-size lump to Jenna's throat, but she maintained her composure and took a picture of Ash and Amber hugging.

Amber's gaze returned to her reflection. No doubt she wanted another glimpse of herself in the dress. "The saleswoman said having my brother here wasn't normal, but I told her you were my best friend and I wanted you to see it first. Well, second, after Jenna."

"First." She lifted her camera. "I'm the

photographer. I don't count."

"Yes, you do," Ash said. "I'm happy to be here with both of you."

Jenna stood taller, a silly reaction, but something about him, in spite of everything, got to her. If Cupid was shooting arrows, his aim was getting better — and that worried her. Time to get out of here before she took a direct hit.

"Well, I've taken enough pictures." She took her camera apart as if defusing a ticking bomb, carefully, but quickly. "I'll get out of your way so you can have time alone."

Amber's smile disappeared. "Oh, I was hoping you could join us for lunch."

"I'm sorry," Jenna said. "But a client is picking up photos at noon."

Amber's brow arched. "Are you free later in the week? I'd like to show you the church and reception site so you can get ideas for group shots."

Jenna glanced at the calendar on her cell phone. "I have time on Thursday or Friday."

"Great, I'll text you." Amber's smile returned. "Thanks for taking the photographs."

"Least I can do for one of my brides." Jenna glanced at Ash, only to find him looking at her. A spurt of anticipation was her cue to leave. "I'll see myself out."

She escaped so quickly she hoped no one noticed. But she had to do something. Ash was already on her mind. She couldn't allow him back into her heart.

CHAPTER TEN

Ash stood outside Westside Christian Church on Thursday morning. Amber's wedding was a week from Saturday. He hoped the weather would improve.

The gray stone church seemed to disappear into the overcast sky. The weather resembled wintertime, but rainstorms were not unusual in June. The air had changed since he'd arrived at work earlier. He smelled rain. A downpour was on the way. The question was when. Sooner or later?

Maybe he should cancel.

He rolled his shoulders, trying to loosen tight muscles. Amber had gone Bridezilla. A slight exaggeration, but the wedding was affecting her brain and thought process. Otherwise she would have never asked him to meet Jenna where he'd broken up with her.

Big mistake. Then and now.

He should have said no to his sister. He

115

would have, except he wanted to see Jenna. Badly. A few minutes after church on Sunday or at the bridal salon earlier in the week hadn't been enough. He would have never agreed to brunch if he'd known she wasn't going. He'd skipped the singles group meeting since he knew she wouldn't be there.

Ash checked his cell phone. Almost time. Too late to back out. He tapped his toe, the knot in his stomach growing by the second.

"Hey." Lines creased Jenna's forehead. "Where are Amber and Toby?"

"Neither could make it. They asked me to show you around."

"Oh."

The one word didn't tell Ash much. The tight lines around the corners of her mouth did. She wasn't happy with the change of plans. He didn't blame her.

"Don't you have to work?" she asked.

"I put in enough hours that my boss doesn't mind if I take a morning off. Ready?"

She nodded.

Ash opened the door to the church. "Westside hasn't changed much."

He expected Jenna to show some emotion stepping inside.

She entered without hesitation, then pulled out a lighting sensor and her camera.

116

"I need to take readings."

He sat in a pew. Better than following her around like Peaches the puppy, even if he wanted to do that. "I'll wait here."

Jenna walked up the center aisle the way she had at their rehearsal. Except he wasn't waiting for her at the front with his heart lodged in his throat.

She measured the lighting and took pictures, then headed down the far side. She climbed the stairs to the balcony used for overflow seating.

"Stand in front of the altar, please," she called down.

He did. Memories of the time when he'd stood here with Jenna by his side hit like a fastball to a batter's helmet. The disintegration of his political aspirations had eaten away at him and made him nauseous. He'd known he couldn't go through with the wedding. He'd needed to take action, place blame, save face.

So he'd broken up with Jenna, then and there, not privately, but publicly, in front of family and friends. What had he been thinking? Gossip had spread like a wildfire. Not about him — everyone had taken his side — but about Jenna.

"Move a foot to your right," she instructed from above.

He did. "How's this?"

"Perfect. Stay there."

A minute later, she walked up the aisle. She aimed the lens at him. "Smile."

"Why do you want my picture?"

"To test the lighting. You could be a groom in your dark suit and tie."

He glanced down at himself. "Work clothes."

"Well, I can Photoshop in a bride and make this look like a real wedding." Her playful tone made him wonder if she'd put the past behind her. "Do you have a request for who she should be?"

You.

His heart slammed against his chest. The answer was so clear he thought he'd spoken the word aloud. She didn't appear to have heard him, so maybe he hadn't. A good thing.

Forget being friends. All this time he still wanted her. Only her.

He wanted Jenna to be his bride. Was it too late for a second chance?

Ash had his family, a great job, money, and his health. God had been good to him. Was it okay to ask for more . . . for Jenna?

"I've got what I need here." She lowered her camera. "Where to next?"

Ash cleared his dry throat. "The country club."

Half an hour later, he walked the grounds with Jenna. The darkening skies overshadowed the manicured lawns, trimmed shrubs, and tall trees.

She took a picture, then wrote in a small spiral pad.

"Any ideas?" he asked.

"A few."

"Dinosaurs?"

"Being chased by a T. rex is fun, but overdone. So is having groomsmen as superheroes beneath their tuxes. I'm trying to think fresh. Maybe something *Star Wars*-related with the upcoming new movie release or flying sharks. That's the beauty of Photoshop. Lots of options."

"I can't wait to see what you come up with."

"Me too."

She pointed to her left. "The gazebo will be a nice spot for photos."

"At night they turn on miniature white lights."

"That must be lovely." She took a picture of the gazebo. "It's pretty enough in the daylight."

"Not with the gray skies."

"The weather is perfect for photographs.

No shadows or backlighting. Nice contrast between the green grass and white wood." She snapped more pictures. "If you want constant sun, move to Arizona."

The clouds opened up. Big, fat raindrops fell.

Jenna covered her camera with her shirt and dashed to the gazebo. He followed.

The roof protected them from the downpour, but they were already wet. Water dripped from her ponytail. She dried her camera with the underside of her shirt.

He shook water from his hair. A good thing he'd ditched his suit jacket after visiting the church. His shirt would dry faster.

Rain pelted the roof, coming down harder. Thunder sounded. Jenna shivered.

"Cold?"

"Wet. I'll dry." Jenna wore a camera strap across her body. She checked the display. "But I don't think we're going anywhere for a while."

He didn't mind spending more time with her. "Is your camera okay?"

"Yes, thanks for asking." She stepped toward him and raised his tie. "This didn't fare as well."

Water splotches darkened the plum fabric. "The puppy drool dried. Rain will too."

"This is your fault for mentioning the gray

skies." Jenna smiled.

"You brought up Arizona."

Another clap of thunder sounded. She stepped closer to him. "We're both to blame."

He placed his hand on her shoulder and gave a reassuring squeeze. "We're safe here."

Jenna hadn't let go of his tie. She nodded.

"You'd rather be inside."

She nodded.

"You don't like storms."

"Hate them."

He hadn't known that. "Why?"

She stared at the wood floor.

"Tell me, please."

"One time, Colton and I were left alone during a thunderstorm. Driving rain. High winds. The electricity went out. A tree branch hit the house. Everything shook. A window broke. Scary when you're a little kid."

"Or a big one." Ash raised her chin with his fingertip. "Jenna . . ."

Her eyes were bright and warm. So beautiful.

His heartbeat rivaled the rumble of thunder.

She parted her lips.

An invitation? Ash needed to find out. He lowered his head.

She met him halfway and kissed him.

Warm and sweet. Jenna's kiss took him to the place he'd forgotten — home. He wrapped his arms around her. She went eagerly toward him, as if they hadn't been apart for two minutes, let alone the past two years. She fit against him perfectly. Her hands moved up his neck, and she wove her fingers in his hair. He soaked up the taste and feel of her as if he might not get this chance again.

Ash had missed this, but more importantly, he'd missed her. He wanted Jenna in his life. Today, tomorrow, always.

The way she kissed back suggested she might feel the same way. *Thank you, God.* Maybe Ash hadn't messed up completely. But he couldn't afford to make any mistakes.

Not a second time.

He wanted to get closer but drew the kiss to an end.

Her eyes were wide, her face flushed, and her lips swollen. Beautiful, but Jenna's true beauty came from the inside.

She blinked. "What —"

Ash placed his finger against her lips. "Shhh."

"We kissed."

She was adorable. "Yes, we did."

"But we're not a couple."

"Not yet."

Worry filled her eyes. "Ash . . ."

"This is unexpected." But welcome. "The rain isn't letting up, so let's figure out what's going on and what we want to do about it."

Jenna started to speak, then stopped. "Okay."

That was more than he'd hoped to hear. He'd expected a no. Hope surged. There must have been a reason he hadn't thrown away her wedding gift. He fought the urge to kiss her again. He had to be patient, careful. This time things would work out between them. He was positive.

Sitting on the floor of the gazebo, sheets of water falling from the sky, Jenna leaned back on her hands to keep from touching her mouth. Her lips tingled. Her body missed Ash's warmth. And worse, she wanted another kiss.

Crazy, or a smart way to forget about the storm? She couldn't decide.

No doubt crazy.

The rain wasn't letting up. Lightning streaked the sky. Thunder boomed. She inched closer to Ash.

Fear. Not attraction. At least that was what she told herself.

"So what did you want to talk about?" Jenna asked.

"Us."

"O-kay." But she wasn't. Her fingernails dug into the narrow space between the floorboards. She crossed her legs and raised her chin. Maybe she would look more confident than she felt.

Ash took a breath, then exhaled slowly.

Nerve endings stood at attention. Too bad they weren't soldiers who could protect her. Well, her heart. She worried nothing could now.

"I've been doing a lot of thinking. I realize I messed up long before I didn't believe you." Regret dripped from his words like the water running down the gazebo's support beams. "When we met, I started dating you for the right reasons, but everything got mixed up with the campaign."

That wasn't what she'd thought he was going to say. "The campaign?"

"Yeah." He scrubbed his face with his hand as if trying to wipe off dirt. "Running for office took over my life. Everything I did was questioned to the minute detail. From what I wore to who I dated."

"You mean me."

He nodded.

She knew where this was going now. "I

124

was a liability."

"No, you were an asset."

Jenna drew back. "Your father —"

"Your working-class background was a boon to the polls. Voters related to you in a way they couldn't with my family."

Jenna appreciated his honesty, though his words stung. "Who would have ever thought I could be considered a trophy wife?"

He gave a half-hearted laugh.

Good, she thought. They needed to keep their senses of humor.

Ash drew imaginary circles on the wood. "Seeing you again made me realize the glossy election flier with the photo of the perfect-together engaged couple was no more real than two people who had only dated a few months finding themselves pushed to settle down before the primary election. I'm . . . sorry."

"Me too." Jenna rubbed her thumb over her fingertips. She didn't look Ash in the eyes. He wasn't the only guilty party. "The whole reason I attended your church's singles group was to make contacts in another part of town. I wasn't looking for a boyfriend, but a higher-end clientele. When we started dating, my business took off with new customers. The additional income made life easier for once. Only everything blew up after you called off the wedding. My new clients disappeared. I had nothing. I realized I'd made your life, your friends, mine. I had no connections with anyone outside of my family. My faith was so weak."

"That's not true. I've seen you working with the youth."

"Before, when I was with you, I wasn't like the way I am now." Admitting the truth was almost painful, but a weight lifted off her shoulders. Her heart felt lighter. "You were my catalyst for change. For finding Pastor Dan and his church. For falling in love with God. I can't believe I'm telling you this, but being dumped at the altar was the best thing that ever happened to me."

He smiled close-mouthed, a thoughtful gleam in his gaze. "At least something good came of that."

"Lots of good." She hoped he heard the sincerity behind her words. "We just had the wrong — misguided — intentions."

"If I could go back . . ."

"It's okay." Lightning flashed, followed immediately by a roar of thunder. She rubbed her arms. Focused on Ash. "You mentioned being friends. That's one step we skipped the first time."

"Does that mean there's going to be a second time?"

Jenna's chest seized, the beat of her heart seeming to stop. She knew how she wanted to answer. Did she dare?

He held her hand. Tingles exploded from the point of contact.

"Are you willing to give us a second chance? Be friends with the possibility of more? That's what I want."

No air remained in her lungs. She drew in a short breath so she could answer. "I want to believe things could be different."

"They will be. I promise." He leaned toward her. "I know I've apologized, but I want you to know I've changed. I regret what I did, and I'll never do it again."

Those were the words Jenna needed to hear. Peace settled over her. A smile tugged at the corners of her mouth.

"What do you say?" he asked.

Hope filled her heart. This time would be different. "I'm up for a second chance."

Taking a second chance put a permanent smile on Jenna's face. Dinners, a movie, texts every day, a video chat before saying good night. She couldn't have asked for a better start to her and Ash's friendship.

Watching a DVD together last night had reaffirmed what Jenna knew in her heart — she wanted Ash to be a part of her life again.

As a friend . . . as more.

But something stood in the way. The wedding dress hanging in her closet had to go.

Jenna had told Ash not to look back. Her turn. She didn't need a reminder of the past. Not when she wanted to live in the present and look forward to the future. And she knew exactly who to call to take the dress off her hands.

An hour later, Kerri arrived alone. "Are you sure about this?"

"Positive." Jenna had never been more certain. "Hanging onto the wedding gown makes no sense. If you don't like the dress, that's okay, but I thought since you were looking for one I'd offer it to you."

"I'm honored. Shocked, really."

"We're about the same height, but you're thinner so you'll need alterations done. Come on." Jenna had hung the dress in the bedroom closet. She removed the gown from the cover. "Here you go."

Kerri gasped. She covered her mouth with her hands. "What a gorgeous dress."

"Try it on."

She reached for the dress with a hesitant hand. "I could never afford —"

"Just see if you like the gown." Jenna headed out of the bedroom. "I'll wait in the hallway. Let me know if you need anything."

Several minutes later, Kerri called Jenna into the bedroom. "What do you think?"

"Oh, my. Gorgeous." A lump burned in Jenna's throat. Tears stung her eyes. Seeing Kerri wearing the wedding gown felt oh-so-right. "The dress looks better on you than me."

Kerri wiped her eyes. "It's perfect, but —"

"The dress is yours." The words tumbled out of Jenna's mouth without regret. Full of relief. "My gift to you."

Kerri's eyes widened to the size of half-dollars. "Don't even kid."

"I'm not." Jenna grinned at her friend's shocked expression. "Take the dress. The number of the woman who did my alterations is on the bag. She can take in the waist and bodice."

Tears streamed down Kerri's face. Happy ones, based on her smile. "Thank you. This is so much more than I imagined. An answer to my prayers."

"Mine too." A weight lifted off Jenna's shoulders. Nothing held her back now. "I can't wait to see how the dress looks in photographs."

Kerri wiped her face with the back of her hand. "I'd better be careful. I don't want to cry all over the lovely lace."

Jenna didn't tell the bride-to-be that she

had cried on what would have been her wedding day. Only the tears hadn't been joyful ones like today.

"Trust me. A few tears won't hurt the dress."

After Kerri left with the wedding dress, Jenna danced around her house until she reached her bedroom. She stared at the empty spot in her closet where the gown used to hang and giggled like a schoolgirl.

The past was behind her. Finally. She thought she'd moved on, but she hadn't. Not really. Now . . .

She touched the gold cross she wore around her neck, a birthday present from Pastor Dan and Trish.

Thank you.

Two words could never give back what she'd been given, but the words were all she had.

The doorbell rang.

Ash? They were planning to have dinner.

Jenna walked with a bounce to her step. Full of anticipation, she opened the front door. Not Ash. "Judge Vance?"

"Hello, Jenna." He wore a dark suit with a blue shirt and tie. The wrinkles on his face had deepened, and his hair was whiter. "May I come in?"

"Please do." She motioned him inside. "Would you like something to drink? Coffee or tea?"

"This isn't a social call."

Her muscles tied into knots tighter than the ones she'd learned rock climbing. "I don't understand."

"I'll make this brief." He removed a white envelope from his suit jacket's pocket. "Inside is a check. It's yours if you agree not to photograph Amber's wedding."

What? Jenna stared at him. "The wedding is next weekend. We have a contract."

"Contracts can be broken." Judge Vance sounded more like an ambulance-chasing lawyer than a respected judge. "Say you're sick or your brother has been injured and you need to fly to him."

"I can't lie. I won't." She couldn't believe this. "Finding a last-minute photographer would be too stressful for Amber and Toby."

"I have a backup on retainer." Judge Vance handed Jenna the envelope. "Look inside."

"Judge —"

"Go on."

She raised the flap and took a peek. A check made out to her. She counted the zeroes. Ten thousand dollars. She gasped. Nearly dropped the envelope.

"A lot of money. All you have to do is not

show up at Amber's wedding and stop seeing Ash."

"Ash?" Jenna's stomach felt as if it were going through the washer's spin cycle and she might throw up. "This has nothing to do with Amber's wedding."

"No, it doesn't." Judge Vance didn't sound guilty or remorseful. "I respect you, Jenna. You've done well for someone from such . . . humble beginnings. But Ash needs more, a woman with a similar background. A woman who can handle the demands of being the spouse of a high-profile attorney and political candidate."

"Ash isn't interested in running for office."

"He'll change his mind."

"That's his decision. As is who he dates."

The judge's face reddened. "I'm not letting my son throw his life away on a woman like his mother. One who will never adjust to the better lifestyle Ash would provide. You'll end up miserable and hating each other."

Jenna handed back the check. "I don't want your money. I'm not your ex-wife. Your concerns are misguided. I'm going to photograph Amber and Toby's wedding. And I have no idea what will happen with Ash, but he makes me happy, and I believe he'd say the same thing about me. I'm hopeful things will work out differently this time."

The judge's nostrils flared. "You're making a big mistake. I can make your life difficult."

"I'm sure you can." Jenna squared her shoulders, not about to be intimidated. Once she might have cowered, taken the money, and walked away without a word. No longer. She wasn't alone. She didn't have to handle this by herself. She touched her cross around her neck. "But I'm not afraid."

What was Jenna doing at the law office? Ash waited by his doorway. They'd planned to have dinner tonight, but he wasn't going to complain about an afternoon visit.

Jenna turned the corner, saw him, smiled. "I could use a hug."

"You came to the right place." He wrapped his arms around her, brushed his lips over hair. She smelled like grapefruit. So nice. "What's up?"

"We need to talk in private."

He kissed her cheek, led her into his office, and closed the door. "Tell me what's going on."

She took a breath. "Your father stopped by my house."

"That's great."

"Not really." She dragged her upper teeth over her lower lip. "He offered me ten thousand dollars if I wouldn't photograph Amber's wedding and if I stopped seeing you."

"That's . . . impossible." Ash tried to make sense of what Jenna was saying. Tried and failed. "You must have misunderstood his intentions."

"I heard him quite clearly." Her voice trembled. "He had a white envelope. Inside was a check made out to me for ten thousand dollars. He suggested reasons I could use to cancel on your sister. He wanted me to lie."

"I'm sorry, but there's been some kind of mistake."

"No mistake. He doesn't want us dating. Said I'm too much like your mom. He threatened to make my life difficult if I didn't do as he asked."

Ash stiffened. "My father is a respected judge. He's on the church's financial council. He would never pay off anyone, let alone threaten them."

Jenna's mouth gaped. "You don't believe me."

"I believe you talked with my dad, but there has to be some sort of misinterpretation of what he meant."

She covered her face with her hands. "You're doing it again."

Ash touched her shoulder, only to have her jerk away from his touch. "What?"

"Not trusting me."

"I trust you."

"Then why don't you believe what I say happened?"

"My father isn't like that."

Raw hurt flashed in her eyes. Ash took two steps back.

"You said things would be different. Promised . . ." Her lower lip quivered. "I thought you'd changed."

"I have."

"You don't believe me. Again."

Each word punched his gut. "That's not true. I'll speak with my father. Find out what happened."

"You still need proof?"

Ash hated how disappointed she sounded. He wanted to fix this.

Jenna headed to the door. Her pace accelerated with each step.

"Wait. Where are you going?" he asked.

"Home." Her hard look froze his heart. "I'll photograph Amber and Toby's wedding per our contract, but please don't contact me again."

CHAPTER ELEVEN

That night, Jenna sat next to Sam on her living room couch. She tried concentrating on the movie playing, but couldn't. Two pints of ice cream, two spoons, and a box of tissues — all but the spoons courtesy of Sam — sat on the coffee table.

Goosebumps covered her skin. She was cold down to her bones, freezing though a fleece throw covered her. "I don't know if I should cry or scream."

Sam grabbed another scoop of double-chocolate chip. "Have more ice cream. That's step number one. Then we'll egg his house."

"The judge would have us arrested."

"Only if the judge found out. I'll make sure we don't get caught."

"I'd probably start crying and be no fun. Sorry."

"Just a thought."

Her heart hurt, a familiar aching tightness. She wiped her tired, swollen eyes. "I can't believe I let Ash do this again. I thought I was being smarter this time, more careful. I should have known he hadn't changed."

"Don't be so hard on yourself." Sam put his arm around her the way Colton would do if he were here. "You had feelings for the guy. You were hoping for the best."

"Hoping and praying. I wanted things to work."

"Did you fall in love with him again?"

Had she? "I don't know. It's only been a couple weeks."

"Doesn't take long."

"Speaking from experience?" Jenna asked.

Sam focused on the ice cream. "We're talking about you."

"I don't know what or how I feel about Ash, only that I want the hurting to stop. I also feel like I should pray for him. Is that weird?"

"Not at all."

She closed her eyes. *Please help Ash. Help him find his way like you helped me.*

"Feel better?" Sam asked.

"A little." She stared at her chocolate mint chip. "I don't know how I'm going to get through the rehearsal dinner and wedding."

"I'll come along as your assistant," Sam offered.

"You'd do that?"

He mussed her hair. "Of course. You're one of my best friends. Though I only know how to take pictures with my phone."

She laughed.

"Wait. Is that a smile I see?" He grinned. "Yes, that's definitely a smile. Progress. This calls for more ice cream."

"I don't think I could eat another bite."

Sam winked. "More for me, then."

"Help yourself." Jenna had a feeling food would be the last thing on her mind until she survived the next two days. But she'd signed a contract and would be professional dealing with the Vance family. Even if her heart was broken and all she wanted to do was cry.

After the rehearsal dinner, Ash unlocked the door to the house where he and Amber had grown up. His annoyance level had reached an all-time high. Jenna had barely said a word tonight except to give instructions, and she'd kept her face hidden with the camera.

Talk about awkward.

But what was he supposed to do? His father had denied her accusations, agreeing she'd misconstrued the intent of his visit. She'd cut off all communication. Ignored Ash's texts and calls. Frustrating. Maybe he could speak to her tomorrow.

"The rehearsal went well." His father handed over his jacket to be hung. "Let's hope the wedding goes as smoothly."

"It should." Ash headed to the closet. "The wedding coordinator and DJ are top-notch. They'll keep things on schedule."

"That photographer has nerve showing up tonight," his dad said.

"You mean Jenna."

"One step above trailer trash. Like your mother."

"What are you talking about? Mom wasn't like that." Ash had never heard his father badmouth his mother. She had been pretty and kind and made the best cookies in the world. But she'd cried a lot and hadn't left the house much. His mom never would have tackled a ropes course or half the things Jenna did. "And Mom and Jenna are nothing alike."

"Maybe not now, but Jenna will turn into a woman just like your mother in a few short years. I know you're upset over what happened, but this might turn out for the best."

"I miss Jenna."

"I'm sorry you're hurting. But you'll feel better eventually."

Ash wasn't so sure. Nothing provided relief. If he'd felt dissatisfied before Jenna reentered his life, he was completely on edge and unhappy now.

He opened the closet door and hung up his dad's jacket. Something crinkled. He checked the inside pocket. A white envelope.

He had a white envelope. Inside was a check made out to me for ten thousand dollars.

Warning bells sounded. Ash removed the envelope. The flap was unsealed. He felt as if he was trespassing, but he looked inside and saw a check for ten thousand dollars made out to Jenna.

No. No. No.

Emotion clogged Ash's throat. His vision blurred. He almost lost his balance.

Jenna had been telling the truth. But he hadn't believed her. He'd made excuses for his father. Trusted his dad. But now that Ash had proof . . .

He shouldn't have needed proof.

His lack of faith in her had ruined everything again. But he wouldn't wait two years to right the wrong. Ash carried the envelope to his father. "Dad, we need to talk."

CHAPTER TWELVE

Jenna took pictures of Amber and her bridesmaids preparing for the wedding ceremony. The smells of hair spray and perfume filled the dressing room. Music played from an iPod docking station. The strawberry-blonde flower girl danced bare-foot.

The wedding coordinator, a twentysomething woman named Ruby, flitted in and out of the room on her three-inch heels. She clapped. "Only an hour to go."

Jenna glanced out a window. The sunny blue sky matched the festive atmosphere inside. Rain and gray clouds would fit her mood better. But this wasn't the time to throw herself a pity party. Jenna knew He would see her through. Time to be the photographer that the bride and groom expected her to be.

Picture Perfect Photography.

She would give Amber and Toby perfect

images of their love on this special day and creative, fun ones too. If a flying shark happened to be eating the brother of the bride . . .

Jenna fiddled with the camera settings, pasted on a smile, and faced the women preening in mirrors. She used the reflections to show off their dress backs and faces at the same time. See . . . she had this.

Amber wore her flowing white fairy-tale princess dress. The bridesmaids dressed in lavender cocktail dresses.

Two women took pictures of each other. That gave Jenna an idea. "I want everyone to take a selfie, then give me your phones with the picture on them."

The women did.

Using Amber's wedding dress train as a backdrop, Jenna arranged the phones, then took photos of the selfies. Satisfied with the results, she handed back the phones. "Thanks."

A knock sounded.

Amber hurried toward the bathroom in a swish of white, luxurious fabric. "That better not be Toby."

The maid of honor, a pretty blonde named Elizabeth, answered the door. "Ash. Mr. Vance. What are you doing here? Your knock sent Amber into hiding."

"Can we speak with Jenna out in the hallway?" Ash asked.

Jenna wanted to ignore the request, but Ash was paying her. No sense causing a scene. She made her way out. "Be right back, ladies."

In the hallway, Ash stood next to his father. Their black tuxedos highlighted their similar heights and different accessory colors. His father wore black. Ash had on the same lavender vest and tie as the other groomsmen.

Handsome, yes, but looks would never make up for Ash's lack of trust and faith in her. Nothing could.

"What's up?" She tried sounding nonchalant when all she wanted to do was bolt. A runaway bride was one thing. She'd never heard of a vanishing wedding photographer. Jilting a couple at the altar would not be good for business.

Ash looked at his father.

"I owe you an apology." Judge Vance's tone was contrite. "I should have let my son decide what he wants, not try to make those decisions for him. I've treated you unfairly twice. First when I told Amber I'd buy her a new car if she stopped your wedding."

That had been Amber's reason? A car? No wonder she hadn't wanted to tell anyone.

The revelation left Jenna speechless.

"And the other day," the judge continued. "I was trying to protect my son. His mother comes from a background similar to yours. I saw history repeating itself and stepped in to stop him from being hurt. I hope you'll see it in your heart to forgive me someday."

The judge walked away. His shoulders hunched.

She watched him go, feeling sad. "Your father loves you very much."

Ash nodded. "He was trying to protect me the best way he knew how. Not that his reason excuses his actions."

Jenna could see the situation more clearly now. "He didn't want you to suffer the same pain he did, but his methods were wrong."

"I was wrong. I've said 'I'm sorry' so many times you must not believe me."

"Words are easy to say."

Ash brushed his hand through his hair. "I mean them. I let pride get in the way of seeing the truth. Believing my father wasn't capable of . . . well, everything he's done to you."

"Don't worry about me." She wasn't sure where the words came from, but she believed them with her whole heart. "You need to forgive your father and yourself."

"What about us?" Ash asked. "We tried

starting over, but maybe if we tried again . . . if you can forgive me . . . ?"

"I accept your apology, but it's hard to forget what you've done when you keep doing it." Her throat clogged. She swallowed, but that didn't help. "I care about you, Ash. I always have. But you promised. You claimed you wouldn't do the same thing again. But you did. You wouldn't believe what I said until you had proof. I need to know the man I'm with trusts me. That he'll be on my side, no matter what."

"Jenna —"

"Not now." She raised her hands, palms facing him. "You're paying me to take pictures of your sister's wedding. I can't do that out here."

"Later, then." The hope in his voice matched the sentiment in his gaze.

"Maybe." That was all Jenna could give him. "It's going to be a long day."

Hours later, Ash loosened his tie. The four-tiered cake had been cut and served. The tossed bouquet had hit Jenna on the forehead. One bandage later, she was back taking pictures. Bridesmaids had stuck their shoes under a table and walked barefoot.

He looked at the smiling guests and crowded dance floor.

A perfect wedding. Exactly what Amber had wanted. He couldn't be happier for his sister and Toby, now Mr. and Mrs. Matthews.

Funny how Amber was married while Ash was still single. And at this rate would remain so. A vise tightened around his heart. He had only himself to blame.

I had no connections with anyone outside of my family. My faith was so weak. Before, when I was with you, I wasn't like the way I am now.

Jenna's words reverberated through his head. Made his heart hurt more. What she said described him.

You were my catalyst for change. For finding Pastor Dan and his church. For falling in love with God. I can't believe I'm telling you this, but being dumped at the altar was the best thing that ever happened to me.

Dissatisfaction with his life, with everything, made Ash itch. He wanted what Jenna had found — unwavering faith and a place to belong. Was it too late to change?

Amber touched his shoulder, then hugged him, not the half-armed air hug she was famous for, but an honest-to-goodness not-letting-go hug like they'd shared when she was little. "Isn't today wonderful?"

He let go of her. "The best."

146

"Thanks for your help." She rose up on her tiptoes and kissed his cheek. "I appreciate everything you've done, given what a mess I made of you and Jenna."

"I would have lost her on my own. I just did."

"Try, try again."

"What happened belongs in the past," he said.

"No, it doesn't. You make a cute couple. That's why I've been trying to get you to spend more time together."

"The dinner at the café and wedding site tour."

"I was hoping for lunch after the bridal salon visit, but that didn't work out." Amber beamed. "Still rather brilliant with shades of Jane Austen's Emma, don't you think?"

"You're not a matchmaker. Don't do it again."

"You didn't seem to mind at the time."

"I do now." Jenna's present burned a hole in his pocket. She might not want it, but he needed to give her the box. Maybe she could see the gift as a thank-you, not a good-bye.

"Change your mind," his sister suggested. "We'll figure out a plan."

Amber was so young and in love. He was happy for her, but she didn't understand how complicated things were with Jenna. "Go find your husband. The two of you should be leaving soon."

"I will, but I have to say something first. Since Jenna came back into your life, you've been the happiest I've ever seen you. I think there's a correlation between her and your good mood."

"Maybe," Ash said. "Or maybe not."

Amber stuck out her tongue at him. "I'm trying to help. I still feel awful for what I did."

"Don't. This is nobody's fault but mine. Jenna and I were in no position to make a marriage work two years ago. Not the way God intended." He kissed Amber's forehead. "Go find Toby so you can start your honeymoon."

She walked away. Her gown swooshed with each step. His little sister was a married woman, a wife.

Ash should get used to being a confirmed bachelor. The only woman he wanted didn't want him.

He saw Jenna standing on the other side of the room and joined her. "Toby was correct. You are the right photographer for this wedding."

Jenna fiddled with her camera. "Thanks."

Ash wanted so much more than her gratitude. He wanted a second — make that third — chance. "Jenna —"

"I'll e-mail a link when the proofs are ready." Her tone was polite, measured. "Amber and Toby are getting ready to leave. I need to photograph their exit."

Always the professional. Ash wouldn't stand in her way. "Go."

What was he going to say, anyway? *I'm sorry? Forgive me again?* He hadn't a clue what to do. But maybe God would know. Ash closed his eyes, and for the first time in a long while he prayed, a heartfelt prayer of thanksgiving and gratitude for all he had, and a petition for what he didn't have. But he realized that wasn't right, and instead he prayed that God's will be done for him, for his family, and for Jenna.

The sun dipped below the horizon. White lights twinkled in the darkness, illuminating trees and the gazebo at the Sweetwater Country Club. Jenna stood off to the side where she had a panoramic view of the bride and groom's exit.

A lively song played over the speakers. Amber and Toby danced their way to a waiting limousine. Laughing guests blew bubbles at the happy couple.

Jenna captured the departure with more

pictures than she could count. Her job was finished, and she couldn't be happier with the photographs she'd taken or more relieved to know she could finally go home. She'd negotiated a tight-rope of emotions today. Each time she saw Ash she thought she might fall, but she hadn't.

Thank you, Lord.

In the hallway outside the ballroom, Jenna packed up her gear, everything from lighting to the photo booth props she'd set out during the reception.

Guests exited the ballroom with their favors — white boxes containing lavender-infused jam, lavender-infused honey, and a lavender satchel. All three items were made by Toby's mother, a woman who reminded Jenna of her own mom.

She wanted to hear a friendly voice, but with the three-hour time difference she'd have to wait until tomorrow. Maybe she could still catch Colton.

"Long day."

Ash. The one voice Jenna didn't want to hear. Friendly, yes, but the sound made her nerve endings twitch. She placed the lens in its protective case. "Weddings usually are."

"I see why your parents suggested eloping."

Her fingers trembled. She tightened her

grip on the lens case. She didn't want to look at him. "Makes sense for certain situations, but if every couple eloped I'd be out of a job."

He handed her a small, square, gold box. "This is for you."

"You're paying me. You didn't have to buy a gift too."

"Open it."

His firm tone surprised her. She lifted off the top, then removed a small piece of white padding. A silver charm — a frame similar to the ones she used with her photo booth props — was inside.

His thoughtfulness tugged at her heart. "So pretty. Thanks."

"The back is engraved."

She looked up at him, noticed his intense gaze. "You shouldn't have gone to so much trouble. I'm just doing my job."

"I wanted you to have this."

She flipped over the frame. Words were etched into the sides: *Jenna and Ashton* on the top, *June 22, 2013,* on the right side, *A Picture Perfect Love* on the bottom, and *1 Cor. 13:4–7* on the left side.

She reread the date. Her mouth opened, but no sound came out. She tried again. "That was going to be our wedding date."

"This was your wedding present."

"You kept it?"

"Every time I thought about throwing away the box, I couldn't. I want you to have it. To see that even if I wasn't completely solid in my intentions, I did care two years ago. I still care about you."

Air rushed out of her lungs. Nerve endings tingled. She prayed for strength.

"A picture perfect love says it all," he continued. "That's what I thought we had the first time around, but I was wrong. The only perfect things are the photographs you take and hang on your studio walls, but whether the poses are orchestrated or candid, they aren't real. Real love can be messy. Mistakes are made. But no matter what, the love remains. As His does with us. Mine has with you."

His sincerity brought tears to her eyes. "Ash . . ."

He held her hand. "You want someone to believe in you and trust you. I've failed you twice when it counted most. Pride blinded me to the truth. But that doesn't change the love I feel for you. It's far from perfect, like me, but if you'll give me another chance, I'm committed to you and a future together. What we have is special. I won't let my pride or my father or anything else get in the way. I will stand by you, no matter what. You're the woman I want next to me at the altar because I can't imagine life without you in it."

Jenna wanted to believe. She forced herself to breathe.

He continued, "Whether you forgive me or not, keep this frame to remind you that love is the most important thing. I realize that, thanks to you. Real love, mind you, not the glossy wedding-day love. You deserve unconditional love. An everlasting love, not one that just looks good in a frame."

Her trembling hand clutched the charm against her heart. "Thank you for the present and your words. You made mistakes, but so did I. Seems like both our hearts needed to refocus. I may have forgiven you, but it wasn't sincere. I hadn't forgotten what happened. I kept dwelling on what could go wrong. But I'm letting all that go. God has humbled me with your gift. I forgive you. I hope you forgive me."

"Always." Ash's gaze locked on hers. "I love you, Jenna. Truly love you. That much I have learned from all of this."

Joy overflowed from her heart. "I love you."

He lowered his mouth to hers. She gave in to the kiss, feeling as if she'd come home. The gentle kiss spoke of possibilities and the future.

Their future.

She backed away. "We have to go slow. Do it right."

"I agree. We have the rest of our lives to be together. Let's build a solid foundation that will last for the next fifty or sixty years."

Jenna sighed. "I like the sound of that."

"Me too. And I know what should come first." He pulled out his cell phone and held it out in front of them. "Smile."

"A selfie?"

"You'll see." The phone clicked, capturing the photo. He typed on his screen.

She peered over his shoulder, but he wouldn't let her see. "What are you doing?"

"Just a minute." He showed her his phone. "What do you think?"

He'd uploaded the selfie to a social media account with the following caption: *Back together again. This time for good.*

Love swelled inside Jenna. Her patience to see what God had planned had paid off. She brushed her lips across Ash's. "That's about as perfect as it gets."

ACKNOWLEDGMENTS

Thanks to my editor, Becky Monds, as well as Becky Philpott, Karli Jackson, and the rest of the team at HarperCollins Christian. I so appreciate this opportunity! I'm thrilled to be a part of the Year of Weddings series!

A special thanks to my line editor, Jamie Chavez, for the time you spent on this project and all the back-and-forth emails.

A shout-out to my agents Christina Hogrebe and Annelise Robey at Jane Rotrosen Agency for thinking of me when they heard about this project and making it happen. I cannot thank you enough for all that you do and have done for me over the years!

Thank you to my dear friend Terri Reed for your support, friendship, and prayers as we've traveled the road from unpublished to published authors and beyond. I hope you know what a blessing you are in my life.

Thanks to my sweet friend Kimberly Field

for reading this manuscript, offering encouragement and help when I needed it most. You're another one of my blessings, and I pray we can meet in person someday!

A high five to my Panera Write-In Group — Amy, Delle, Marilyn, Melania, and Peggy. Next to attending church on Sunday, meeting with you is the other thing I look forward to each week. Thanks for getting together so we can socialize and get words written too!

A big hug to my oldest daughter for helping me brainstorm my hero's first name by telling me the names of the guys in your favorite band.

And finally, lots of love to my readers. You're the best! I pray that God blesses each one of you the way you have blessed me.

DISCUSSION QUESTIONS

1. When unexpected events happen, like Jenna's cancelled wedding, people say that God has a plan, but Jenna didn't believe her friends. What would you have thought if you were in Jenna's situation? How accepting are you if God's plan differs from the path you're taking? Do you question God's plan?

2. Jenna admits to hitting rock bottom and turning away from God after Ash breaks up with her and leaves her facing a mountain of wedding debt. How has your faith been tested? Did you find yourself turning away from God? If so, how did you find your way back to your faith?

3. Ash didn't believe Jenna when she had nothing to do with posting his photo on Facebook. He publicly called her a liar. Do you think there was any more Jenna could have done to convince Ash she was telling the truth? Can you share a time

when you have been falsely accused of something? How did it make you feel?

4. Jenna eventually came to see the break-up with Ash as a blessing that made her stronger as a person and in her faith. Share an experience that was perceived at first to be a bad thing, but later turned out to be a blessing. How did you realize what happened was a blessing?

5. Jenna thought she'd forgiven Ash and moved on with her life, but seeing him again made her question if she had put the past behind her. As Christians, we're told to forgive. Can you share a time you had trouble forgiving someone? If so, do you know what was holding you back from forgiving them? How did you resolve the issue?

6. Ash believed his family instead of trusting his fiancée. Why do you think it was so hard for him to accept Jenna was telling the truth without proof? Based on the evidence Ash had, would you have believed Jenna was guilty? Why or why not?

7. Jenna was able to do the trust exercise with the people she didn't trust by putting her faith in God and letting go. Have you ever done a trust exercise like that? How does it make you feel when you give over all your trust to God?

8. After Jenna has forgiven Ash, their relationship is again tested when he doesn't believe she's telling the truth until he has proof. If you were Jenna, how would you feel? Do you think you could forgive someone a second time for falsely accusing you? Even if they apologize again when the truth comes out, would you give them a third chance? Why or why not?

ABOUT THE AUTHOR

Melissa McClone has always been a fan of fairy tales and "happily ever afters." She holds a degree in mechanical engineering from Stanford University but eventually decided to follow her dream and write full-time. She lives in Washington with her real-life hero husband, two daughters, indoor cats, and a forty-eight-pound Norwegian Elkhound who thinks she's a lap dog. She also loves to ski, rock climb, and read.

VISIT HER ONLINE AT
WWW.MELISSAMCCLONE.COM.
TWITTER: @MELISSAMCCLONE
FACEBOOK: MELISSA MCCLONE

■ ■ ■ ■

I HOPE YOU DANCE

ROBIN LEE HATCHER

■ ■ ■ ■

*To the One who causes His children to
take up their tambourines
and go forth to the dances of the
merrymakers.*
— JEREMIAH 31:4

CHAPTER ONE

Summers were made for weddings. Skye Foster had believed that for the past twenty years — ever since she was six and a guest at a distant cousin's wedding. This July she would have a small part to play in the wedding of Charity Anderson and Buck Malone. A wedding Skye knew would be the most beautiful and romantic ever held in Kings Meadow.

When she closed her eyes, she could imagine it perfectly. The couple, standing in the gazebo with pastor, bridesmaids, and groomsmen, repeating their vows in the golden glow of an Idaho summer morning. The bride in white satin and lace, and the groom in a coat and tails. White folding chairs set up in the park, filled with friends and family. Women dabbing their eyes with tissues. The cutting of the many-layered cake. The music. The dancing.

Ah, yes. As far as she was concerned, no

wedding was complete without dancing.

She imagined the band playing a romantic country waltz. She imagined herself stepping into the arms of a tall, lanky cowboy, feeling the warmth of his hand as it closed around hers. She imagined moving around the dance floor, the fluttering of her heart in time with their steps.

It was all so romantic.

Taking a deep breath, she tilted her head back and mentally tried to see the face of the cowboy who turned her around the floor with such expertise. But here, at last, her imagination failed her. In her daydream, there was nothing but shadows beneath the brim of his Stetson.

She released a sigh and opened her eyes again. It was hard to envision a romance when she didn't even have a boyfriend. At the rate she was going, she would never get to plan a wedding of her own. But that didn't stop her from wishing for it. Only now was not the time.

With another sigh, she set aside the latest issue of *Brides* magazine that had come in the mail, grabbed the keys to her truck, and left the house.

First stop on her agenda was the Clippity Do-Da Hair Salon. It was time for a trim. Her mother, Midge — the owner of the salon — would plead with Skye, as usual, to let her try something different. And Skye would, as usual, refuse her. Long and straight was her style. She liked it and wasn't about to change it.

Next up she had an appointment to meet the vet at the pasture where she kept her two horses, Snickers and Milky Way. Snickers had started limping a few days ago and didn't seem to be improving, even with rest and the use of liniment. Skye hoped it wasn't serious. The gelding was the best barrel-racing horse she'd ever owned — there'd been five over the years. He'd made her the queen of more than one rodeo by the time she turned twenty. Snickers had more heart than stamina these days, but that didn't matter to Skye. She loved him to pieces.

It took only minutes to drive to the east edge of town. On a Wednesday afternoon Skye was able to park on the street right in front of the salon. As she got out of the pickup, high-pitched voices called her name. She looked toward the corner and saw two teenage girls, books in their arms, apparently headed for the library. She knew them, of course, just as she knew almost everyone else in Kings Meadow. Krista and Sharon

Malone, daughters of the high school principal.

"Hey!" she called back with a wave of her hand.

The girls moved on out of sight, and Skye pushed open the door to the salon, a tiny bell ringing above her head. The main room — smelling of perm solution and fruity shampoo — was completely empty. No stylists. No customers.

Her mom looked out from the stockroom. "Skye! Is it that time already? Gracious. I thought I would have my inventory done before you got here."

"Where is everybody?"

"Slow day. Lori doesn't work most Wednesdays, and Becca finished with her last client an hour ago, so she went home. When I'm done with you, I'm doing the same thing." She took a cape from a drawer and snapped it in the air, draping it around Skye as soon as she was in the chair. "What are we doing today?"

"Just trim the ends and shape my bangs."

"How much off?" Her mom lifted a segment of hair.

Skye swallowed a smile, knowing what was about to come. "An inch. No more."

"Are you sure?" Her mom placed her fingers, like a pair of scissors, up a good six

170

inches from the ends. "Because I think if we —"

"I don't want short hair, Mom, and you *aren't* going to change my mind."

Her mom met her gaze in the mirror. "Don't you get tired of it always looking the same? You've had the same look since you were twelve, when you wouldn't let me braid it anymore."

"I haven't always had bangs."

Her mom groaned in frustration. "I give up."

Skye laughed. "I wish I believed that."

"Can I at least wash it for you?"

"I'm kinda in a hurry. I've got to meet Dr. Parry at the pasture. He's taking a look at Snickers's leg, and then I have to get home to shower and change and have a bite to eat before it's time for my adult class. I'm teaching them the two-step tonight."

"How many couples have you got coming?" Her mom picked up the scissors and began trimming away the split ends.

"Four couples. They've been a great group. I'm having a lot of fun with them." She drew in a deep breath. "And next week I begin giving private lessons to the Anderson-Malone wedding-party members."

"Already?" Her mom's eyes widened as

she met Skye's gaze in the mirror again.

"It's less than two months until the wedding. That's hardly any time at all."

"Seems like yesterday when you wondered if Buck Malone might be interested in you."

Skye almost shook her head, but remembered in time to stay still. "That was last summer. Almost a year. Besides, he'd already fallen hard for Charity, so I was way wrong."

"You never minded, did you?"

"Not even a little. And when you see Charity and Buck together, you know they were meant for each other."

Her mom gave her a smile of encouragement. "You'll meet somebody too. You're still young, honey. You've got lots of time."

Skye didn't say so, but she'd begun to feel her biological clock ticking. If she only wanted one or two kids, it wouldn't matter so much, but she had her heart set on a half dozen babies. Minimum. She'd always wanted to be part of a big family. Since her parents had chosen not to give her lots of siblings — only an older brother and sister — she intended to create that large family for herself. With the help of that still-elusive husband.

"Close your eyes," her mom said. As soon as Skye obeyed, her mom took the scissors to her bangs, leaving them long but giving them shape. *Snip. Snip. Snip.* "All right. You're done. Hardly worth the time of coming into the salon, far as I can tell."

Skye laughed. "You wouldn't want me cutting my own hair, would you?"

"Heaven forbid! Remember what you did when you were five?"

"Yeah, but like you said, I was *five.*" As soon as the cape was off, Skye stood and gave her mother a kiss on the cheek. "Love you, Mom."

"I love you, too, baby girl. I hope Snickers is all right."

"Thanks. I'll let you know."

She stepped outside a few moments later, intent on getting over to the pasture before the vet. So intent was she that she almost mowed down an unexpected passerby on the sidewalk.

"Whoa, there," a deep voice said. Strong hands gripped her upper arms and steadied her.

Skye looked up into the face of a stranger. He was rugged looking with a bit of mischief in his blue-green eyes and one of those I-haven't-shaved-for-a-few-days beards that she liked on cowboys. He wasn't movie-star handsome, but there was something about

173

his looks that made her heart behave erratically.

Who is this guy?

"Sorry, miss." Grant Nichols released his hold on the young woman's arms and took a step back. "Hope I didn't hurt you."

She shook her head, and her straight black hair waved across her narrow shoulders.

"Maybe you can help me. Is there a dance studio around here?"

Her eyes widened. Big, brown, doe-like eyes. "Yes." She pointed. "Around that corner and to the right."

"Thanks."

"But it's closed now."

He almost said a curse word but managed to swallow it. The BC Grant — the Before Christ version — had cursed all the time. Breaking himself of that habit had been tough. It was just one of the reasons he'd kept to himself most of the time since arriving in Kings Meadow. God had delivered him of other bad habits, but the impulse to swear had hung on for dear life for the past four years.

"Maybe I can help you," she added, watching him closely. "I'm the owner of the studio."

Every other thought fled. "You're Skye

174

Foster? Just the gal I'm supposed to see. I'm Grant Nichols. One of Buck Malone's groomsmen. He told me to talk to you about those lessons you're giving the wedding party."

"Oh. Of course. I recognize your name, but we've never actually met. Have we?"

"No, we haven't." *And I'm sure sorry about that.*

"Well, it's nice to meet you now. As for the lessons, they'll start next week. We'll meet every Tuesday night until the wedding."

"That's my first problem. I work on Tuesday nights. Buck thought you and I might be able to work out a different schedule for me."

"I suppose I could do that." She tipped her head slightly to one side. "But if that's your first problem, what's your second?"

"Miss Foster, I've got two left feet."

She laughed.

Man, what a smile. Perhaps he'd been too successful at keeping himself separate from the general population if her smile was what he'd been missing.

"I'm sure that's not true, Mr. Nichols. Anybody can learn to dance."

"Oh, it's true. Ask every girl who's ever had the misfortune to coax me onto a dance floor. They're probably still sporting bruises and broken toes, years later."

She shook her head again. Then she reached into the back pocket of her jeans and fished out a business card. "Listen, I have an appointment that I can't be late for. Call me at this number. If I'm not in, leave a message and I'll call you back. And don't worry. We'll find a time that will work, and I'll have you dancing like a pro by the wedding. I love a challenge."

He took the card and read it. *Skye Foster, Two-Step Dance Studio.*

"Please excuse me, Mr. Nichols —"

"Call me Grant."

"Okay, Grant. But I've gotta run. I'll talk to you soon."

She stepped around him and hurried to the silver Toyota Tacoma parked at the curb. She hopped into the cab with no problem, despite looking too petite to drive such a rig. The engine started, and Skye drove away.

Grant stood there for a few moments, feeling winded by the encounter. Then he grinned. He'd dreaded taking the lessons, and only his friendship with Buck had made him agree to it. But suddenly it didn't seem like a terrible idea after all. The weeks until

the wedding might turn out to be a whole
lot of fun.

CHAPTER TWO

Skye loved bridal showers almost as much as she loved weddings, and the best part about the shower taking place in half an hour was how surprised the bride would be. Charity Anderson hadn't a clue what was coming.

The two women sat at a table on the patio outside the Friendly Bean coffee shop, sipping lattes from Styrofoam cups. On this Saturday in mid-June it was sunny and breezy, inviting residents of the valley to be outdoors. Thus, all of the patio seating was taken. Which meant it was difficult to have a private conversation. Other customers kept coming over to their table to say hello and to give their best wishes to Charity. As if none of them had said it to her before today.

When the latest well-wishers Mayor Ollie Abbott and his wife walked away, Skye repeated the question she'd asked before they'd been interrupted. "So when you get back from your honeymoon, where are you going to live?"

"In Kings Meadow until November. Of course, Buck will be gone a lot in August and September, but it'll be nice for me, being right next door to Mom and Dad. Then in November we'll go down to Boise to stay until early spring." Charity shrugged. "I'm not sure how long we'll do it that way. We may decide to move back to Kings Meadow full time. Did I tell you we converted the back part of the garage of my house in Boise into a workshop for Buck? Demand for his custom-made saddles has really gone up in the last year."

"I'm not surprised," Skye said. "His craftsmanship is amazing. I don't think I could even afford one of his saddles. Good thing I'm not competing this year, or I'd be tempted to go into debt to get one." She made a show of checking her watch. "Do we have time to run over to my place for a minute before we need to be at Sara's?"

Charity nodded. "Sure."

"Great." Skye drank the last of her beverage before standing. "And thanks for coming over here with me. I need to buy a new coffeemaker. Mine's disgusting. Trust me. The coffee is *so* much better here than at my place."

They tossed their empty cups into a nearby receptacle and then crossed the street to where Charity had parked her SUV. As Skye got in on the passenger's side of the Lexus, she wondered what on earth she could say to get Charity to come into her house. She wished she'd figured that out sooner.

It wasn't a long drive from the Friendly Bean to Skye's cute little rental on the hillside. But an idea came to her at the same moment Charity turned onto her street.

"Hey, would you mind coming inside? Just for a sec. I've got this video of a dance I'd like to teach the wedding party, but I'm not sure it will fit in with your other plans."

Charity pulled into the car-length drive-way. "Sure, I can come in."

Skye breathed a silent sigh of relief. So far, so good. She got out of the car and glanced up and down the street. No vehicles that didn't belong or made the neighborhood look too busy on a Saturday morning. Even better. Although she did wonder how far away most of their friends had had to park.

She reached into her pocket and pulled out her house key. Not that she would need it. She'd left the door unlocked so the guests could get inside while she and Charity were getting coffee. But she pretended for the bride's sake. She gave the door a little push to open it, then moved back and politely waved for Charity to go in first.

"Thanks."

Charity had made it only one step inside when cries of "Surprise!" filled the air. She looked over her shoulder at Skye, as if she needed an explanation.

Skye grinned. "It's a bridal shower. Surprise!"

When she stepped into the house beside Charity, Skye couldn't believe how many women had managed to squeeze into her small living and dining rooms. Borrowed folding chairs filled every available space between sofa and stuffed chairs. Crepe paper had been draped from wall to wall and over doorways. A sheet cake sat in the center of the table, a punch bowl nearby.

Charity leaned to the side and asked, "Whose idea was this?"

"Mine. Sara's. Your sister's. Half the women here. We all wanted to do a shower, and Terri insisted it be a surprise."

"Terri and her surprises. She's crazy for them."

"Why don't you tell her yourself? She's right over there."

Terri stepped out of the hallway into full view, and Charity's face lit up as she went to hug her sister. Once Terri let go, Charity was passed from person to person, collecting kisses on her cheeks and more warm hugs around the neck.

Skye beamed with pleasure. It was going to be a great bridal shower.

Of all of the various kinds of cooking Grant did for Leonard Ranch Ultimate Adventures — advertised as "luxury mountain glamping" — his favorites were the cookouts where he was waiting with a great meal when a string of horses and riders rounded a bend in the trail. He loved the surprised looks on the guests' faces, and folks were often impressed by what he accomplished with a fire burned down to the perfect temperature, a good-sized grill grate, and a large, well-seasoned cast-iron skillet.

Magic!

At that moment the guide, Buck Malone, was helping the greenhorns in his party take care of their mounts so that the humans and horses could, as Buck put it, "graze together." Grant turned his attention to the rainbow trout and thin slices of lemon cooking in the skillet. Another minute or two and the food would be ready. On the edge of the grill grate a tinfoil container — filled with baby potatoes, red onions, bell peppers, and mushrooms — had reached the perfection stage. Later, the guests would enjoy peach halves and brown sugar that had been grilled together, also in tinfoil. The dessert would be topped with the vanilla ice cream that was currently stored in one of the coolers with dry ice.

Grant was thankful for this job, one of two he worked in Kings Meadow during the summer. June through September, whenever Ultimate Adventures had guests — excepting Sundays and Mondays — Grant's days were spent at Chet Leonard's ranch or in the mountains nearby. Several evenings a week, he was also the cook at the Tamarack Grill on the western edge of town. For the past two years, the owner of the restaurant, Skeeter Simmons, had increased Grant's hours back to full-time duty once the Leonards' glamping season ended. Skeeter had promised to do the same again when October rolled around, and Grant was more than a little grateful for it.

He pulled the skillet away from the fire. "Come and get it!"

After that, Grant was too busy to think of anything beyond the food he'd prepared and the guests he served. It wasn't until an hour and a half later that he was alone once again at the cook site. As he returned supplies to the crates and bins in the back of the Leonard pickup truck, his thoughts wandered to other things.

He'd received a phone call from his older brother last night. Vince still lived in Montana, not far from the ranch where Vince, Grant, and their eight younger brothers and sisters had been raised. Vince had called with the news that his wife, Segunda, was going to have another baby. Their fourth. If there was one thing the Nichols family knew how to do, it was to reproduce like rabbits. At the age of thirty, Grant was already an uncle to fourteen kids — all under the age of eleven — and in addition to Segunda, his youngest brother's wife also had a bun in the oven.

Every time one of his parents or siblings called Grant, the same two questions eventually came up: When was he going to get married? Shouldn't he think about starting a family soon?

No, thanks.

The pressure to marry and have kids was one of the reasons Grant had left Montana. He'd wanted some mileage between himself and the rest of the Nichols clan. He loved his parents and every single one of his siblings, as well as his nieces and nephews. But he had no plans to add to the family numbers. He already felt as if he'd raised a passel of kids. As the second oldest in the family, he'd been called upon to help with his brothers and sisters on a daily basis when they were all still at home. Maybe someday he would find the right woman and decide to get married, but he still wouldn't want any kids of his own.

The right woman.

The memory of Skye Foster popped into his head — and it wasn't the first time it had happened since he'd met the dance instructor. She was a little thing, both in height and weight. A bale of hay probably weighed more than she did. He ought to know. He'd pitched plenty of hay bales as a kid on his dad's ranch. But it was her big brown eyes and that bright smile of hers that he remembered most.

With the last of his gear put away, Grant got into the truck cab and started the engine. But he didn't drive away from thoughts of Skye as he headed toward the ranch complex. He had to admit, he was looking forward to seeing her again. He'd be happier, though, if dance lessons weren't part of the bargain. All he could do was hope he wouldn't stomp on her feet too hard or too often or fling her into the wall. Earlier today, Grant had expressed similar concerns to Buck.

"Don't worry," his friend had answered. "Skye's tougher than she looks. She's run half-ton horses around barrels to beat the clock since she was eleven or twelve years old. I imagine she can steer you where she wants you to go." Buck had grinned. "She made a regular twinkle-toes out of me."

They'd both laughed hard over that comment.

Grant decided to not worry about it. His first lesson with Skye Foster would be on Monday afternoon. He would know soon enough if there was any hope for him on the dance floor.

Or with Miss Foster.

Charity and her mother, Sophie Anderson, were the last to leave at the end of the bridal shower.

At the door, Charity gave Skye a tight squeeze. "This was so nice of you to do for me," she said softly. As she drew back, she glanced at her mother. "I had no idea you're both such good liars. And Sara too. I didn't suspect a thing."

"I'm glad we fooled you," Skye answered. "I thought for sure I'd give something away before we got here."

"Well, you didn't, and it was great fun." Charity moved through the open doorway onto the front stoop. "See you Tuesday night?"

"Yeah. See you then."

Skye waited to close the door until Sophie's Suburban and Charity's Lexus disappeared around a corner at the end of the street. Almost at once, exhaustion swept over her. She dropped onto the sofa with a sigh, thankful the other ladies had insisted on helping clean up before they left. The shower had been a great success, which delighted her to no end. But what she wanted most now was a nap. She closed her eyes, and visions of white wedding gowns filled her imagination as she drifted off to sleep.

CHAPTER THREE

Grant had been invited to Sunday dinner with the Leonard family. During the summer, it always felt strange to be at the ranch and not be cooking for the guests of their glamping enterprise. Strange, but nice for a change.

Other than his dad, there wasn't any man Grant admired and respected more than Chet Leonard. Nearly twenty years Grant's senior, Chet had an easygoing way about him, even when life threw him curveballs. He also had a strong work ethic and an even stronger faith. It was the latter that had made him so important as a friend and mentor.

Grant had been a brand-new believer when he'd moved to Kings Meadow. Despite the best efforts of his parents, he'd known next to nothing about the Bible and forgotten whatever he'd learned as a kid in Sunday school. At twenty-six he'd been partial to beer, cigarettes, swearing a blue streak, and wild women — in no particular order. A lot of his sinful habits had fallen away the night he'd given himself over to God. A lot of them, but not all. He'd still been a rough-around-the-edges Christian when he met Chet. The older man had taken an interest in Grant and had been guiding him ever since.

Now, an hour after polishing off hamburgers, potato salad, baked beans, and cherry-topped cheesecake, the two men sat on the back deck, shaded from view by huge, decades-old trees. Both of them held open Bibles on their laps.

"I understand what you're saying." Grant leaned forward. "And I love the honesty of the psalmist. But this verse seems to be talking about killing babies. How can that be right in God's sight?"

"The Bible is full of hard sayings, Grant. I believe God wants us to wrestle over the words we don't understand and go to Him for answers." Chet closed his Bible and moved it to a small table. "I also figure some things will remain a mystery, or we would have no need for faith."

"And it's impossible to please God without faith," Grant said, feeling a pleasant calm steal over him.

Chet nodded. "Yep."

Grant thought about asking another question, but realized he had his answers for now. Then Chet's attention was drawn to the driveway leading to the highway. Grant's gaze followed, and he saw a silver pickup approaching the ranch complex. He knew that pickup — and his pulse quickened. Unless someone else was driving it, Grant wouldn't have to wait until tomorrow to see Skye Foster.

In unison the two men stood and reached for their hats. By the time the truck began to slow as it approached the barnyard, Chet and Grant had left the deck and rounded the corner of the house.

The driver's side door of the Tacoma opened, and a moment later Skye dropped to the ground. Clad in boots and jeans, her hair covered with a straw cowboy hat, Grant thought her just about the cutest gal he'd ever laid eyes on. She kind of . . . sparkled.

Now there was a word he'd never before used to describe a woman.

Skye grinned when she saw the two men approaching. "Hey, Chet." If she remembered Grant from their meeting outside the hair salon, she didn't greet him by name, although she did nod at him. "Hope I'm not interrupting anything. Kimberly said it was okay for me to come out this afternoon."

"It's fine, Skye." Chet tipped his head toward Grant. "Have you two met? Skye Foster, Grant Nichols. Grant, Skye."

"Yes, we've met," Skye said. "Hi, Mr. Nichols."

"Just Grant, please. Good to see you." He touched his hat brim in her direction.

Her smile broadened before she looked at Chet again. "I'm thinking about buying another horse. For competitions. I was hoping you might have a good prospect for me."

"You've retired Snickers, I take it."

Grant noticed a flicker of sadness in Skye's eyes.

"Yeah," she answered. "He deserves to take it easier from here on out. He's still got plenty of life in him, but his barrel-racing days are over."

"What about your mare?"

Skye laughed softly, the sadness gone. "Milky Way? Oh, I love her to death, but I'm never going to use her to rodeo. Not if I want to win."

"I've got a few that might be right for you. One in particular." Chet motioned with his head toward the barn, and Skye fell into step beside him as he set off in that direction. Grant stayed where he was, feeling like a fifth wheel.

Chet stopped and looked back. "Coming?"

"Sure." Grant hurried to catch up with them.

To Skye, Chet said, "Grant's got a great eye for horses."

The praise felt good coming from the man Grant respected so much. It felt even better that Chet had said it to Skye Foster. Grant felt a need to impress her. And it wasn't because he liked her looks — which he most definitely did. It was something more than that.

Skye felt her heart skip a beat or two when she saw the blue roan at the far side of the paddock. "Oh, my," she whispered.

Chet Leonard chuckled. "He's young yet. Turned three earlier in the spring. But he's quick. Shows a lot of promise. He's got speed and great confirmation."

Skye had been saving up for several years for another horse. Not that she truly *needed* another. She could retire from competing in rodeos, the same way she'd retired Snickers. After all, she'd taken this summer off and it hadn't killed her. But oh, my. There was something about taking barrels as fast as a great horse could go that couldn't be described with words. It had to be experienced. And once it was, it was hard to say *Never again.*

"Come on." Chet opened the paddock gate. "Let's get a closer look at him."

Skye knew she should ask Chet the selling price for the gelding. Too much and she would need to look elsewhere. But she wanted that closer look he'd offered, so she kept the question to herself.

As they approached, the horse tossed his head and then trotted across the width of the paddock. He was even more beautiful in motion than he'd been standing still. When he reached the far corner, he spun about and trotted toward Chet and the others.

"Hey, fella." Chet rubbed the gelding's head.

The horse nickered and bobbed his head.

Skye ran her hand over the gelding's coat while walking a slow circle around him. She listened as Chet shared some details. The names of the sire and dam. Date of birth. Training received. It was all important information, but Skye's gut told her everything she needed to know. This guy was meant to be hers. She felt it in her bones. Same way she'd known about Snickers a decade earlier.

"What do you call him?" she asked once

she'd made her full circle and now stood looking into the horse's eyes.

"Nana Anna dubbed him River when he was a yearling. Said he's the same blue-gray color of the boulders and rocks that line the rivers up here. The name stuck."

As if knowing the humans were discussing him, River shook his head and snorted.

"He's glorious." Skye rubbed his muzzle.

Chet said, "Thought you'd like him."

"Who wouldn't?"

Grant spoke. "I remember the first time I saw this guy. That same summer when Ms. McKenna named him River. If he'd been for sale back then, I'd've bought him myself. If I could've scraped together the money, that is."

Skye turned, and when her gaze met with Grant's, she felt the strangest connection with him. Because they both liked the blue roan? Or was it something more?

Chet took a long step back from the horse. "I haven't listed him for sale yet. For a while I thought one of my boys might want him for rodeo events. He's championship mate-rial. But they'll both be in college come August, and they won't be here to take on the training of a new horse. So now it's time to sell him. I'd just like him to go to some-one who knows what they're doing." He looked at Skye. "Somebody like you."

She knew then that Chet was going to offer her an incredible deal for the three-year-old gelding. She wouldn't have to look elsewhere or settle for a horse she didn't like quite as much as this beautiful blue roan. She would want to ride him first, put him through his paces, but she knew in her heart what her answer would be.

"Hey," Grant said. "Skye and River. River and Skye. With those names, I'd say you two were meant to be together."

The thought hadn't occurred to her, but it seemed to confirm everything else she'd been feeling. She smiled at Grant, grateful, as if he'd given her some sort of gift.

But she couldn't begin to describe what the grin he sent back made her feel. It was simply . . . amazing.

CHAPTER FOUR

Skye opened the last of the blinds on the front windows of her dance studio, letting in the late-afternoon sunlight, then paused for a moment to capture her hair in a ponytail. Before she moved away, she saw Grant pull up to the curb in his Jeep.

It can't be that time already.

She glanced toward the big clock opposite the wall of mirrors. Grant was fifteen minutes early. She wasn't ready for him yet. Still, it pleased her that he appeared eager to start the lessons, despite his so-called two left feet.

He pushed open the door and stepped inside. When he saw her, he grinned. "I'm early."

She had the same indescribable reaction to his smile that she'd experienced yesterday. "I noticed." She turned and headed for the iHome stereo, needing a little distance so she could think straight again. "You'll have to wait while I get organized. Tell me. What kind of music do you like?"

"Country, mostly. And I listen to a lot of praise music when I'm cooking by myself."

Grant Nichols was an interesting combination, Skye thought as she scrolled through her iPod. He had an eye for horses, according to Chet, and he had the look of a real cowboy. Something more than the clothes he wore. A kind of western inner attitude. He made his living in the kitchen and made no apologies for it as some men would. However, he was ashamed of his dancing abilities. Still, because of his friendship with the groom, he was willing to try to change that.

And how cool is it that he listens to praise music while he works?

She stopped scrolling and selected a Vince Gill album. An extra-slow waltz number was in order for this first lesson, and this album had one that was about seventy beats per minute. Perfect for a novice. When it was ready to play, she turned toward Grant again.

"We're going to start with the country waltz. Ever done it?"

He shook his head. "Not really."

"Okay. Just a few basics. We'll count it out like this: One. Two. Three. Four. Five. Six.

One. Two. Three. Four. Five. Six." She went to stand in front of him. "No leaning forward. Keep your own balance. Imagine a string pulling you up from the top of your head." She put her right hand in his left, then positioned his right hand on her back. "Your knees shouldn't be stiff. We want to compress into the floor so that our actions are nice and smooth as we move in a circle."

Confusion filled his eyes. "Compress into the floor? What does that mean?"

"Just keep your knees flexible. You'll get the hang of it."

"What about spins and going backward?"

She smiled, hoping to encourage him. "That's a ways off. All we want right now is to glide. Let's try it without music first, shall we? I'll count off six, and then we'll begin on the next one. Okay?"

He nodded. His hand tightened on hers. To the point of pain.

"Relax your grip, Grant. You're going to do fine."

He released a humorless laugh.

She counted to six, then, "And one —"

Grant's boot came down hard on her toes.

Ouch! Somehow she managed to only think the word, but she couldn't keep from wincing.

He froze in place. "See. I told you. I'm a

lost cause when it comes to dancing."

"Mr. Nichols." Skye showed him her best serious-teacher expression. The one she'd perfected for her elementary school students. "Do you give up so easily on everything you try?"

"What? No. But this is different. I've *tried* this before."

"Not with me you haven't."

Grant opened his mouth as if to say more, then closed it.

Skye smiled at him. "Very good. Let's try again. One. Two. Three . . ."

The lesson didn't end up being the worst experience of Grant's life, although it hadn't ranked up near the top of his best experiences either. He hadn't battered and bruised his teacher. Not to an extreme degree, at any rate. She could still walk to the stereo after the final dance. They could both be thankful for that.

Music off, Skye turned toward him. "That went well."

And she said it with a straight face.

Grant about choked on a laugh. When he recovered, he said, "You're cute when you lie, Skye Foster." As soon as the words were out of his mouth, he regretted them. If he'd insulted her —

199

Her laughter spilled forth unabated. Not insulted. Amused.

Everything about Skye seemed wonderful to him. Her sense of humor. Her glorious smile. Her boundless energy. Those expressive, big brown eyes. Her luxurious black hair. Sure, he didn't know lots about her yet, but that was the great part. He couldn't wait to learn more. To get to know her better and better.

"Would you have dinner with me, Skye? Tonight at the Tamarack."

Her smile faded by degrees.

His heart felt like it might break in the same way. "Sorry. Maybe you're involved with someone else. I didn't mean to —"

"No," she answered, the word breathy. "There's no one else, Grant. And I'd like to have dinner with you."

Relief rushed through him. "Great. I don't eat out often. I already spend a lot of time at the restaurant, cooking. And it's not much fun to eat out alone."

"I know. I feel the same way."

"Do you?" He couldn't imagine why she would ever have to eat alone. The men of Kings Meadow must all be married, engaged, or blind. That was the only explanation that made sense to him.

"Give me a minute to close things up. Or

I can meet you there if you'd rather. My truck's parked in the back."

No way was he leaving the studio without her. "I'll wait for you. We can go in my Jeep, and I'll bring you back afterward."

Grant leaned a shoulder against the wall and watched as she closed the blinds, checked the lock on the back door, and turned off the lights. All of that done, she removed the band that had held her hair in a ponytail and let it tumble free.

Like an ebony waterfall.

He nearly chuckled at the thought. He wasn't a poetic sort of guy, but Skye seemed to bring it out in him. She made him feel things he'd never felt before.

"Okay." She turned to face him. "I'm ready."

He pushed off the wall. "All right." Outside, he took the key from her hand and poked it into the lock, turning the deadbolt in the door. Then he escorted her to his Jeep and helped her into the passenger's side.

The drive to the Tamarack Grill didn't take much more than five minutes, and since it was still early, the waitress — Cynthia Rogers — offered them their choice of seating.

"Outside?" Grant asked Skye.

She nodded.

"Follow me," Cynthia said with a smile.

The interior of the restaurant had a rugged, western motif. Varnished logs, complete with bark, had been used as supports throughout. The floor was made of large planks of wood, possibly pulled from an old barn. Definitely not the usual hardwood flooring used in homes. Instead of paintings, rusty farm utensils, ropes with frayed ends, and antique spurs hung on the walls. Even a couple of pans used in gold mining. There was a bar on the far right side of the large room, but the entire restaurant — inside and out — was smoke free.

When Grant started working at the Tamarack upon his arrival in Kings Meadow, the menu had been heavy with deep fat fried foods. Little by little he'd managed to convince the owner to add some more innovative choices. Not that he didn't like a burger and fries himself every now and then.

The outdoor seating overlooked the gurgling creek that ran through town. Trees lined the banks of the stream, their leaves applauding in a light breeze. Plenty of shade made the area pleasant, even on a warm summer's day.

At their table, Grant held out a chair for Skye and then went to the opposite side to take his own seat. He could have sat on either side of her, but he wanted an easy view of his companion while they talked and ate.

"Would either of you care for something from the bar?"

Grant glanced at Skye, who shook her head. "No, thanks."

"Anything besides water?"

He looked at Skye a second time.

"Iced tea," she answered.

"I'll have the same."

Cynthia scribbled on her pad, then grinned at him. "Back in a jiff."

When they were alone again, Skye leaned forward and said in a near whisper, "She likes you."

"Cynthia?" He shook his head. "No. Just friends."

"Hmm."

Now seemed a good time to change the subject. "So tell me about yourself, Skye. Have you always lived in Kings Meadow?"

"Yes. Except for a couple of years when I was at BSU. I didn't go back my junior year." She shrugged. "There wasn't anything I wanted to do except teach dance and race barrels, so I decided to open my studio. I'll go back and get a degree eventually. Just not yet. What about you? What brought you here?"

"Long story. I wanted to leave Montana, and a friend of a friend of a friend told me the Tamarack Grill needed a new cook."

Curiosity filled her eyes. "Why did you want to leave?"

Another long story, one he wished he didn't have to tell. But the truth was the truth. He was stuck with his past. "I was a bit of a hell-raiser in my teens and early twenties. More than a bit, really. Caused my folks all kinds of grief. But when I finally reached the end of my rope" — he paused and looked toward the creek for a moment before continuing — "When I reached the end of my rope, I found Jesus waiting for me there. I was different after I let Him take control, but I wanted to move to a place where not everybody knew what I'd been like before."

Skye had been raised by parents who were Bible-believing Christians, and she'd become one herself at a young age. She was used to talking about God over a meal or at a Bible study. But it wasn't often she met a guy who introduced faith into a conversation this early in a relationship.

Relationship? That might be rushing things. She wasn't sure this could even be called a first date. It had happened so last minute.

"I didn't plan to stay in Kings Meadow for long," Grant continued. "But I liked it here. Right from the start, I liked it. Felt at home. Like it was a place where I could put down roots and change my old ways. I made some good friends, like Buck Malone and Chet Leonard. Men I respect. And now that I'm also working as the lead chef for Ultimate Adventures, I reckon I'll stick around."

"I'm glad."

He grinned. "Thanks."

She hadn't meant to say that out loud, but she couldn't take it back. "Do you still have family in Montana?"

"Do I ever."

"What does that mean?"

"Really want to know?"

She nodded, her curiosity piqued.

"Okay." He held up his left hand in a fist. "My brother Vince is the oldest. I'm next." Up went his index finger, then his middle finger. "We're followed by Martina, Chelsea, Ridley" — He held up his right hand too — "the twins, Tommy and Tina, then Joshua, Brittany, and finally Heather, the youngest. She's sixteen." All fingers and thumbs were now extended.

"Ten of you? Wow."

"Yeah." He chuckled softly. " 'Wow' kind of describes it."

"Anybody made you an uncle yet?"

"I'll say. Fourteen nieces and nephews. The oldest of them is ten. And there are two more on the way."

Skye swallowed a second wow, but she couldn't swallow the envy she felt. "Your family get-togethers must be something."

"You have no idea."

He was right about that. She had no idea what it would be like. Neither of her parents had siblings, and her brother and sister, although both married, seemed in no hurry to give their mother the grandchildren she longed for. There were no large family reunions, and there never had been any because there wasn't a large extended family. Just a small group of five. No, she had no idea what it would be like to have nine siblings and fourteen nieces and nephews. But she would like to know.

Maybe she could find out with Grant.

A yummy, warm feeling spread all through her, and she was afraid she would blush and give away her thoughts.

But Cynthia returned with their iced teas and stayed to take their dinner orders. It gave Skye enough time to pull herself together. After that, their conversation turned to horses, followed throughout the meal by a variety of other topics.

For Skye, getting to know someone had never felt this special.

CHAPTER FIVE

On Wednesday afternoon, Skye hitched the horse trailer to her truck and drove out to the Leonard Ranch. Once there, she presented Chet with a cashier's check that represented every last cent she'd had in savings — and more than a few pennies from her checking account as well. Then she put a halter on River and led the gelding out of the paddock and into the barnyard.

Before she had a chance to open the back of the trailer, the sound of an approaching vehicle drew her attention around. Her heart skipped a beat or two at the sight of the familiar Jeep. Only then did she realize she'd hoped she would see Grant while she was at the ranch.

She waved at him and smiled. Through the dusty windshield she saw him grin in return.

He stopped the Jeep a good distance away and hopped out. "This is the day, huh?" He set a hat on his head.

"Yeah. This is it."

"He's a beauty." Grant strode toward her, but he looked at Chet. "We're done up there until suppertime, boss. I'll head back up at four."

"Sounds good," Chet answered.

Grant's gaze swung back to Skye. "Want some help loading him?"

Skye didn't need help getting this horse or any horse into a trailer. Not even ornery ones. But she said, "Sure. Thanks."

Grant lowered the gate of the trailer to the ground, then stepped out of the way as Skye led River toward the ramp. The horse eyed the trailer with suspicion. She prepared for a refusal. But at the last moment River walked up the ramp as if he'd been getting in and out of trailers every day of his life.

"I should've known that's how you'd be," she said softly, patting the horse's neck.

Grant leaned his shoulder against the back of the trailer and looked inside. "A lot of help I was."

"It was nice of you to offer anyway." She secured River's lead rope, gave the gelding another pat, and then headed out of the trailer.

Grant lifted the gate and latched it closed.

Ask me out again, Skye thought as she

stared at his back. *Ask me, please.*

He turned around and smiled that easy smile of his. "How'd the lesson go?"

"The lesson?"

"Last night. With the rest of the wedding party. Any left feet in that group as bad as mine?"

"Not quite *that* bad," she said, somehow keeping her expression bland.

"Ouch!"

"I know. Ouch!"

Face toward the heavens, he laughed. It was a great laugh. Full of honest delight. Skye felt pleasure clear down to her toes.

Grant bumped the brim of his hat with his knuckles, pushing it higher on his forehead. "Why don't I ride along with you? Just in case River gives you more trouble getting out than he did going in."

His help wouldn't be needed, and they both knew it. But it pleased Skye that he'd given her an almost plausible excuse for him to join her. Besides, his spontaneity was one of the things she liked about him. Just one of an increasing number of things she liked about him.

"Sure," she answered. "I wouldn't mind a little backup. Just in case."

"Want me to follow in my Jeep so you don't have to bring me back?"

She shook her head. "No. It isn't that far. I'll bring you back."

"Great."

While Grant went to the right, Skye rounded the left corner of the trailer, headed for the cab of her pickup. She stopped when she saw Chet standing not far off, a knowing smile curving his mouth. She'd completely forgotten he was there.

"Looks like you're all set," he said. "I'll get those papers to you by next week."

"Thanks. I'm not worried about them. Whenever it's good for you."

Was she blushing? Her face felt warm. Oh, how she hoped she wasn't blushing.

"Well." Chet's smile grew a little. "Good luck to you and Grant when you unload the horse."

She gave him a quick nod before opening the door to the cab and climbing in. Grant was already on the passenger's side, but she didn't look in his direction. Her plan was to wait until her embarrassment cooled.

She kept her speed under fifteen miles an hour on the long dirt driveway. No point jostling River around any more than necessary. No point filling the cab with dust either, since both of their windows were open.

When they reached the highway, she

stopped and looked both ways. This was a quiet stretch of road, but she never took chances when it came to her horses.

"Clear this way," Grant said as he stared north.

"Thanks."

The road was clear to the south as well. She stepped on the gas and pulled onto the highway.

After a few minutes of silence, Grant said, "Buck told me you put on quite a shindig for Charity last weekend."

"I didn't do all that much."

"Not what I heard."

They were simple words that felt like a huge compliment, and her heart fluttered with pleasure. She decided to change the subject. "Is the town where you grew up as small as Kings Meadow?"

"Definitely. A wide spot in the road is more like it. Care to hear how I walked to school through the snow, ten miles and uphill both ways?"

She laughed. "No."

"Shucks. I thought that story might impress you. It worked for my dad and grand-dad."

"You'll have to try something else to impress me, then." *Like kiss me.*

The thought made her go tingly all over.

She'd never felt like this about a guy. She'd had boyfriends, of course. But this was different. Did Grant feel it too?

What was it about being in Skye's company that made Grant feel like a million bucks? Since meeting her, she'd been his first thought when he awakened in the mornings and his final thought when he fell asleep at night. And ever since their dinner together, he'd thought of her most of the hours between waking and sleeping as well.

His dad had told him once that when Grant met *the* girl, he would know it. At the time Grant hadn't believed there was such a thing as *the* girl. At the time he hadn't thought he'd ever want to settle down with any woman. Why limit himself to one entrée when he could try every choice at the all-you-can-eat buffet?

But once again, the man who'd thought that way was BC Grant. He'd changed, and the way he looked at women had changed. And something about Skye Foster was changing him even more. For the first time in his life, marriage wasn't a remote possibility.

Hold your horses. You hardly know her.

He looked over at Skye as she slowed the truck before turning onto a narrow, winding road that took them closer to the mountains. A few minutes later, she pulled into an area where the wild grasses had been flattened by truck and trailer wheels. Not exactly a parking lot, but the next best thing.

When Skye got out of the truck, a couple of horses in the nearby pasture came trotting toward the wood and barbed-wire fence. Arriving at the gate, the brown-and-white paint nickered a welcome.

"Snickers?" Grant asked as he closed the passenger's door behind him.

"Yes." She went to the gate and stroked the gelding's head. "I've brought you a friend, boy. Think you can show him the ropes?"

The Appaloosa thrust her head over the top of the gate too. Skye moved to the mare and repeated the stroking motions. "You'll be nice to him. Right?"

Grant slipped his iPhone from his shirt pocket. It didn't make calls most anywhere in Kings Meadow — no cellular company thought it worthwhile to invest in this area off the beaten path — but that's not what he wanted it for. The phone had a great camera. He held it out in front of him, pointed it toward Skye and her horses, and snapped several pictures.

She looked at him, smiling. "What are you doing?"

"Taking pictures."

"I know that. But why?"

He strode over to her and held the screen so she could see the last photo. "Because you are in your element."

Her gaze lifted to meet his, but she didn't speak. After a few seconds, her eyes widened and her smile faded.

It was hard not to focus on her mouth, harder still not to lean down and kiss her. He hadn't known her long enough to do that. The old Grant wouldn't have cared that it was too early in their relationship. If he kissed a girl and scared her away, no worries. He would meet someone else soon enough. But the man he was today cared a lot. He wanted to do everything right, and he sure didn't want to risk losing her before he'd had a chance to see where these feelings of his might go.

Clearing his throat, he took a step back. "Shall we get River unloaded?" He returned the iPhone to his pocket.

"Yes. Let's." Her reply had a breathless quality.

For the second time, he had to fight back the urge to kiss her.

Looking at the ground, she hurried past

him. Had she sensed his desire? Had he blown it already?

Skye didn't wait for Grant to join her before lowering the gate and stepping into the trailer. River came out with the same ease as he'd entered. The blue roan might be young and have lots of training still ahead of him, but he had intelligence and a calm nature. That boded well for both horse and rider.

Grant went to the pasture gate and unlatched it while Skye led her new gelding toward him. "Snickers," he said. "Milky Way. Get back. Get back now." He slowly swung the gate inward, keeping his eyes on the two horses. But they seemed willing to wait until River was set free before crowding in to inspect him.

Skye led the blue roan several yards beyond the gate before stopping, patting his neck, and saying something Grant couldn't make out. Then she turned the horse loose. He trotted a short distance away. Head high, he whinnied. Snickers replied and walked toward the newcomer. Milky Way held her distance.

"Looks like they're gonna get along fine," Grant said.

Skye glanced in his direction and nodded. "Do you own this property?"

"No," she answered as she returned to the gate. "I rent it. Dad and Mom used to have some land south of town where we kept our horses when I was growing up. But they had to sell it when the economy took a downturn. That time was hard on a lot of folks around here."

"Your mom's a beautician —"

"Stylist," she interrupted. "If you call Mom a beautician, it makes her feel old."

He grinned at her. "Stylist. Sorry. Definitely don't want to make your mom feel old. She wouldn't like me much. What does your dad do?"

"He teaches history at the junior high school and coaches track-and-field."

"So you're a teacher like your dad?"

Her expression said she was pleased by the comparison he'd made. "Not quite like my dad. He had to get his college degree to do what he does. I just took dance lessons every year from the time I was six until I was seventeen."

"What kind of dance?"

"All kinds. Tap. Ballet. Ballroom. Country. Miss Cooper taught everything." As she spoke, she walked to the back of her truck and began to unhook the trailer. "My dance teacher was really great. I was never going to be a prima ballerina or anything, but she

217

wasn't after perfection from her students. She simply wanted to impart the joy of dance."

"From what I've seen, she succeeded."

Grant stepped forward to help lift the trailer off the hitch. When his hands landed on the bar beside hers, she looked up, a flicker of surprise in her eyes. Surprise and something more. Their heads were close. To kiss her, all he needed to do was sway forward a few inches. But before he could take action, she looked down again. With a strong yank, she freed the trailer from the hitch without his help.

Next time, Miss Foster. Next time I get the chance to kiss you, I'm taking it.

CHAPTER SIX

On the following Saturday, the groom, best man, and four groomsmen — including Grant — climbed into Ken Malone's mini-van. They were on their way to be fitted for morning jackets and all the accessories — trousers, shirt, waistcoat, pocket square, and cravat — for the wedding. Grant had been in enough of his siblings' weddings to know what to expect once they got to the men's store in Boise. But none of their weddings had been quite as formal as the Anderson-Malone wedding would be. Wearing tails would be a first for Grant.

The Malone brothers sat in the front of the automobile, Ken driving and Buck in the passenger's seat. Behind them were Grant and Tom Butler, the Methodist minister. Buck's soon-to-be brother-in-law, Rick Jansen — who'd driven to Kings Meadow from Sun Valley that morning — had the third row of seats to himself. From all appearances, Rick planned to sleep until they reached their destination.

Once on the highway, with Ken and Buck talking baseball, Grant said to Tom, "I guess you don't find yourself serving as a groomsman very often."

"It's a first, actually. I'm enjoying the experience."

"Even the dance lessons?"

Tom chuckled. "Even the dance lessons. But we're all sorry you can't be there the same night as the rest of us."

"It's okay. Skye and I found a time that works for both of us." He schooled his features, trying not to sound overly interested. "She goes to your church, doesn't she?"

"Yes, she does. All the Fosters do. Good family."

Grant nodded as his gaze drifted out the window at the passing terrain. His thoughts drifted too. Back to Kings Meadow. Back to Skye. It had only been three days since he'd gone with her under the pretense of helping unload her new horse, but those three days had seemed extra long.

Why didn't I pick up the phone and call her?

He'd wanted to. It almost scared him how much he'd wanted to. He'd never felt this way before, as if he were headed over a waterfall in a raft, not knowing if he would survive the drop but willing to take the risk because of what he might find at the bottom. Skye liked him. He was fairly certain of that. The last thing he wanted to do was spook her by moving too fast. By coming on too strong.

By kissing her too soon.

Her image filled his mind. Did she *look* like the kind of gal who would spook that easy? The question made him grin.

Not on your life.

On her knees, Skye scrubbed the shower grout with a toothbrush. Attacked it, more like. Frustration had been building in her for the past three days, and she was letting it out with a fit of cleaning.

She'd been certain Grant would call her. But her home phone hadn't rung on Thursday or Friday. It had been just as silent this morning.

Maybe I misread him.

No. No, she hadn't misread Grant. He was attracted to her. Maybe she was a little out of practice. She hadn't had a steady boyfriend in a while. But she hadn't lost her senses completely. She knew when a guy was interested. Grant Nichols was interested.

Maybe he's shy.

No, that didn't make sense either. He wasn't shy around her. Not at all. He was friendly and inquisitive. And when he looked at her —

Pleasure skittered up her spine at the memory.

Skye sat back on her heels, and with the back of her rubber glove she pushed her bangs off her forehead.

"I like him so much," she whispered. Then she straightened, eyes widening. "Maybe he doesn't know I like him."

As if in response, the long-awaited ring of the telephone came to her from the other end of the house. She shot to her feet, yanking off the rubber gloves and dropping them in the sink before rushing out of the bathroom and down the hallway to the kitchen. She grabbed the phone without even taking time to check the caller ID.

"Hello?" She squeezed her eyes closed and held her breath, hoping.

"Hi, Skye."

Disappointment sliced through her at the familiar voice. "Hi, Charity."

"I was wondering, would it be all right if Mom and Dad joined our group on Tuesday nights? I know they didn't sign up for the lessons. They go dancing all the time as it is. But now Mom says it sounds like we're having too much fun without them."

"Sure. They're welcome to come. Everybody can get better with a few lessons, even if they know what they're doing."

"Terrific. And while I've got you on the phone, can I just say thanks again for the bridal shower? It was so much fun. Buck says the bride's the one who gets to have all the fun." Charity laughed softly. "I gave him a couple of twenties and told him not to party too hard while he and the guys are in Boise."

What guys? Skye pressed the receiver tighter against her ear. "What's he doing in Boise?"

"Today's the day they all get fitted for their morning suits."

"Grant too? I thought he worked on Saturdays."

"Mmm. I guess Chet gave him the day off. I'm glad, 'cause it will be good to mark this off the wedding to-do list."

Skye's entire body seemed to lighten. Grant was with Buck and the other groomsmen. He couldn't or wouldn't call her when he was down in Boise. Of course, that didn't explain away the silence of the phone on Thursday and Friday, but Grant worked two jobs. Perhaps he'd tried to call her when she wasn't in. Some people didn't like to leave messages. Maybe he was one of them.

"Skye? Are you still there?"

"What? Yes. Yes, I'm still here. Something was . . . about to boil over on the stove." She winced as the lie slipped off her tongue. "Sorry."

"Sounds like you're busy. I won't keep you any longer. See you Tuesday."

"See you Tuesday. Bye."

Skye returned the handset to the phone cradle but didn't move away from the kitchen counter. There wasn't much point hanging around the house, waiting for the phone to ring again. Not with Grant in Boise for what sounded like at least several hours.

The grout could wait. She needed some fresh air.

Grant wasn't a tuxedo or morning suit kind of guy. But he had to admit the party of men looked handsome in gray tailcoats and trousers with accents of lavender.

As he stared at his reflection in the mirror, he wondered if this was the type of wedding Skye Foster would want. Not him. If he ever got married, he would want it to be by a cowboy preacher with the wedding party and guests all on horseback. Maybe have a big barbecue for the reception.

He gave his head a shake, uncomfortable with the direction of his thoughts. He and Skye hadn't even had an official date yet. They were a long ways from romance, and even if romance happened between them, they were still a long ways from talk of a wedding — *if* that time ever came.

"I've got everything I need, Mr. Nichols," the tailor said, holding out his hands toward Grant's shoulders to help remove the jacket.

"Thanks." He shrugged out of the tailcoat, then went into a nearby dressing room. It didn't take long to shed the rest of the wedding finery and get back into jeans, boots, and cotton shirt. Funny, how much more himself he felt with the right clothes on.

When he came out of the dressing room, he found the other men waiting for him.

"Lunch is on Charity," Buck said with a grin. "Where do you want to eat?"

Ken suggested a popular pizza parlor on State Street.

As they headed for the car, Tom said, "Buck, now that it's getting closer, how do you think you'll like living down here?"

"I've gotten used to the idea," Buck answered. "I'm no fan of the traffic, but since both Charity and I will be working out of the home, I guess we can avoid the worst of it. And we'll be back in Kings Meadow from spring until after hunting season."

"Sounds like a good compromise."

"It was an easy one to make, once I realized how much I loved her."

Up to that moment, Grant had only listened with half an ear. But now Buck's remark reminded him of something his brother Vince had said to him some years ago. *"I'd do anything for Segunda. You know, climb the highest mountain. Swim the deepest sea. Just so long as she agrees to marry me."*

He pictured Skye once again. Would he want to climb the highest mountain and swim the deepest sea for her? He'd been on his own for a long time. He hadn't needed to make any compromises. He'd only had himself to think about. Was he ready to put someone else's needs ahead of his own?

He didn't know the answers, but he intended to figure them out. The sooner, the better.

CHAPTER SEVEN

Skye glanced at her watch and quickened her pace. She was late for church. Again. The congregation would be singing the opening hymn by now. She would have to slip into the back and hope nobody noticed her tardiness.

Rounding the corner, she looked toward the front doors of the church. Her heart flip-flopped. Grant Nichols stood on the steps. His jeans looked new, his black hat obviously one he kept nice for dress occasions. When he saw her, he came down the steps to await her.

"I thought maybe you weren't coming," he said as she drew near.

"I'm late." As if he didn't know that already.

Voices raised in song drifted through the closed doors.

He grinned, his eyes saying, *You're right. I already knew you were late.*

"What are you doing here?" That sounded rude. "I mean, don't you go to Meadow Fellowship?"

Grant shrugged. "I thought it was about time I heard Tom preach. Mind if I sit with you?"

Oh, the hammering of her heart. Could he hear it above the singing from inside?

"No," she answered in a breathless voice. "I don't mind. But we'd better hurry."

He cupped her elbow with his hand and guided her up the steps, opening the door with his free hand. She slipped into the shadowy narthex, and he followed right behind. Just as they were about to move into the sanctuary, the strains of the amen filled the air.

Skye hurried toward the back pew, hoping to reach it before the congregation sat down, hoping no one would notice how late she was. *How late* we *are.* The thought made her tingle from head to toe.

She stepped into the pew and turned, her gaze sliding to Grant as he moved in at her side. He removed his hat, and when they sat, he placed it on his left knee.

How long had it been, she wondered, since a man had come to church to be with her? Never. Not really. When she was younger, she'd sat with the boys from youth group. Later, she'd often sat with rodeo friends who came to church as a group. But coming to church to be with her? That hadn't happened until now. Of course, Grant had said it was to hear Tom preach, but instinct told her that she was the real reason — and it felt good.

Grant saw her looking at him and smiled. There was that tingling sensation again. She looked toward the pulpit, lest he see what she felt.

Skye had dreamed of marriage, a husband, and lots of children since she was a girl in pigtails. But she'd longed for all of that under God's covering and blessing. Was it beginning to come true at last?

The service passed in a blur. Skye had a difficult time concentrating on the words spoken and the songs sung. She tried to focus, but it seemed an impossible task.

The congregation rose for Tom Butler's closing prayer, and when he said "Amen," the sanctuary buzzed with voices as people began to depart. Friendly invitations to Sunday dinner were spoken. Hugs were given. Laughter erupted from small groups.

"So," Skye said to Grant, "what did you think?"

"I liked it. Tom's a good preacher. Figured he would be." He stepped backward out of the pew, then waited for her to exit and walk with him.

Skye felt warmth color her cheeks. So strange. She didn't blush easily. Why now? Why this? Before she could answer her own questions, her mom's voice intruded.

"Skye, you *are* here."

As her parents approached, Skye answered, "Yes, I was running late, so we sat in the back."

The word *we* drew her mom's gaze to Grant.

"Mom. Dad. This is Grant Nichols. Grant, my parents, Midge and Rand Foster."

The two men shook hands and exchanged a greeting while her mom turned questioning eyes upon Skye. She returned the look with a small shake of the head. A shake that said, *Don't pry.*

"So," her mom said, as if she hadn't understood the silent warning, "what are you two doing for Sunday dinner?" Her gaze took in both Skye and Grant.

Skye wanted to sink into the floor.

Grant didn't look bothered. He answered, "Mrs. Foster, I was planning to ask your daughter to go for a drive. It's a fine summer day. I thought we'd get something to eat up in McCall." He glanced over at Skye. "Interested?"

The embarrassment over her mom's question vanished as she nodded to Grant.

"Well, you two have fun," her mom said. Then she leaned in to kiss Skye's cheek before whispering, "Call me later."

Grant once again cupped Skye's elbow, and they followed her parents out of the church, all of them pausing long enough to speak to Tom Butler before passing through the open doors. On the sidewalk, her mom and dad said good-bye to them and walked toward the church parking lot.

Grant tipped his head in the opposite direction. "I'm parked down thataway. You ready? Do you need to go home first?"

"No. I'm ready."

"Great."

He stepped around to her left side so that he walked closest to the street. Skye wondered if he treated all women with this much care and respect. But as soon as the thought came to her, she knew the answer was a yes. He was that kind of man. It was obvious that was how he'd been raised.

She glanced at him, curious to know more about that. "Have your parents come for a visit since you moved to Kings Meadow?"

"Nope. Not yet. You know how hard it is for a rancher to get away for any length of time. Dad takes care of most of the ranch work himself. I've got brothers who pitch in, of course, but they've got other jobs, and all but one have families of their own." He gave a slight shrug. "So I go home for visits when I can."

They arrived at his Jeep, and he held the door for her as she got in. What was it about his polite actions that made her feel pretty and feminine? And so very eager to know what would come next.

Northbound traffic was light on this summer Sunday afternoon, and Grant was content to drive in silence with Skye at his side. The windows were down, and the wind tugged at their hair. The air smelled fresh and sweet. He glanced to his right and saw a smile curve the corners of her mouth.

That's a good sign.

When he had to slow down for a series of curves in the winding road, he said, "I've got a friend who recently opened a restaurant in McCall. I thought we'd eat there. Unless you're too hungry to wait that long."

"I can wait," she answered. "There're not a lot of choices between here and there anyway."

He sensed her gaze upon him. It was insane, the way it made him feel. The way *she* made him feel. And it surprised him how eager he was to dive headlong into the insanity.

"Okay to have some music?" she asked, already reaching for the audio control.

His Jeep was over twenty years old, but he'd had a new stereo system put in the previous year. Even with the windows down, the speakers put forth a great sound. The playlist was a mixture of classic country and hits by current recording artists, and he knew he'd chosen well when Skye began to sing along. Soon Grant's voice joined hers.

The miles seemed to melt away beneath the spinning tires as they sang their way toward their destination. When they tired of singing, they chatted about this and that. Grant always enjoyed learning something new about Skye. And even when they fell silent, it was comfortable instead of awkward. Before Grant knew it, they had reached the outskirts of McCall. He eased off the gas as the speed limit dropped, ten miles per hour at a time. Skye reached over and turned off the stereo.

At last, they entered the resort town. His friend, Andy Davidson, had given Grant clear directions to the restaurant's location. Easy to follow — a right, a left, and another left. After the last turn, at the end of a short road, he saw the sign on a new building:

THE SUNDOWN.

"There it is," he said to Skye.

"Good. I'm famished."

After parking the Jeep, Grant hopped out and hurried around to open the door for Skye. He offered his hand, and she took it without hesitation. As if they'd been holding hands for years. He was sorry when she let go.

"How do you know the owner?" she asked as they walked toward the entrance.

"Andy's from Montana too. We met at the university in our freshman year."

"And you bonded over your common interest in food and cooking?"

Grant chuckled. "No. He was a business major. He planned to be a CEO of one corporation or another by the time he was thirty. But the first business he invested in was a little hole-in-the-wall restaurant, and he found he liked running it. So he bought a place that was bigger and better and liked it even more. Then he inherited this piece of property from a relative and decided to tear down what was on it and build the Sundown."

"I've never heard of it."

"Not surprised." He pulled the restaurant door open and waved her inside. "It just opened a couple of weeks ago."

"Has he tried to steal you from Ultimate Adventures and the Tamarack Grill?"

Before Grant could answer in the affirmative, Andy appeared, walking toward them with an arm outstretched.

"Great to see you." Andy shook Grant's hand with gusto. "Have you thought about my offer?" Without waiting for an answer, Andy looked at Skye. His eyes sparkled with appreciation, and his voice deepened as he said, "You must be Miss Foster. A pleasure to meet you. I'm Andy Davidson."

"It's nice to meet you too."

"Was good of you to drag Grant out of Kings Meadow. I've been after him to come up to McCall for months, but he's always busy."

Skye glanced in Grant's direction. "This was all his idea. I had nothing to do with it." She smiled, and the warmth of her gaze made him feel like a hero out of one of his sisters' romance novels.

After a period of silence, Andy cleared his throat. "I've got the best table in the house all ready for the two of you." He motioned for them to follow.

Andy hadn't lied. It was a great table. At the back of the restaurant, up five steps, then up another five, the table looked out over the lake. Sunlight glimmered off the water in sparks of gold and silver. Waves created by breeze and boat motors lapped at the shore below them.

"It's beautiful," Skye said.

Andy grinned at them both and then walked away. Moments later, the waitress came to take their beverage order.

As soon as the waitress was once again out of hearing, Skye leaned toward Grant. "So he *has* tried to steal you away from Kings Meadow," she said in a hushed tone.

He shrugged, liking that she'd overheard Andy's question. Not that he wanted to be prideful, but still . . .

"You aren't going to leave, are you?" There was earnest concern in her voice now.

He matched her posture, his gaze holding hers. "I've got a few good reasons not to leave." A slow smile curved his mouth before he added, "At least I hope so, Skye." Another few heartbeats. "Do I?"

The room seemed to spin. Skye's heart raced. The conversations of other diners dimmed.

"I've got a few good reasons not to leave . . . At least, I hope so, Skye . . . Do I?"

She found it hard to draw a breath as the words repeated in her head. Was he asking about her? About her feelings? Was she one of those good reasons for him not to leave Kings Meadow?

Before she could think of what to say, the waitress arrived with their beverages. Skye felt a sudden and strong dislike for the girl and her lousy timing. Oblivious, the waitress asked, "Are you ready to order?"

Skye glanced at the menu, settling on the first thing she saw. "I'll have the lemon-crusted chicken."

"Any sides?"

She shook her head. *Hurry up. Go away.*

The waitress looked at Grant.

"I'll have the pan-seared trout, please. Garlic mashed potatoes for the side."

The waitress smiled. "I'll have these right out." She walked away in the direction of the kitchen.

Skye feared the interruption had ruined the mood, but when Grant's gaze returned to her, the intense look in his eyes made her pulse gallop a second time.

He drew his chair closer to hers. "Skye, I've never known anyone like you. Never felt this way before. There's something . . . something special going on here." He pointed to himself, then to her. "Between you and me."

She swallowed.

"Do you feel it too?" he asked, his voice low.

Yes, she mouthed, but no sound came out.

He didn't smile, as she'd expected him to. Instead, his dark brows drew together in a frown. "There's something you should know about me, Skye."

"What's that?" she whispered.

"I . . . I haven't always lived the way I should. I partied hard for a lot of years. Wasn't very respectful of the girls I dated. Never thought it mattered because I didn't have any intention of settling down." He ran a hand over his hair. "God got my attention a few years back, and I've been trying to live right since. It's one of the reasons I came to Kings Meadow. To move away from the man I used to be. I didn't come here to . . . to get into a serious relationship. I never had plans to fall in love with anybody."

Serious relationship? A warm thrill passed through her. *Fall in love?*

He reached across the corner of the table and took hold of her hand. "I don't know for sure where this is going. Maybe it won't go anywhere. But I'd sure like to find out. Wouldn't you?"

She nodded.

He leaned in slowly, his gaze on her mouth. Unable to breathe, she waited for their lips to meet. The sensations, when it happened, were delicious. She wanted it to last forever. It ended in seconds. But brief as it had been, she knew she would never be the same.

CHAPTER EIGHT

Skye was still asleep the next morning when the phone rang.

"Hello?"

"You were supposed to call me when you got back yesterday."

"Hi, Mom." She pushed hair off her face. "I . . . forgot." It was the truth. Her mind had been in a muddle after Grant brought her home late in the afternoon.

"So . . . tell me about your young man."

"It's a little early to start calling him that."

"Is it?"

She remembered the brief kiss in the restaurant. She also remembered the second, slower kiss they'd shared, standing on her doorstep.

"Skye?"

With her free arm, she drew a pillow to her chest and held it close. "Oh, Mom. He's really special. I know nobody's perfect, but I think Grant's perfect for me."

"Tell me about him."

Eyes closed, she launched into a litany of all she'd learned about Grant since the moment they first met. Every wonderful, thrilling, fascinating, charming thing she knew about him.

"My goodness," her mom said when Skye fell silent at last. "He does sound perfect. Doesn't he have *any* flaws?"

Trying to sound more serious and less starstruck, she answered, "He isn't a very good dancer."

"Hmm."

"But we're working on that." Eyes open again, she laughed. She couldn't help it. She was too happy to hold it in for long.

"Your dad and I would love to get to know him. More than to just say hello in church. Could we have you two over for dinner sometime soon?"

"Sure. That'd be great." Skye shoved aside the pillow and sat up. "Sundays and Mondays are his days off. He's pretty busy the rest of the time. Working two jobs and all."

"Well, how about next Sunday after church?"

"Okay. I'll ask him if he's free and let you know." She glanced at the clock and quickly counted the hours until she would meet Grant at the dance studio. Anticipation

241

caused her insides to spin.

Her mom deftly changed the subject, and they chatted for a few more minutes before saying good-bye.

After dropping the phone back into its cradle, Skye was tempted to fall back into bed and pull the sheet over her head. Going back to sleep sounded like the best idea, but something told her it wouldn't happen, even if she tried. Not with Grant's image planted firmly in her mind. She would blame her mom's call, except she'd been dreaming about him when the phone rang.

Smiling, she got out of bed and headed for the shower. Fifteen minutes later, wet hair wrapped in a turban, she stood in front of the bathroom mirror, dressed in her underclothes, and applied makeup. Normally, she was in too much of a hurry to care. A little eye shadow. A bit of mascara. A quick brush of mineral foundation. Even when competing, she'd never been one to primp too much. But today she didn't want to look normal or even settle for pretty. She wanted to look beautiful. For Grant.

Is it real? Can this be happening?

She lowered her hand, still staring at her reflection.

God, I think Grant's the one. I hope he is. Did You bring us together so we can build a future together?

A husband. A home. Babies. Meeting Grant, loving Grant, could mean all of that.

Blessed is the man whose quiver is full of the children of his youth. Isn't that what You say, Lord?

There was that luscious swirl of sensations in her midsection again.

"Mmmm."

She dropped the makeup brush into a bin in the middle drawer, then reached for the blow dryer. If she didn't hurry up, she wouldn't be ready for that lesson with Grant this afternoon.

Grant stood by the river, skipping smooth, flat stones across the surface of the water. He'd come here to think, not long after the sun was up. It was a quiet setting. Far from any homes or ranches. Far from the road that wound its way east. Most fishermen didn't come to this spot, although Grant didn't know why. He'd seen fish swimming near the banks. But he wasn't about to ask any fishermen. He liked knowing he could come here and be alone, to think and to pray.

This morning, his thoughts and prayers were all about Skye Foster.

It wasn't often that he felt as unsure of

himself as he did right now. BC Grant had been arrogant and impudent. The new version of Grant was more levelheaded, more of a clear thinker, more prudent.

Prudent? He skipped another stone. *Not exactly what I'd call what I said and did yesterday.*

Maybe not, but he'd meant it. All of it. He wanted to find out where things might go between them. And he'd meant that kiss too. Those kisses. He was more than attracted to Skye. It wasn't merely the desire of a guy for a beautiful gal. There was more to his feelings than that.

"But can I trust my feelings? The heart's deceitful. Right?"

He tipped his head back and looked beyond his hat brim at the cloudless blue sky, as if expecting to find the answer written in the heavens. It wasn't.

Skye was special. He didn't want to hurt her, but he was afraid he would. This was new territory for him. He'd never expected to meet a girl who could change his mind about love and marriage. Not that Skye *had* changed his mind. Especially not about the latter. Not yet anyway.

But what if she *did* change it and then he discovered — too late — that he wasn't cut out to be one half of a whole? What if he was meant to be a whole all on his own? Hadn't the apostle Paul written that it was better to be single? Grant didn't have to be like the rest of his family, rushing into love, rushing into marriage, rushing into having kids.

He shook his head as he scuffed his boot against the hard ground. He'd been sure of himself yesterday morning. Why all the doubts now?

Maybe because there's already more between us than I know what to do with. Maybe because it scares me, not knowing what's going to happen next.

He released a deep breath. Scared or not, confused or not, he would be with Skye this afternoon. He would hold her in his arms while the music played and while he tried not to step on her toes.

And if opportunity allowed, he would kiss her again.

Skye came around the corner of her dance studio at a quarter before the hour. The Jeep was parked at the curb. Grant leaned his backside against it, his legs braced, ankles crossed, face shaded by his hat brim.

Add a guitar and it'd make a great album cover.

"You're early again," she said with a smile.

He straightened away from the vehicle. "Guess I'm eager to get the footwork right."

Heart tripping, she put the key in the lock and turned the deadbolt.

"Tell me something," he said from nearby.

"What's that?" The words were nearly inaudible, even to herself.

"You park in the back lot, but you don't go in through the backdoor. How come?"

Well, that wasn't what she'd expected him to ask. It left her disappointed, to say the least. She faced him. "Habit, more than anything. And the lock on the backdoor sticks sometimes, so coming around to the front is easier than fighting with it."

"Mmm." He pulled on the bar to open the door. "Maybe I should look at the lock and get it to stop sticking."

"Sure. If you want to."

Skye led the way inside, Grant following right behind. The interior of the studio was bathed in shadows. It was tempting to leave it that way. More romantic. But she forced herself to open the blinds and let in the sunlight. Best if she remembered why they were here. She'd promised Charity the entire wedding party would be the best dancing bunch this valley had ever seen.

"We're going to work on the two-step today," she said, heading for the stereo.

"This is the Two-Step Dance Studio, after all."

"What about that waltz we did last week? I didn't master that yet."

She smiled at the uncertainty in his voice. "You will. We still have time. I want you able to do at least two dances at the wedding. So we'll get the basics of the two-step down this week, and next week we'll start perfecting it and the waltz."

He shook his head slowly but said nothing.

Skye selected a Josh Turner album from her collection of music on the iPod. Punching the control, she fast-forwarded to the last track, "Why Don't We Just Dance." Josh's deep voice came through the speakers.

"Great song," Grant said.

She turned toward him again. "Just listen to it. Get a feel for the tempo. Count it out. One. Two. Three. Four. Five. Six." She patted herself near her collarbone for several bars. "Feel that beat. One. Two. Three. Four. Five. Six. Feel it on your insides."

"Okay. I'm feelin' it."

"We're going to dance to those six beats." She paused the player, plunging the studio into silence. She returned to stand before Grant. "For the man, the first step always starts with his left foot. So put your weight on your right. We're not going to move at first. Just step in place. There are two quick steps, followed by two slow steps."

"How quick?" Unmistakable dread filled his voice.

She couldn't help herself. She took hold of his hands, then rose on tiptoe to kiss him lightly, almost playfully, on the lips. "You can do this. Relax. Okay? Relax."

"Easy for you to say," he muttered — but he was smiling again.

She squeezed his hands before releasing them. "Left is one. Right is two. Left is three, four. Right is five, six. Quick. Quick. Slow. Slow. Ready?"

"As I'll ever be." He took a half step forward. "But when do we get to the part where I get to hold you?"

She laughed. "When you earn it."

"Knew there had to be a catch."

Her mom had always said that falling in love was exhausting because of all the highs and lows involved, but that being in love for the long haul was like a good fire on a cold winter night, full of comfort. Skye wasn't sure about the second part, but the first part was wrong. She found falling in love exhilarating. It was all highs so far.

"Teacher?"

"Hmm."

"I don't think I can wait."

And he didn't. He grabbed the brim of his hat, pulled it off his head, and tossed it aside. Then he placed his index finger under her chin, tipped her head back, and lowered his mouth to hers. Skye felt the kiss all the way down to her toes, and she was grateful when he wrapped his arms around her, lest she crumple into a helpless heap at his feet.

I love you, Grant. I know it's happening fast, but I love you.

He ended the kiss and drew back, though not far. His breath still warmed her cheek. She opened her eyes to look up into his.

"Miss Foster," he said, voice low, "I've completely forgotten the steps."

"Strange, Mr. Nichols. So have I."

CHAPTER NINE

On matters of a romantic nature, Grant would have preferred to talk to Buck Malone. A year ago, Grant's good friend had been a lot like him when it came to thoughts of marriage. Although for different reasons than Grant, Buck hadn't been interested in settling down with one woman. Meeting Charity had changed his mind.

But Buck was in the backcountry for the next week with a large group of riders, and Grant couldn't wait until his return. He needed advice now. When he arrived at the Leonard Ranch on Thursday, he went looking for Chet. Grant found his boss in a stall in the barn, doctoring a wound on a yearling's chest.

"Mornin'," Grant said as he leaned his arms on the top rail.

Chet glanced up, then returned to his task. "Morning."

"What happened to this young fella?"

"Not sure. Looks like he tangled with barbed wire. But I had the boys look for loose wire or a downed fence, and they couldn't find anything."

Grant placed a boot on the bottom rail. "Any changes in our plans for the rest of the week?"

"Nope. You'll be doing all of your cooking at the chef's patio. No trail rides. Lunch and dinner today. Dinners only the rest of the week." Chet straightened and patted the yearling's neck. "Do you need help? Sam's around if you want him to join you."

"No, thanks. I'm good." He took a few steps back as Chet reached for the gate. "But I was wondering if you had a minute to talk."

"Sure. What's up?" Chet came out of the stall.

"I . . . I . . ." Grant took a slow, deep breath. "It's about Skye Foster."

Chet cocked an eyebrow. "What about her?"

"Well, I —" Why did he feel so tongue tied? *Spit it out already.* "To tell you the truth, Chet, I think I'm falling in love with her."

"Yeah?"

"No. Not quite right. I think I've *fallen* in

251

love with her. Past tense. Already happened."

"And the problem is . . . ?" Chet leaned a shoulder against the stall.

Grant removed his hat and ran a hand over his hair. "I don't know that there is one. But it all happened so fast. I've never known anyone like her before. And I knew plenty of girls before I came to Idaho. I hooked up with someone different at every party, without any intention of ever seeing any of them again. That's why I haven't dated since I got here. I thought it better to give all women a wide berth while I turned my life around. I didn't want to fall into my old patterns."

"I know. I thought it was a sound plan."

"Chet, I never planned to get married. I figured I'd stay a bachelor the rest of my life."

His friend chuckled. "But you're thinking about marriage anyway."

"Yeah. I guess I am. I mean, that's the only place love can lead for a Christian couple. Right?"

"I'd say that's true. If that's what God has for you and Skye."

Grant walked to the far end of the barn and looked out at the paddocks beyond the open doors. *"If that's what God has for you and Skye."* If marriage was what God wanted for them, then everything would work out. The things he worried about now wouldn't matter anymore.

Chet arrived at his side.

"When I'm with her," Grant said softly, "I don't have any doubts. Except about my dancing." They both chuckled. "When I'm with her, all I want is to stay with her. To be with her all the time. To hear her laughter. To listen to her talk . . . about *anything.* She's interesting and funny, and we like the same music and books. We both like the outdoors. She'll always want to own horses and so will I. Having them will probably keep us strapped for cash, but neither of us will care. We don't have expensive tastes. It's like —" He shrugged. "It's like we were meant for each other."

"Maybe you are."

Grant finally cracked a smile. "But you're not going to tell me what to do, are you?"

"No." Chet shook his head. "You'll have to wrestle through your questions with God. I'm not in the matchmaking business." He chuckled again. "But I will tell you this: when I fell in love with Kimberly, I didn't think it was going to work out between us. Unlike you and Skye, we had lots of differences that seemed certain to keep us apart.

But God has a way of cutting through the stuff we think is impossible. He'll do the same for you, if you're listening to Him."

"And you don't think this has happened too fast between us?"

"It all depends, I suppose. But I've known more than one couple who fell in love in a matter of days or weeks and who are still married after thirty or forty or even fifty years. I know another couple that courted for years, and they were divorced before the first year was out. I'm not saying you should rush. I'm saying there's no set timetable. God's timing is what matters. Not yours."

Strange, the calmness that fell over him. As if all of his questions had been answered. As if all of his worries had been swept away.

"Thanks, Chet. You've been a big help."

Skye rode River out of the arena and walked him toward the lean-to. Once there, she dismounted and quickly set about removing his saddle and bridle.

"You're going to be a champ," she said as she slipped his halter on. "Aren't you, boy?"

The horse's ears flicked forward and he turned his head away from her. She had to follow right along with him in order to fasten the buckle. That's when she saw Grant walking toward her.

An already perfect day got instantly better.

"Hey, Skye." Small clouds of dirt rose behind his boots as he walked.

"Hey, Grant." Her heart did a little trill in her chest.

They had spoken on the phone several times since his last dance lesson, but this was the first she'd seen him in person in several days. It surprised her, how the sight of him made her feel.

"River looked great out there," he said, stopping nearby.

"You saw?"

"Some. I stayed in my Jeep. Didn't want to take a chance of disturbing him." He paused. "Or you."

One more thing to love about Grant. He knew better than to interrupt a horse in training. He was willing and able to be patient.

She said, "I thought you were working all day at the Leonards'."

"I am. But I wanted to see you before I start cooking again."

She didn't know if she should be delighted or worried. Was it something urgent? Or was it something he'd rather not say over the phone? Such as he couldn't go to her parents' home for Sunday dinner. Her mom would be disappointed if that was what he'd come to say.

"Come here, you." He took hold of her upper arms and drew her to him. "There. That's better." He embraced her, holding her close.

"I'm all horsey."

"I like horsey." He kissed her on the forehead.

"And gritty."

"I'll take my chances." He lowered his head so their lips could meet. A long, slow, luscious kiss.

River snorted hard, spraying them both.

They broke apart. Neither of them spoke. Then, in unison, they laughed.

"River," Grant said, "you're a real killjoy." He reached for Skye's left hand and drew her away from the lean-to and the horse. "I've got something important to say, and I need your full attention."

She sobered. "Okay. You've got it." Her mouth went dry, and she found it hard to swallow.

"Skye Foster, since the day I met you, I haven't been able to think straight."

Now she didn't seem able to breathe.

"But I feel like I know you better than some people I've known my whole life. I told you last Sunday that I wanted to see where things might go between us. That's not quite true anymore."

"It isn't?" she whispered.

"No, because I already know where it's going. I already know what I feel." He took a half step closer to her. "Call me crazy if you want, but . . . I love you."

He loves me?

"I've never said that to a woman before. Never said it to anybody who isn't a member of my family. Never."

You haven't?

"I'd like you to become a member of my family, Skye. Will you marry me?"

Vision blurred by unexpected tears, Skye's happiness bubbled over into laughter. Grant took a step back from her, and she realized he thought she was laughing at him, at his proposal.

"Wait. Grant. No. I mean, yes. Yes, I'll marry you."

"You will? Wahoo!"

He picked her up underneath the arms and spun her around and around. Her legs flew out like swings at the carnival. The first thing he did when he set her down was kiss her again. Only the kiss was different this time. The kiss claimed her for his own. She felt winded by the time he straightened.

"I've gotta get back to work," he said. "I

don't want to, but I've got to."

"I know. It's all right. Go."

"I don't have a ring for you yet."

"It's okay."

"Can I come to your house tonight when I'm done at the Tamarack? It'll be late."

She grinned. "That's okay too. I'll wait up."

It was close to midnight before Grant pulled his Jeep into Skye's driveway. The light above the front stoop was on, shedding a warm yellow glow several feet in all directions. Another light inside the house told him he was expected.

He hopped out of the vehicle and strode to the front door. Rather than ring the bell, he rapped lightly. The door opened in seconds. Skye looked up at him, eyes sleepy. Or would he call them dreamy?

"Hey, beautiful."

"Hi." She shoved tousled hair back from her face.

"You were asleep."

"On the sofa."

He cupped the side of her face, leaned forward, and kissed her. "I shouldn't have asked you to wait up."

"Yes, you should have. I needed to see you. I needed to know I wasn't dreaming earlier today."

"You weren't dreaming."

Holding on to the front of his shirt, she drew him over the threshold. He caught the open door with his fingertips and swiped it closed. He became instantly aware of how alone they were in this little bungalow. He remembered how easy it could be — with the right words, with the right look in his eyes, with the pressure of his lips — to help a girl let down her defenses.

Careful, he warned himself. *Be careful.*

"Would you like something to drink?" she asked, intruding on the silence. "There's Coke in the fridge, or I could make some decaf."

He wasn't thirsty, but a little distance between them might be a good thing. "Decaf would be great."

"I'll get it for you."

She turned and headed into the kitchen. He followed a few moments behind. On the opposite side of the kitchen bar, he sat on a stool and watched as she filled the carafe with water and poured it into the coffee-maker's reservoir.

"Did you tell anybody?" he asked at last.

She faced him but stayed where she was. "No. I didn't know if you wanted me to yet." She tipped her head slightly to one side. "Did you tell anyone?"

"No." He smiled. "But it was hard not to with so many people in and out of the kitchen tonight. I thought I'd explode with the news. I didn't expect that. Then again, I didn't expect any of this. People tried to tell me it would be like this. My parents. My brothers and sisters. Have I mentioned the Nicholses are a romantic lot? I didn't think I got that particular gene, but I was wrong."

"Not sure you told me about them being romantics. However, I can tell your parents raised you with good manners. When I'm with you I feel . . . protected." She returned his smile. "Cherished."

Who knew it would feel this good to hear her say something like that? And it made him determined to keep her feeling protected and cherished, determined not to hurt her or abuse her trust in even the smallest of ways.

"Grant?"

"Hmm." It was hard not to get off the stool and go take her in his arms again.

"Let's wait to tell anybody here in Kings Meadow until after we have dinner with my parents on Sunday. Is that all right with you? I'd like the two of us to tell them in person first."

The sounds and scent of coffee brewing

filled the kitchen.

"Sure. That's fine with me. Do you think they'll take it all right? It happening so fast, I mean."

She nodded. "I think so. As soon as they really get to meet you, they'll know we're right for each other."

"I'll wait to call my parents until Sunday night."

"Will they take it all right?"

He chuckled. "All they'll want to know is when do they get to meet you and how soon is the wedding." Surprise shot through him when he realized how he wanted to answer them. "Can I tell them it will be soon?"

Her large, dark eyes widened, all traces of sleepiness long gone. "How soon?"

"How about at the end of September or early October?"

She walked toward him, stopping with the bar still between them. "Yes. The colors will be turning by then. A perfect backdrop for a wedding. It will be beautiful."

"*You're* beautiful." He leaned across the kitchen bar and kissed her. "It may sound corny, Skye, but you've made me the happiest guy on earth."

CHAPTER TEN

The way Skye felt, she couldn't believe the entire congregation couldn't see the truth for themselves. It was a wonder everyone didn't come over at the end of the service and start shaking Grant's hand and congratulating them both.

But if anyone guessed she and Grant were engaged, no one let on, and the couple made it to her parents' home with their secret still intact. The next half an hour was pure agony while her mom and dad asked Grant questions and he answered them. But Skye could only hold back the announcement for so long.

When a lull in the conversation occurred, she reached over and took hold of Grant's hand. "Mom. Dad. Grant and I have something to tell you." She tightened her grip. "We're getting married."

"What?" her dad exclaimed.

Her mom shushed him. "Let her talk, Rand."

"We know it seems fast," Skye said. "We've only known each other a few weeks. But we're sure, Dad. We love each other. And we aren't rushing straight to the altar. We thought this fall would be a good time for the wedding."

Grant cleared his throat. "Sir, I love your daughter." He looked at her father with a steady gaze. "I'm as sure of that as I've ever been sure of anything. I promise I'll take care of her, be a good husband to her, cherish her always. You've got my word on it." He put an arm around Skye's shoulders and hugged her close.

Her dad was quiet for a long while, then said, "Neither one of you are kids. You're old enough to make decisions for yourselves. I don't know you well, Grant, but I respect the men who are your friends. That says a lot about you. And Skye, you know your own mind. I never had to worry about you the way I worried about your brother and sister. You were always more focused and self-disciplined than they were. So if this is what you want, then God bless you. I hope you'll both be as happy as your mom and I have been all these years."

Tears slipped down Skye's cheeks as she

got up to hug her father. When she turned toward her mom, she saw that she was sniffling. Happy tears, judging by the smile on her lips.

After they'd exchanged a hug, too, her mom said, "I'd best get that roast out of the oven before it turns to charcoal."

"I'll help." Skye took two steps toward the kitchen, stopped, and turned to look once again at Grant. After several heartbeats, she mouthed the words, *I love you.* Then she left the room, her heart tripping with joy.

The meal was over, but they lingered at the dining room table over cups of coffee. Grant felt accepted by Skye's parents. No small thing. It was easy to envision a future full of friendly dinners like this one.

Midge rose from her chair and began to clear the table. Skye got up to help her. Soon, running water and the clatter of plates and clink of glasses could be heard from the kitchen.

"I'll get the rest of these dishes," Grant said to Rand.

When he arrived at the doorway, he paused to look at the two women, mother and daughter, as they worked. It reminded him of home and his mom and sisters.

"I can hardly wait to meet Grant's family," Skye was saying. "Especially his mother. She raised ten kids, Mom. Ten. She must be full of advice, and I plan to ask her all kinds of questions when we get to meet. You know how I've always dreamed of having a big family like the one Grant grew up in. Oh, Mom. I can hardly wait until we have babies of our own. We'll have a big old house with a rope swing in the tree in the backyard and ponies for the kids to ride when they're little."

Grant went cold all over. He knew Skye and her mother continued to talk, but their voices were more like a buzz in his ears now.

He and Skye had crammed a lot of information, questions, and answers into the short time they'd known each other. Whenever together, they'd talked. About everything. How was it possible she'd never said anything about wanting a big family like his? Never a clue that she was eager to add to the overpopulation of the world. But then, he couldn't lay the blame at her feet. He should have made his own sentiments clear when he proposed. Or better yet, before he proposed. Why hadn't he thought to tell her how he felt about it?

A sick knot formed in his gut.

Midge Foster caught sight of him in the doorway. "Oh, thank you, Grant. That was nice of you to bring those to us."

Feeling stiff, he moved forward and set the dishes on the counter next to the sink.

As he turned, Skye touched the back of one of his hands with her fingertips. "I'll help Mom clean up, and then we can go."

He nodded.

To her mom, Skye said, "We're going to call Grant's parents with the news after we leave here."

"Grant, I look forward to meeting your parents. I hope your whole family can come down for the wedding."

The whole family. Thirty-two of them, counting spouses. Where would they all stay if they did come? Kings Meadow didn't have a motel. Only a bed-and-breakfast that had three available bedrooms. He knew because that's where he'd stayed upon his arrival in town.

His head began to throb.

Maybe he hadn't prayed about this marriage idea enough. Maybe he hadn't heard God's answer after all. He'd given Rand Foster his word that he would take care of Skye, that he would make her happy. They weren't even wed yet — not even home yet — and he was about to break that promise.

Tension emanated from Grant. Almost like

266

a third entity in the Jeep.

When Skye dared to glance at him, his eyes were locked on the street ahead, his mouth set in a hard line. His hands gripped the steering wheel as if he might try to break it in two.

Something had gone awry, and she didn't know what. There had been joy and laughter at her parents' home throughout the dinner. Announcing their engagement plans had gone even better than she'd hoped it would. But something had changed before they left the house.

She didn't have the courage to ask Grant about it. She would have to wait until he told her of his own accord.

However long that'll be.

As soon as the Jeep stopped in her driveway, Skye opened the passenger door before Grant, per usual, could come around and open it for her. His tension had become her tension, and she couldn't stand to wait for him. Wordlessly, she led the way up the narrow walk.

"I'll be out in a minute," she said over her shoulder as she headed to her bedroom. Once inside, she closed the door and leaned against it, her breath rapid and shallow. *Calm down. You don't know anything's wrong. Not for sure.*

He loved her. That was what mattered. That was all that mattered. Wasn't it?

She pushed off the door, stepped over to the mirror above her dresser, and stared at her reflection. Forcing herself to take a slow, deep breath, then another, she pushed her hair behind her shoulders.

Yes, that was better. Foolish to stand in here, imagining the worst. Better to go out and talk to Grant. That was what people did when they were married. They talked things through. Might as well begin now.

Drawing one more deep breath, she left the bedroom and walked the short hallway to the living room. Grant stood at the window, staring outside, his thumbs tucked into the back pockets of his jeans.

"Are we ready to make that phone call?" she asked, trying to sound normal, not sure she succeeded.

He turned toward her. "We need to talk first."

Dread became a lump in her chest. "Okay." She expected him to move to the sofa where they could sit, side by side, as they discussed whatever was on his mind. He didn't. He stayed near the window, the light at his back, casting his face in shadows.

"I heard . . . I heard you talking to your mom. In the kitchen before we left. I heard you say you want a big family. I saw how much joy that idea gave you. You came alive when you talked about it. It was written all over your face."

She nodded, glad that he understood her so well, still afraid because she didn't know what he would say next.

"Skye, we never talked about kids. I don't think I can give you what you want."

This time she shook her head, confused.

"I never planned on having kids of my own," he said softly. "No big family for me. I can't."

"Can't?" Was there a medical reason? Because if —

"Won't." The single word dashed her brief hope. "I decided a long time ago. No kids."

Tears welled, and she rubbed them away. "You decided," she whispered, the words like a dagger to her chest.

"Maybe I'd better go so you can think about it. So we both can think about it. I'm sorry, Skye. Real sorry. It's just . . . I don't know . . . I just —" He broke off, his frustration obvious, and walked to the door. Without looking back at her, he said, "I'll call you."

The instant the door closed, she sank to the floor. Tears flowed down her cheeks, but she didn't sob. Didn't make a sound. She hadn't the strength for more than one single thought.

So this is what a broken heart feels like.

CHAPTER ELEVEN

Grant arranged for time off from both of his jobs and was on the road to Montana before dawn the next morning. It was a little better than a six-hour drive, taking the route through the mountains and not counting any stops for fuel or food. He pulled into the barnyard of the Nichols family ranch just after one o'clock in the afternoon.

Before he could close the door to his Jeep, his mom was running toward him from the house. "Grant! Grant's here!" she shouted to anyone within hearing distance. In the next instant, she was hugging him. "Oh, son, you're home again. You're home. It's been too long."

"Hey, Mom."

"Why didn't you let us know you were coming?" she asked as she drew back from him.

"It was a last-minute decision. Spur of the moment."

His dad appeared out of the barn. A second or two later, Vince came around the corner of the house. More hugs were exchanged. More questions about his impromptu visit. His answers were evasive, although honest.

He might have fooled his parents as per the nature of his visit, but not his older brother. "Care to tell me what's up?" Vince asked as soon as they were alone in the room they'd shared as boys.

Grant dropped his duffle on the bed. He'd had all those hours of driving to think about what had happened with Skye. Not only what had happened yesterday but from the first moment he'd met her. Thinking hadn't solved the dilemma. Maybe talking about it would. Maybe.

He sat on the bed. "I met a girl," he began.

After that the words poured out of him. Vince listened, never trying to interrupt. Not even once. He didn't make a sound until Grant ran out of words. All he said then was, "Wow."

" 'Wow'? I was hoping for something more than that."

"Wow, I had no idea you were such a bonehead. How's that for something more?"

Grant wasn't sure how to respond.

"Look, bro. I know being part of a big

family isn't always easy. And being the oldest two kids meant a lot of stuff fell on our shoulders, yours and mine, when we were growing up. But you're no prize, you know. Yeah, you've turned your life around in the last few years. I'm proud of you for it. But you've got more work to do in that head of yours. You think Mom and Dad had too many kids? You think your brothers and sisters all married too young and had their own kids too fast? Who made you the judge?"

Wasn't Vince ever going to draw a breath?

"Maybe you oughta take another look at this family, Grant. Yeah, we're big and noisy. Yeah, at any family gathering there's probably at least one baby crying and another needing a diaper change. But there are also husbands and wives there, supporting each other, loving each other, helping each other. Because of the examples of our parents, we've got strong marriages that we keep working on so that they'll stay strong. And there isn't a single one of your brothers and sisters who wouldn't do just about anything for you if you needed them. If you were in trouble, there'd be an entire tribe coming to your rescue. How many people in this world are lucky enough to say the same?"

Defensive, Grant said, "I never said I

didn't love and appreciate my family."

"Then start taking note of your blessings. And then check with your brain and your heart to see if you even know what you want anymore. Don't stay a bonehead. Grow up!" With those words, Vince strode out of the room.

"What got him so riled?" Grant muttered.

He tried to get angry over his brother's outburst, but he failed. In fact, something in his gut told him they were the words he'd driven all the way from Kings Meadow to hear.

Skye pressed her face against Snickers's neck. She would have wept, but her tears had run dry after four days of doing little else but crying.

Grant's last words to her had been that he would call.

He hadn't called.

He hadn't come to his dance lesson on Monday night.

And yesterday she'd learned from Chet Leonard that Grant had gone to Montana. For a few days? Or for good?

"Skye."

She gasped softly. Now she was hearing voices. No, now she was hearing *his* voice.

"Skye?"

She spun around, and there he stood — black hat, rumpled cotton shirt tucked into the waistband of his jeans, boots covered in a fine layer of dust.

He took a step forward. "Can we talk?"

"If you want." She turned toward the gelding and stroked his neck.

"My brother called me a bonehead. He was right. I am one."

After all the crying she'd done in the past few days, the urge to laugh took her completely by surprise. It even maddened her. She looked over her shoulder and followed him with her eyes as he walked to the opposite side of Snickers.

"I was wrong not to sit down and talk it through, you and me, right then, Sunday night. I panicked, I guess. I love you, but all of a sudden I saw my whole world spiraling out of control."

"I'm sorry," she said stiffly. "I didn't mean to do that to you."

"No. You misunderstood. That's not what I meant." He ran a hand over his face. "Man, I'm making a mess of it."

Skye couldn't argue with that.

He leaned against Snickers's side. "But maybe it was for the best, me going away for a few days. Maybe I needed my one and only big brother to knock some sense into me. Maybe he's the only one who could."

"Did he?" Hope rose in her chest.

"Yes."

"Like what?"

"Like looking at all the ways God's blessed me through that big, noisy, interfering, exasperating family of mine. Like holding one of my nieces in my arms and realizing the absolute miracle of new life. Like how much I love you. Really love you. Deep down in my bones love you." His arm snaked across the horse's back, and he clasped Skye's right hand in his left. "Skye, I don't know if I'd ever be ready to have as many kids as my folks did. But when the time's right, I wouldn't mind starting with one . . . as long as you're the mother."

"Oh, Grant," she whispered.

"Stay there."

He hurried around Snickers and stopped before her. She thought he was about to hug her, but instead he drew her into a dance hold, his right hand in the small of her back, warm, strong, reassuring.

He stared down at her. "I want to dance with you for the rest of my life, Skye." He started to sway side to side. "But you know I've got two left feet. I'm going to need you to teach me the steps, and you know I'm gonna stumble every now and again. Probably step on your toes. Think you can handle it?"

Soft laughter escaped her. "Grant, remember what I told you the first time we met? I love a challenge." She pressed her cheek against his chest. "As long as we dance together, we're going to be just fine."

EPILOGUE

Through tear-blurred eyes, Skye watched the wedding party — bride and groom, parents of the bride and groom, best man and maid of honor, groomsmen and brides-maids — waltz around the dance floor. Who wouldn't cry at such a beautiful moment?

Everything about this wedding had been sublime, just as she'd imagined it would be — the bride and groom speaking their vows in the gazebo, the morning sun bathing the world in a golden July glow, the guests filling row after row of white folding chairs, the cutting of the cake, the music, and now the dancing.

The waltz ended. Skye looked for Grant. He'd been with the wedding party a moment before, dancing with one of the brides-maids. But now she couldn't see him. Where had he gone? Then, seemingly out of nowhere, he stood before her. Still wearing his suit jacket but with the addition of a gray cowboy hat covering his hair.

"Care to risk your feet, Miss Foster?" A slow grin curved his mouth.

"I'm a brave woman, Mr. Nichols."

"Yes, you are."

She stepped into his arms as the band began to play "I Hope You Dance."

Perfect.

She loved the way Grant made her feel as he folded her smaller hand within his larger one. There was a sense of security in his other hand against the small of her back. Her heart fluttered as they moved in time to the music.

Heavenly.

She tilted her head back and looked up at him. Beneath the brim of his gray Stetson, she saw the love in his eyes and the warmth of his smile. No shadows could hide him from her. She saw him as clearly as he saw her, and the knowledge made her tremble with more happiness than she had ever dreamed possible.

Skye had learned something important over the summer. Dreams for her future were all well and good, but the present — whatever that present looked like — was what she was meant to embrace, to savor.

Here, in the arms of the man she loved,

was the only dance, the only moment, that mattered.

ACKNOWLEDGMENTS

I have enjoyed reading each one of the Year of Weddings novellas as they have released, and I was delighted to be invited to participate in the second year, especially since it allowed me to return to Kings Meadow once again.

And a special thanks to Ami McConnell, who championed all of the stories set in Kings Meadow.

DISCUSSION QUESTIONS

1. Skye was in love with the idea of love. Did she have unrealistic expectations of romance and/or marriage? In what ways did her faith in God protect her from making poor choices?
2. Grant's past relationships with women before he was a Christian weren't respectful or healthy. What did he do right to change his behaviors? What could he have done better?
3. Skye and Grant both fell in love quickly. Do you believe in love at first sight? Why or why not?
4. Grant's history with his family was loving but made him reluctant to marry and have kids of his own. How has your family history impacted your marriage and/or your plans for the future?
5. Skye makes assumptions about her future with Grant that nearly end their relationship. What assumptions have you made in

your relationships (romantic or otherwise) that you need to talk over with a loved one?

6. In the end, Skye realizes the importance of living in the present. In what ways have you allowed memories of the past and/or dreams or fears for your future to spoil the present? What steps can you take to live more fully today?

ABOUT THE AUTHOR

Robin Lee Hatcher is the bestselling author of seventy-five books. Her well-drawn characters and heartwarming stories of faith, courage, and love have earned her both critical acclaim and the devotion of readers. Her numerous awards include the Christy Award for Excellence in Christian Fiction, the RITA Award for Best Inspirational Romance, *Romantic Times* Career Achievement Awards for Americana Romance and for Inspirational Fiction, the Carol Award, the 2011 Idahope Writer of the Year Award, and Lifetime Achievement Awards from both Romance Writers of America (2001) and American Christian Fiction Writers (2014). *Catching Katie* was named one of the Best Books of 2004 by *Library Journal.*

Robin enjoys being with her family, spending time in the beautiful Idaho outdoors, reading books that make her cry, and watching romantic movies. She and her husband make their home on the outskirts of Boise, sharing it with Poppet, the high-maintenance papillon, and Princess Pinky, the DC (Demon Cat).

■ ■ ■ ■

LOVE ON A
DEADLINE

KATHRYN SPRINGER

■ ■ ■ ■

To Wendy Lawton
It's important for an author to have
a good agent, but it's a blessing
for an author to have an agent
who is also a good friend!
This one is for you ☺

CHAPTER ONE

"Have you finished that special feature on the historical society's fashion show yet, Mac?"

Mackenzie Davis smiled up at her editor as she discreetly hit the Send button. "It should be in your in-box, Mr. Buchanan."

Right about . . . now.

"Great!" Grant Buchanan stepped into Mac's cubicle and held up a sheet of paper. "Because I've got the perfect story for you."

"Great," Mac echoed, trying to match the editor's enthusiasm. The last time Grant claimed he had the "perfect" story for her, she'd been sent to interview the cheerleading squad about their upcoming fall fundraiser. Forcing Mac to relive certain moments she'd rather forget.

Like all four years of high school.

"I guarantee this will have the whole town talking." Grant continued to hold the piece of paper just beyond her reach, the proverbial carrot dangling in front of a hungry reporter's nose.

"Senator Tipley agreed to an interview?" Mac was the one who'd found out the politician planned to spend a week at a friend's cabin a few miles north of Red Leaf. She was also the one who'd hinted that *someone* should set up a meeting with Tipley to discuss his stand on proposed cuts to Wisconsin's tourism budget. And Mac wanted — no, *needed* — that someone to be her. The interview would be her ticket out of Red Leaf.

"Senator — no, this is better." He slapped the paper down on the desk, creating a breeze that ruffled the collage of multicolored Post-it notes stuck to Mac's bulletin board.

She glanced down and the one-word subject line shattered the front-page byline dancing in her head. "A . . . wedding?"

"That's right." Grant looked so happy, one would think he'd come up with the concept. "What do you think?"

Probably not a good idea to tell him what she was thinking. Not when Mac practically had to beg the man to hire her in the first place.

In a world where people had instant access to the headlines on their cell phones and tablets, the *Red Leaf Register*'s survival depended on low overhead costs — Grant's wife, Beverly, and her twin sister worked for free — and good old-fashioned loyalty. The weekly newspaper had been around as long as the town itself because really, where else could people list their children's accomplishments or find out the stats for the men's summer baseball league?

Grant hadn't been looking for a reporter, but the fact Mac had a minor in photography seemed to tip the balance in her favor. Kind of a two-for-the-price-of-one special. It probably hadn't hurt that she'd turned in her résumé on the opening day of fishing season, either.

Mac hadn't cared. She needed a job and working for the *Register* would give her experience. An opportunity to write stories — *serious* stories — that would capture the attention of a larger newspaper. Except . . . no one in Red Leaf seemed to take her seriously. After being assigned to attend the garden club's monthly meetings instead of the city council's, Mac realized that in her editor's eyes — and in everyone else's — she would always be little Mac Davis. The coach's daughter.

And right here, in black and white, was the proof.

Trying to hide her disappointment, Mac dropped her gaze to the first sentence of the e-mail and her heart stalled. "Hollis Channing" — she practically strangled on the words — "is getting married? In Red Leaf?"

Grant's eyebrows hitched together over the bridge of his nose. "Brides traditionally return to their hometown to tie the knot, don't they?"

"Yes, but the Channings moved away years ago." Ten, to be exact. Not that Mac was counting.

"The family never sold the house on Jewel Lake after Dr. Channing passed away, so maybe they still feel some sort of connection to the town," Grant pointed out. "It doesn't really matter *why* Hollis chose to get married here. The *Register* is going to be there every step of the way."

"But . . ." Mac pushed out a laugh even though the expression on her boss's face told her that he wasn't joking. "Newspapers don't *cover* weddings. At least, not unless you're a celebrity."

"Or marrying one." Grant smiled. "Hollis is engaged to Connor Blake."

"Connor Blake the *actor*?" Mac recognized the name immediately. Critics who'd previewed *Dead in the Water* were already predicting that Connor's big-screen debut about a rookie cop who takes on a powerful drug cartel would be a runaway hit at the box office when it opened in three months over Thanksgiving weekend.

"That's right." Grant spread his hands apart, framing an invisible headline in the air. "Future Academy Award Nominee Marries Daughter of Prominent Local Family."

Given the recent buzz surrounding Connor Blake, Mac couldn't refute her editor's claim. But Hollis, a local? That was a bit of a stretch.

"The Channings live in Chicago," Mac muttered.

"Doesn't matter. This is going to sell newspapers. Lots of newspapers. People love all that hoopla, happily ever after, blah, blah, blah," Grant went on, revealing the heart of a true romantic. "Don't you remember how big the wedding reenactment went over last fall? It was the highlight of the historical society's open house."

How could Mac forget? Grant had given her that assignment too. Annie Price and county deputy Jesse Kent's wedding reenactment at historic Stone Church, meant to honor the young couple who'd founded the town, had been scripted — except for the part when Jesse actually proposed during the ceremony.

295

Grant expected Mac to do a follow-up story when the couple exchanged their real vows at the end of September, but she wasn't sure she'd be in Red Leaf that long. In fact . . . Mac skimmed through the rest of the e-mail and found an escape clause.

Yes! Thank you, Lord!

"According to this, Hollis's wedding is the last weekend in August." Mac tried to hide her relief. "I might not be here."

Not if everything went according to plan. It had to. Mac refused to consider the alternative.

"Well, you're here now, aren't you?" Grant didn't look the least bit disturbed by the reminder, which Mac found . . . disturbing. Did everyone assume she'd come back to Red Leaf to stay?

When she'd returned to her hometown to take care of her dad after he'd suffered a mild heart attack, it was supposed to be a temporary arrangement. And yet here she was, a year later, monitoring his diet. Making sure he got his prescriptions refilled and didn't overdo it. It was the last one that proved the most challenging.

Red Leaf's beloved Coach — even Mac called him by his title — wasn't going to let a little thing like a blocked artery prevent him from doing what he loved. Coaching football and teaching PE at the high school. And because Mac loved her dad, she'd put her dreams on hold and moved back into her old bedroom with the glow-in-the-dark stars pasted on the ceiling, the shelves lined with books instead of sports trophies.

"There's going to be an outdoor ceremony and reception at Channing House, so I want you to get some shots of the property today. We'll run them on the Local Scenery page in this week's issue, get everyone talking about it — and next week, we'll run part two of the story." Mac could almost see the subscription sales rising in her boss's eyes. "Interview the caterer. The florist. The guy in the penguin suit who's going to stroll around the grounds with a violin. Anyone connected with the wedding."

"That seems kind of intrusive." Even as Mac voiced the comment, she remembered this was Hollis Channing they were talking about. The girl who'd been taking selfies a decade before there'd been a name for it.

"Intrusive? Here's our personal invitation." Grant rapped his knuckles against the e-mail. "I'm sure there will be other newspapers angling to get the details, but the *Register* has an edge."

"An edge?" Mac realized her vocabulary was shrinking in direct proportion to her level of control.

Grant leveled a finger at her nose. "You."

"Me?" Mac squeaked.

"You lived next door to the family for years. You must have been friends with Hollis and her older brother, right?"

Wrong, Mac wanted to howl.

When Hollis hadn't been ignoring Mac, she'd made her life miserable.

And Ethan . . . Ethan Channing had broken her heart.

After searching underneath practically every stone that lined the overgrown walkway for the spare house key, all Ethan Channing had to show for his effort was half a dozen night crawlers. Useful for catching a stringer of perch on Jewel Lake but not for opening a front door.

You can't go home again. Isn't that what the old adage claimed?

Ethan dropped a set of rusty hinges on the ground and smiled. Not true. A person *could* go home again . . . Sometimes he just had to choose an alternate route.

Like a window.

He slung one leg over the sun-bleached ledge and eased his body through the narrow opening. The thick carpet muffled his landing but didn't stop his knees from buckling as he took in his surroundings. He hadn't simply found a way into the house. He'd stepped back in time.

The study looked exactly the way Ethan remembered it. The faint scent of lemon furniture polish remained trapped in the air, along with a whole lot of memories.

Three months after his father's funeral, with the ink barely dry on Ethan's high school diploma, his mom had closed up the house and they'd moved back to Chicago, where her extended family lived.

Lilah Channing preferred city living over small towns, a complaint Ethan had heard on a regular basis while he was growing up.

He still wasn't sure why his mother hadn't sold the house in Red Leaf. She wasn't known for being overly sentimental, and when she wanted to get away for a weekend, she booked a spa vacation or a shopping trip to New York.

His cell phone rang, shattering the silence.

"And so it begins," Ethan muttered as he saw his sister's name flash across the screen. "Hi, Hollis."

"Where are you?"

"I'm fine. Thanks for asking. How are you?"

"I'll let you know after you answer the question," came the impatient response.

Ethan smiled. "I'm at the house."

A high-pitched scream pierced his eardrums. "Really? How does it look?"

"It's still standing." Ethan heard a rustling sound behind the wall and wondered how many four-legged critters had built tiny condos in the insulation during his family's absence.

"What about the boathouse?"

"I haven't been down there yet."

"What's taking you so long?" Hollis demanded.

"I'll walk down to the lake before it gets dark." Ethan went over to the bank of windows that overlooked Jewel Lake. Branches littered the yard, debris left over from a summer storm, and cattails crowded the shoreline where the dock had been.

Ethan frowned. Was it his imagination or did the boathouse look closer to the water?

"You aren't saying much. Is it . . . terrible?" For the first time a note of uncertainty crept into his sister's voice.

"We probably could have used a little more time to get things in order," Ethan said carefully. Like two months instead of two weeks.

"That's why my awesome big brother is there. To make sure everything is absolutely perfect — and to keep Mom from turning the wedding into a three-ring circus."

In spite of the neglected condition of the property, Ethan knew which of the two assignments presented the greater challenge. "No pressure there."

"I want to be sensitive to Connor's feelings. He's gone out of his way to keep a low profile."

And then the poor guy had fallen in love with Hollis, whose mother didn't know the meaning of the words. Considering the guest list for his mom's annual Christmas party wasn't a whole lot smaller than the population of Red Leaf, it hadn't gone over well when the couple broke the news that they wanted to exchange their vows with only a few close friends and family members in attendance.

"There's still time to elope." Ethan was kidding. Kind of.

"Hey, you were the one who gave me the idea, remember?"

"I remember mentioning Red Leaf. *You* were the one who decided it would be a good place for your secret wedding."

"Funny you should mention secrets," Hollis said sweetly.

Ethan winced. "Good-bye, Hollis."

"Ethan? I . . . I know everything seems like it's happening pretty fast. But Connor and I . . . we just want to start our life. Is that crazy?"

Sunlight spilled through a seam in the clouds and turned the surface of the lake to gold. Ethan felt something in his soul, something that had felt off-kilter a long time, settle back into place.

"No," he said quietly. "Not crazy at all."

Not when he'd waited ten years to start his.

CHAPTER TWO

Mac took a shortcut through the hedge of maple trees that separated the sliver of land her father owned from the Channings' sprawling lakefront property.

Like Coach, the handful of people who lived on Jewel Lake had crafted their houses out of logs and fieldstone in an effort to blend in, rather than compete, with the natural beauty of their surroundings.

Not Monroe and Lilah Channing. They'd built their home like the third little pig in the nursery rhyme. Out of brick. It rose from the shoreline like a miniature fortress, complete with twin turrets and a wall of windows that faced the lake.

Ethan's mother had waged a campaign against the native flora, gradually bending it to her will until the yard resembled a golf course. A large patio — also brick — fanned out toward the water, and an adorable wooden gazebo with gingerbread trim had been built on the hill overlooking the rose garden. Since no one in the family ventured that far from the house, Mac decided the gazebo was more like an expensive yard ornament, its sole purpose to fill a bare spot on the property.

Well, not its *sole* purpose. Shaded by a hundred-year-old oak tree whose branches stretched over the property line, the gazebo had become Mac's favorite hideaway when she was growing up. How many times had she sneaked inside and stretched out on one of the built-in benches, listening to Hollis and her friends' laughter as they sunbathed by the lake?

She and Hollis might have been next-door neighbors, but contrary to her boss's assumption, they'd never been friends.

Mac traced it back to an unfortunate incident at Hollis's seventh birthday party, when Mac had declared she'd rather eat a minnow than have Betty Sadowski from the Clip and Curl Salon paint her fingernails pink. It was the truth, but in retrospect Mac realized she could have stated her preference a little more . . . tactfully.

That was the trouble with having been raised by a man who'd lost his wife to leukemia a week before their only daughter's third birthday.

Coach spent more time on the field or at the gym than he did at home, and he never dissembled when it came to his players. He was fair but blunt, traits he'd passed on to his only child. It wasn't until Mac was in junior high that she realized she didn't fit in with Hollis and her friends, whose primary method of communication seemed to be giggling and shaking their . . . pom-poms.

Coach had done his best, but by the time Mac was a freshman in high school, she'd attended more sporting events than dances.

Nope. Not going there.

What was it about Red Leaf that resurrected every painful moment from her past? She was no longer an awkward teenage girl, harboring a major crush on the most popular boy in school.

You're a reporter. This is a story. You have to separate feelings from facts.

But that didn't stop Mac from wincing when she swept aside a curtain of wild grapevine and saw the gazebo. Harsh winters, the relentless scrape of the wind, and the summer sun had bleached the color from the cedar posts, leaving them as dry and brittle as bones. A thick crust of moss and decaying leaves coated the shingles on the roof.

Mac felt the strangest urge to apologize

for the neglect. Whoever the Channings had hired to tend the grounds had obviously stopped caring at some point. The yard had shrunk to a small patch of green that stopped a few yards short of Lilah's prize-winning rose garden.

Mac took a tentative step inside the gazebo and heard an ominous snap as one of the boards shifted beneath her feet.

Sunlight streamed through the lattice walls, creating an intricate stencil on the floor.

Focus.

Mac raised her camera and the gazebo shrank to one small frame.

And there it was. The tiny heart etched in the corner of the built-in bench. Most girls wanted lip gloss or nail polish for their thirteenth birthday, but Mac had asked for a Swiss Army knife.

The gift had come in handy the night she'd impulsively carved Ethan's initials in the wood, all the while imagining the story she would tell their adorable green-eyed children.

This is the place where your dad and I fell in love. I was a freshman. He was a senior. He was the star quarterback of the football team. I was the coach's daughter. He was gorgeous, smart, and popular. I was . . .

Totally delusional — Mac ruthlessly shut down the memory — that's what you were.

The step creaked again — a sound that immediately caught Mac's attention because she wasn't the one standing on it this time.

She whirled around and her eyes locked on the man standing less than three feet away in the doorway of the gazebo.

Ethan Channing had just stepped out of her dreams and into her life.

CHAPTER THREE

Ethan wrestled down his irritation as the young woman in the gazebo turned to face him.

His mother had threatened to hire a professional wedding planner even though Hollis insisted that she and Connor wanted to keep things simple.

A word that wasn't in their mother's vocabulary. Neither was the word *no.* Ethan loved the woman dearly, but this was exactly the kind of thing she would do. There was no getting around it. His mother was a steamroller in Ralph Lauren and pearls.

Still, it didn't give Ethan license to shoot the messenger. A very attractive messenger — even if she *was* looking at him the way a character in a cheesy horror flick would look at the ax murderer who'd just stepped out of the shadows.

"Sorry." Ethan took a step backward, lifted his hands to show her they were ax-free. "I didn't mean to startle you."

If possible, the woman's big brown eyes got even bigger.

Now she was staring at him as if she knew him . . . and that was when it occurred to Ethan that he knew *her* too.

"Mac?" He tested the name cautiously, still not trusting his eyes. Until she nodded.

"Ethan . . . um . . . hello."

He couldn't believe it. Mac Davis — the scrawny, freckle-faced girl who'd perched on the bleachers taking stats or handed out water bottles during halftime — had been a fixture at every football game. But the nickname no longer seemed to fit.

Ethan's gaze swept over her, confirming that some mysterious metamorphosis had occurred over the past ten years. Mac's hair, once the color and consistency of copper wire, had deepened to a rich mahogany. It spilled over her shoulders, framing a heart-shaped face that Ethan would have, if pressed, once described as cute. He would have been wrong. Mackenzie Davis was . . . beautiful.

The coach's daughter. All grown up. The thought made Ethan smile. Until he realized that Mac wasn't smiling back. She was inching toward the doorway of the gazebo.

"Excuse me. I have to take some photos

while the lighting is still good."

This was probably his cue to let her go with a polite nod. But at the moment Ethan felt more curious than polite. "Photos?"

"For the *Register.*" Mac held up a digital camera as proof.

"You're a photographer?"

"Reporter. I have a lot of competition, though, because everyone in town tries to do my job and they don't ask for compensation."

It was such an accurate description of Red Leaf's thriving grapevine that Ethan couldn't help but grin. "You moved back here after college?"

"Last summer. Before that I was an intern at the Milwaukee *Heritage.*"

"You didn't like it?"

"It wasn't that." Mac hesitated. "The . . . timing wasn't quite right, so I came back."

Ethan suspected there was only one reason why Mac had passed up an opportunity to work for a prestigious newspaper like the *Heritage* and returned to Red Leaf. "Coach? He's doing okay?"

"It depends on which one of us you ask." The shadow that skimmed through Mac's eyes landed like a punch in the center of Ethan's gut.

Ben Davis had been more than Ethan's

high school football coach and mentor; he'd been a friend. A friend Ethan had lost touch with over the years because he'd been consumed with being the best, and it had affected his priorities. Coach had always claimed he was more concerned about producing good men than good football players. In that respect he'd failed the man twice.

"What happened?" Ethan was almost afraid to ask.

"A heart attack, but you know my dad. He acts like all he did was stub a toe. Dr. Heath warned him to slow down a little, but Coach and I can't seem to agree on what that means."

"I'll talk to him."

"No offense, Ethan" — the gold sparks in Mac's eyes told him *she'd* taken offense — "but if Coach won't listen to me, what makes you think he'll listen to you?"

"He won't have a choice." The words slipped out before Ethan could stop them. "I'm taking over Dr. Heath's practice at the end of the month."

"Taking over . . ." Mac choked. "Doctor . . ."

"Channing." Ethan smiled. "But that's strictly off the record for now."

CHAPTER FOUR

A doctor.

What perfect timing. Because Mac was pretty sure her heart had stopped beating the moment Ethan Channing stepped inside the gazebo.

"You look a little surprised." He tipped his head, and the silky swatch of ink-black hair he'd never quite been able to tame dipped over one eye.

Surprised wasn't quite the word Mac would have chosen.

And his smile . . . Mac hadn't realized it was etched as deeply in her memory as the initials *EC* were etched in the wood less than three feet from where he stood.

Oh. No.

She shifted to the left, blocking the bench from view. At least she hadn't been stupid enough to carve *her* initials next to Ethan's the night of the homecoming dance. Ninety percent of the girls who attended Red Leaf

High School had had a crush on the star quarterback, so any one of them could have been the culprit.

"I didn't know Dr. Heath was leaving." Or that Ethan had followed in his father's footsteps and pursued a degree in medicine. But then again, not asking questions when she called home from college had been part of Mac's "leave Red Leaf behind" campaign.

"A group of medical missionaries who are opening a clinic in Haiti asked Dr. Heath to partner with them. He contacted me a few weeks ago and asked if I would consider taking over his practice." Ethan's smile surfaced again. "That's off the record, too, by the way. He wants to tell his patients before a formal announcement is made."

After Dr. Heath told his patients, Mac knew a formal announcement wouldn't be necessary. The news would be all over town before the next issue of the *Register* went to press. Ethan's father and Frank Heath had been close friends as well as colleagues, and after Monroe's death, Dr. Heath had kept the clinic going on his own.

Now Ethan planned to take his father's place.

Mac had assumed he'd returned to Red Leaf for Hollis's wedding. The thought of

313

seeing Ethan on a regular basis caused her heart to stall all over again.

"Do you and Coach still live next door?"

"Yes." The same house. The same room.

The only thing that wasn't the same was that Mac refused to fall victim to Ethan Channing's irresistible charm. Again.

"I really should get going." She tried to duck past him but Ethan snagged her elbow.

"Careful. That's stinging nettle." He guided her around an innocent-looking plant sprouting between the steps. "I'm beginning to think a controlled burn might work better than a bottle of weed killer. I can't believe how neglected the place looks."

That's what happens when you don't come back for ten years, Mac wanted to say.

After Dr. Channing's funeral, it was as if the family had cut all ties with the town. Ethan's mother closed up the house the summer after he graduated, but when no FOR SALE sign appeared in the yard, everyone expected the Channings to divide their time between Chicago and Red Leaf.

The house had remained empty all summer and during football season. Over Christmas break, it had been Willie Meister's plow truck Mac saw in the driveway, clearing a path that no one used. No one returned the following summer, either. Or

the one after that. Mac finally stopped looking out the window when she heard a
vehicle rumble past.

An empty house didn't stop people from
reminiscing about the family, though. The
name *Channing* was stamped on gold
plaques all over Red Leaf, from the door on
the library's addition to the playground
equipment in the park. Photographs of
Hollis in her cheerleading uniform still lined
the walls of the high school, and even now
when Mac went to a football game, someone
inevitably mentioned how Ethan had led
the Lions to victory over the Lumberjacks
during the play-offs his senior year, breaking several state records on his way to the
end zone.

No wonder Grant wanted to make Hollis's
wedding front-page news. It was like the
royal family returning to Balmoral Castle.

A thought suddenly occurred to Mac.
"Are you . . . staying at the house?"

Ethan looked confused by the question.
"Of course."

Of course.

Red Leaf suddenly felt even smaller.

"I know it's kind of big for one person,
but it's completely furnished." Ethan bent
down to pick up a pinecone and sent it sail-
ing into the trees with the practiced skill of

someone who still tossed around a football now and then. "Mom claimed the stuff wouldn't fit in our condo, but I think it gave her an excuse to leave Dad's collection of antique fishing reels and the bearskin rug behind."

One. Person.

Mac swallowed hard. By now she expected there would be a beautiful, accomplished Mrs. Ethan Channing and two-point-four equally beautiful, accomplished Channing children.

She slowed her steps in order to put some distance between them and scanned the property for another "before" shot that would satisfy her editor.

"Do you know where the ceremony is going to take place?"

Ethan stopped so abruptly she almost plowed into him.

"Ceremony?" he repeated.

"Hollis's wedding."

"That's why you're here?" Ethan didn't raise his voice, but something in his tone set off a warning bell in Mac's head.

"I told you I was taking pictures for the *Register.*"

"I thought you were getting some nature shots. An eagle. The sunset." Ethan gestured toward the lake. "How did you even find out about the wedding? It's supposed to be a secret."

"A secret?" Grant hadn't mentioned that. And it didn't sound like Hollis, the girl who'd flirted with the editor of the school newspaper just to get her picture on the front page. Every week. "My editor received an e-mail with the details this morning."

"Who *sent* the e-mail, Mackenzie?" he asked softly.

Mac hiked her chin and forced herself to look him in the eye. "I . . . I can't say."

Ethan took a step closer, invading her personal space. "It was my mother, wasn't it?"

"A good reporter never reveals her source." Even though Ethan's cologne, a woodsy, masculine equivalent of truth serum, was in the process of breaking down her resistance.

"Never?" A slow smile drew up the corners of his lips. "That sounds like a challenge to me."

Mac silently disagreed. Keeping her head on straight and her heart in line with Ethan Channing working in Red Leaf — and living next door — that was going to be the challenge.

CHAPTER FIVE

"Mom did *what*?"

"Contacted the *Register* about the wedding." Ethan held the phone away from his ear and braced himself for the fallout.

"I can't believe it! She knows how Connor feels about his privacy!" Hollis wailed. "We chose Red Leaf because we wanted a quiet place to exchange our vows."

Of course their mother knew that. But she had obviously decided that when it came to her only daughter marrying Connor Blake, a little publicity was better than no publicity at all.

"It will still be quiet." Even without the newspaper story, Ethan couldn't guarantee privacy, not in a town the size of Red Leaf. "I doubt you'll have to worry about paparazzi hiding in the trees."

Just beautiful, brown-eyed reporters . . .

"Ethan? Are you listening to me?"

"Of course I'm listening." And thinking

about Mackenzie Davis, something Ethan had been guilty of doing quite a bit over the past twenty-four hours. Their conversation the night before had ended in a stalemate, but Ethan was already looking forward to the next one.

"You think I'm being silly, don't you?" Fortunately, Hollis didn't wait for his response. "Things have been a little . . . stressful . . . lately. Connor's agent wants him to be more accessible to the public, especially now that the producer is already talking about a sequel to *Dead in the Water*."

"Answering a few questions and smiling for a photograph or two won't put a damper on your wedding day." Ethan tried to put his sister's mind at ease the way he had when they were kids. By giving her a hard time. "The holes in the roof of the boathouse are another story."

He was rewarded with a gurgle of laughter. "I don't know what I'd do without you."

"Are you kidding? You're my favorite sister."

"I'm your *only* sister."

"A minor technicality."

"I guess I should call Connor and break the news that our secret wedding isn't a secret anymore."

"Once you explain that none of the *Regis-*

ter's subscribers live outside the county line, he'll be okay with it."

"I know." Hollis sighed. "I just wish Mom wasn't so determined to give me the wedding of her dreams."

Now it was Ethan's turn to laugh. "Don't worry. She's too far away to hijack your wedding plans."

"She has a cell phone, and she's not afraid to use it. What we need is a distraction." Ethan could almost hear the wheels turning in his sister's head. "You *could* tell her that you've been thinking about turning down the offer from Midland Medical. That would take the attention off my wedding."

Confession time.

"I'm not thinking about it anymore," Ethan admitted. "I called Dr. Langley this morning and let him know I accepted another position."

He'd confided in Hollis about Dr. Heath's offer, but the shriek that followed his announcement was a clue she hadn't expected him to accept it. Not when he'd worked so hard for a place in Dr. Langley's ER. "What made you change your mind?"

"Dr. Heath mentioned how difficult it is to find doctors who are willing to relocate to small towns."

"So you're saying Red Leaf needs you?"

Hollis teased.

"Maybe." Ethan watched a bald eagle circle lazily over Jewel Lake. A few months ago he'd been so focused on his work, he probably would have missed it.

Ethan had missed a lot of things until God — and a patient he'd referred to as "Bed Two" — got his attention.

Red Leaf might need him, but Ethan had a feeling he needed Red Leaf even more.

"It's all about harmony in the relationship." The sequined hem of Sybil Greene's caftan dusted the floor as she swayed in front of the microphone.

Mac was beginning to feel a little seasick.

"Are you getting this down?" a voice hissed in her ear.

"Got it, Mrs. Baker." Mac minimized solitaire on her tablet and tapped out the word *harmony*.

"If you practice these methods, I promise you'll have amazing results." Sybil gestured toward the PowerPoint screen with the practiced grace of a game show hostess and an awed hush fell over the room.

The local garden club had invited the self-proclaimed "plant matchmaker" to speak at their monthly meeting. Sybil claimed if you put certain plants together, they brought out the best in each other. Halfway through the lecture, Mac had come to the conclusion that it was pretty sad when a vegetable was able to maintain a successful relationship and she spent Friday and Saturday evenings alone.

Not that Mac *wanted* to be in a relationship. Number one, looking after Coach and working full-time at the newspaper didn't leave her much time to socialize. Number two, it didn't make sense to invest her time and energy in a relationship when she didn't plan to stay in Red Leaf. And number three —

Ethan's face popped up and Mac held back a sigh.

That was number three.

No matter how much time had gone by, Ethan's face had a tendency to pop into her thoughts at the most inopportune times. Like when she was out on a date. Or watching a football game. The dates were few and far between anyway, but football? When your dad coached the sport? Kind of difficult to avoid.

There'd been moments of weakness when Mac let herself imagine what would happen if she saw Ethan again. But none of the possible scenarios that had played out in her mind had prepared her for the reality.

Ethan had smiled at her. *Smiled.* As if he was genuinely happy to see her. Which led Mac to one simple conclusion, and she didn't need a PowerPoint presentation to prove it. Recognizing someone didn't necessarily mean you *remembered* them. Or a promise you'd made.

Which only made it more aggravating that she hadn't been able to forget *him.*

Applause erupted around the room, signaling the end of Sybil's presentation.

Mac worked her way up to the podium, winding through the mob of enthusiastic gardeners who'd surrounded the platform like groupies at a Newsboys concert.

After snapping a few photos, Mac snagged a lemon bar from the dessert table and jogged across the parking lot to her car.

Eight thirty. More than enough time to make some popcorn — no butter, no salt — and watch a movie with Coach, but not enough time to sneak onto Ethan's property and take the photographs her boss had requested.

Grant had been waiting at Mac's desk when she walked into work that morning, armed with a double shot of espresso and a dozen pastries she'd picked up from the Sweet Bakery. The espresso to counteract a sleepless night — Mac blamed Ethan for that — and the pastries for Grant's bad mood when he found out she hadn't completed her assignment.

"Where are they?" The editor hadn't so much as glanced at the white cardboard box balanced in Mac's hands.

"I, um, haven't taken them yet."

"It's our front-page story, Mac! I need those pictures by tomorrow morning."

"You'll have them." Unlike some people, Mac kept *her* word.

"Great!" Grant grabbed a blueberry Danish. "You come through on this and maybe I will let you interview the senator."

"Really?"

"Maybe," Grant corrected. "I'm planning to go fishing tonight so you can handle the plant mulch maker, right?"

"*Match*maker." Mac had forgotten all about the garden club meeting.

She blamed that on Ethan too.

A pale yellow moon peeked out from behind a cloud as Mac parked the car in the driveway. A light glowed in the living room window, a good sign that her dad had taken her advice to relax after the first day of practice.

"I'm home —"

A muffled cry drowned out the creak of the front door and Mac's satchel hit the floor with a thud.

"Dad?" She sprinted down the hall, a silent prayer — *Please, God, let him be all right* — tumbling from her heart as she skidded around the corner into the living room.

"Hi, sweetheart."

It took Mac a moment to process the scene that greeted her.

Coach, sitting — *upright* — on one end of the sofa, a bowl of popcorn separating him from Snap, their black Lab.

And sprawled in Mac's favorite chair, wearing jeans that molded to the muscular contours of his legs and a faded Red Leaf Lions sweatshirt, was Ethan Channing.

Chapter Six

"Is everything all right?" Coach tore his gaze away from the television long enough to frown at her. "You look a little flushed."

"I thought . . . never mind," Mac gasped. "I'm fine." Now that she knew her dad wasn't having another heart attack.

"You remember Ethan."

Because it was phrased as a statement and not a question, all that was required was a nod. Which was a good thing, because at the moment a nod was the only thing Mac was capable of.

"Your dad mentioned you were covering a meeting tonight." Ethan's easy smile made Mac's heart skip another scheduled beat. "We didn't expect to see you until ten."

Funny. Mac hadn't expected to see *him* at all. "Coach didn't mention we were going to have company."

"Ethan isn't company," Coach interjected. "He stopped by to say hello, and we decided to watch some of the old games. Relive the glory days."

High school hadn't exactly been the glory days for Mac, but it was impossible to miss the light shining in Coach's eyes.

Her dad never played favorites when it came to his players, but Mac could tell he had a soft spot for Ethan. After practice they would hang out in Coach's office and talk about plays and strategies or watch footage from the previous game. Mac didn't mind. It had given her an opportunity to watch Ethan.

"You're welcome to join us." Ethan's smile had grown wider, and with a jolt of horror, Mac realized she was guilty of doing it again.

"It's almost nine." She cast a pointed look at the clock on the fireplace mantel. "I'm sure Coach is tired after the first day of practice."

"Coach is fine," her dad grumbled. "And I don't need two kids ganging up on me, making sure I get enough sleep and eat all my vegetables."

"You're helping me out." Ethan didn't appear the least bit insulted that Coach had just referred to him as a kid. "I'm a rookie doctor — I need the practice. No pun intended."

Mac refused to smile, knowing it would only encourage him. "I thought that news was strictly off the record."

"I made an exception for your dad." Ethan stretched out his legs, looking way too comfortable for Mac's peace of mind. "He's going to be my first official patient. Isn't that right, Coach?"

Coach's gaze slid back to the television. "I'll try to work it around the practice schedule."

A statement, Mac thought wryly, that pretty much summed up her entire childhood.

When the trees turned scarlet and bronze in the fall, the town of Red Leaf turned blue and gold, the windows of every storefront on Main Street proudly displaying the school colors. Following a Red Leaf tradition that predated Mac's years at high school, before every home game the players and cheerleaders would ride to the field on the back of a flatbed truck decorated with crepe paper streamers.

The cheerleaders wore the players' letter jackets over their uniforms, and Mac would hear them arguing in the locker room over whose turn it was to wear Ethan's. Kristen Ballard usually won because she and Ethan were a matched set in terms of looks and popularity.

It didn't seem to matter that Mac had spent hours making posters and the miniature papier-mâché footballs that hung from the tailgate. Even when Coach was the driver, she'd never been invited to sit with the team.

The one time Mac had scraped up the courage to scramble onto the back of the float, Hollis had stared at Mac like she was a stain on her cheerleading sweater and then coolly informed her that there wasn't any room.

It wasn't the first time Hollis had snubbed Mac, but she'd never done it in front of a group of people. People who hadn't come to Mac's defense or *made* room.

At least Ethan hadn't been there to witness her slink back to the front of the truck and take her place next to Coach in the passenger seat . . .

"Have a seat, sweetheart." Her dad set the bowl of popcorn next to a bottle of root beer on the coffee table, freeing up a space on the couch. "This is going to bring back a lot of memories."

That was what Mac was afraid of.

"I —"

A cheer erupted from the television and drowned out the excuse she'd been frantically trying to come up with. Mac glanced at the screen just in time to see the camera zoom in on the cheerleaders, who wore short blue skirts and sweaters as white as their smiles.

Hollis stood at the top of the pyramid, of course, directly under the floodlight. On the scoreboard behind her, the numbers under the home and opposing team were the same.

Dread trickled down Mac's spine. "Which game are you watching?"

"Homecoming 2005. Lumberjacks versus the Lions." Coach chuckled. "Never going to forget that game."

Unfortunately, neither would she.

The camera panned the players sitting on the bench and then paused on a familiar face.

Her face.

"Is there another root beer?" Mac pitched her voice above the cheerleaders' screams. Desperate measures and all that.

"On the coffee table — help yourself." Her dad pointed at the television. "Look! There you are, Pumpkin."

Mac stifled a groan. The nickname described the color of her hair anyway.

She stood on the sidelines, wearing a lion suit because Beetle Jenkins had come down with a case of food poisoning during seventh-hour study hall. It wasn't the first time Mac had subbed as the school mascot, but she hadn't realized the costume was so . . . *big.* And fuzzy.

Mac hadn't realized the camera was trained on her, either. She'd yanked off the headpiece — probably so she could breathe — but instead of an intimidating jungle animal who prowled the sidelines, urging the fans to cheer for their team, Mac looked more like a little girl dressed in footie pajamas who'd just woke up from an afternoon nap. Flushed cheeks. Hair every which way.

Gazing adoringly at the star quarterback as he ran for a touchdown.

And she'd thought homecoming had been humiliating the first time.

Coach shook his head. "You had amazing instincts, Channing."

"I don't know about that." Ethan's gaze shifted to Mac. "I don't think I always saw what was right there in front of me."

The bottle of root beer slipped through Mac's hands, but she caught it before it hit the floor. "I should take Snap for a walk." The *w*-word roused her faithful Lab from his evening nap but Mac beat him to the door.

She'd bolted from Ethan that night too.

331

Only this time — *thank you, God* — he didn't follow her.

Ethan woke up the next morning to the mournful call of a loon. He rolled out of bed and squinted at the clock, amazed to discover it was almost seven. He hadn't slept more than five hours in a row since he'd started at Midland Medical, the hospital where he'd completed his residency.

The competition to fill a spot on Dr. Langley's team was fierce, and sleep had become a luxury Ethan couldn't afford. The doctor expected his residents to give 100 percent so Ethan had given 150 percent. Langley mentored only one resident and he'd chosen Ethan, a decision that had ultimately led to an invitation to join his team.

He still wasn't sure when — or how — to break the news to his mother that he wasn't returning to Chicago. Sometimes Ethan thought her aspirations were even higher than his. He'd overheard his parents arguing once. Heard her telling his father that he was wasting his medical skills in a place like Red Leaf.

Until a few months ago Ethan might have agreed with her.

He'd embraced the long hours. The blare

of sirens outside the hospital that jumpstarted a rush of adrenaline. The pressure of making split-second decisions that had the power to save a person's life. Now he was trading in the challenge of a busy ER for a family practice in the sleepy little town where he'd grown up. A town with grass instead of concrete. Trees instead of skyscrapers.

Ethan lifted the shade that overlooked the backyard.

Lots of trees. Trees that dropped needles and leaves and pinecones.

He was beginning to wish Hollis and Connor had picked a day in December to get married. The number of tasks on Ethan's to-do list suddenly seemed a lot longer than the number of days he had to accomplish them.

He skipped a shower, knowing he'd only have to take another one later, and extracted a T-shirt and his oldest pair of jeans from the suitcase.

A half hour later, armed with a cup of coffee and a bucket of sealer he hoped was just as strong, Ethan climbed the ladder he'd found in the shed. From the roof of the boathouse, he had an unobstructed view of the lake and the yard.

And trespassing reporters.

Mac was striding down the flagstone path to the water, camera in hand, clearly on a mission to take her photographs for the newspaper.

Ethan thought about calling her name, but he had a gut feeling that when it came to Mackenzie Davis, the element of surprise would only work in his favor.

Or not.

Because Mac suddenly veered off course and headed straight for the boathouse. The breeze toyed with a silky ribbon of mahogany hair that had already escaped the confines of her ponytail. In figure-hugging jeans, a plaid button-down shirt, and hiking boots, she looked more like a camp counselor than a journalist.

"What" — Mac parked her hands on her hips and glared up at him — "are you doing?"

Ethan grinned down at her. "Triage."

CHAPTER SEVEN

"Triage," Mac repeated.

"It's when you assess a situation and choose the most —"

"I *know* what the word means. But you're the one who's going to need a doctor when you fall through that roof and break both your legs."

Ethan didn't look the least bit disturbed by the possibility. "The boards are only rotten in a few places." He thumped one of the shingles with the heel of his shoe. "Hollis thought the boathouse would be a good place to set up the food for the reception."

"It still doesn't explain why you're up there."

Mac had set her alarm an hour early so she could take pictures of the venue and have them on Grant's desk before he poured his first cup of coffee. And maybe to avoid Ethan.

Okay. Avoiding Ethan had been her main motivation.

Mac wasn't sure what to expect when she'd cut through the trees between the two properties. Maybe a scene straight from *Father of the Bride* with a swarm of makeover bees already hard at work. Mowing the grass. Pulling weeds. Sculpting hedges into topiary swans.

The last thing she expected to see was Ethan standing on the roof of the boathouse. Alone. Looking like the cover model for the August edition of *Outdoorsman Monthly* in a T-shirt that stretched across his broad shoulders and a pair of jeans so old they'd faded to a soft January blue.

And he healed people to boot.

Sometimes life just wasn't fair.

Ethan swung down from the ladder and landed in front of her in one fluid motion. "I'm the one who's going to fix it."

"You're telling me that you're in charge of cleaning up the yard?" Mac couldn't hide her confusion.

"Actually, I'm kind of in charge of everything."

Everything. He had to be kidding.

"But . . . but what about Hollis? And your mom?"

"Mom started to take over and Hollis

336

started to panic. When I mentioned I was going to meet with Dr. Heath, she decided the lake house would be the perfect place for her and Connor to exchange their vows. But they've been busy so I offered to help."

Too busy to plan her own wedding? But then again, Hollis probably didn't have to.

"At least she hired a wedding planner —" Mac stopped at the look on Ethan's face. "She doesn't have a wedding planner?"

"She and Connor want to keep things simple."

Simple?

Simple didn't sell newspapers.

Mac saw her chances of interviewing Senator Tipley slipping away.

Ethan frowned. "What's wrong?"

"My editor wants to run a story in next week's edition too. He's expecting me to interview everyone connected with the wedding."

"Like who?" The fact that Ethan seemed genuinely curious spiked another wave of panic.

"Like the florist. The . . . the penguin guy. The caterer."

"You lost me at penguin."

"He plays the violin," Mac muttered.

"Do you know someone? I told Hollis I'd take care of the music too."

"Ethan." Mac dragged in a breath. Released it. Slowly. "I don't think you realize what you signed on for. Weddings don't just happen by themselves. You need a cake. A photographer. Decorations."

In a little less than two weeks.

The Hollis Channing that Mac had gone to school with would have taken that long to pick out her nail polish for the event.

"It sounds like you know a lot about weddings."

"Not really. My friend Annie Price is getting married next month." Mac had spent a Saturday afternoon with Annie at Second Story Books, the bookstore she managed, paging through bridal magazines. Every wedding task list she'd seen had had a one-year countdown.

"You know more than I do, that's for sure." The sudden gleam in Ethan's green eyes made Mac nervous.

"Ah . . . I have to be at work by seven thirty. I'll get out of your way as soon as I take a few pictures of the boathouse."

"You know," Ethan mused, "Hollis wasn't exactly thrilled when I told her that Mom contacted the *Register* about her wedding."

"I never said it was your mother."

"You didn't have to." Ethan reached out and the tip of his finger grazed her cheek.

"Your freckles turned pink. Dead giveaway."

Mac was glad he couldn't see her toes curling inside her boots.

"It's —" *What is it again?* "News." *That's right. It's news.* "Everyone in Red Leaf remembers your family, and Hollis *is* marrying an actor."

"Which is one of the reasons they wanted to keep it simple." Ethan's hand dropped to his side and the gleam became a smile that spilled into the corners of his eyes. "So I propose we make a deal."

"A deal."

"You need photographs, and I need some help."

"What kind of help?" Mac asked suspiciously.

"You give me a little guidance and I'll make sure you get your story."

"That's . . . you're trying to *bribe* me?"

"I like to think of it more as a win-win situation. You get the inside scoop on the wedding, and I get someone who knows there's supposed to be a guy in a penguin suit."

And Grant would let her interview Senator Tipley.

It also meant spending more time with Ethan.

"I don't know —"

"I need you, Mac," Ethan said quietly. "It's important to my baby sister that her wedding day goes smoothly. Dad isn't here to make sure that happens so I promised her I would."

Mac heard a disturbing sound. The sound of another interior wall crumbling.

"Fine. I'll do what I can."

Not the most enthusiastic response but Ethan would take it.

Mac started down to the lake, all business, and he fell into step behind her, fascinated with the way the swish of her auburn ponytail matched the gentle sway of her hips.

"You do have a nice view."

"Um . . ." She's talking about the water. "Yes. Nice."

"Where are Hollis and Connor going to exchange their vows?"

"Down by the water." Ethan pointed to a natural curve in the shoreline.

Mac raised her camera. "What time?"

"Six o'clock."

"An evening wedding." She nodded her approval. "The natural lighting will be good that time of day."

Ethan hadn't thought about the lighting at all. He hadn't thought about music or decorations or flowers, either.

Mac snapped a picture. "Do they have a theme?"

"It's a wedding. Isn't that the theme?"

He took Mac's ragged exhale as a no.

"Hollis said all she needs is a groom, a pastor, and a wedding dress."

"I hate to tell you this, Ethan, but your sister lied to you. My friend Annie is having a simple wedding but she's been planning for months to make it special. The two don't cancel each other out."

"I'm open to suggestions." Really open.

"Start by working with what you have." Mac's gaze swept over the property. "Brides pay tons of money for hydrangeas and you've got a whole row of them growing against the foundation of the house. Don't rip the wild grapevine down, have the photographer use it as a backdrop. Put floating lanterns in the lake. Strings of lights in the trees."

"You said you didn't know much about weddings. Where did you come up with all these ideas?"

"I don't know." Mac shrugged, but a wave of color washed over the delicate curve of her jaw and filled the spaces between her freckles. "What about the menu for the reception?"

"Hollis said —"

"Let me guess." Another sigh. "Keep it simple."

"Right."

"How many guests?"

"Mmm. Twenty?" Judging from Mac's expression, Ethan should have made it sound like a statement rather than a question.

He was beginning to understand why Mac had reacted the way she had when he'd said he was in charge of the details. Planning a wedding wasn't exactly part of his skill set.

"Red Leaf doesn't have anyone who caters, but you could talk to Sharon at the Korner Kettle. Her daughter made hors d'oeuvres for the historical society's fashion show last week and they were amazing."

"Jennifer still lives in town?" She'd been the salutatorian of Ethan's graduating class, voted Most Likely to Make the Cover of *Fortune* Magazine.

"She married Mike Abbott and they run his dad's lumberyard together." Mac shook her head. "You'd be surprised how many people stayed in Red Leaf . . . or ended up coming back."

He shot her a sideways glance. "Like us."

"Like you," Mac corrected. "I came back to take care of Coach after his heart attack,

342

but he really doesn't need me anymore. I've already stayed about six months longer than I planned."

"Where do you want to go?" Ethan didn't know why, but the thought of Mac leaving Red Leaf cast a shadow over the conversation.

"A few weeks ago, the editor at the *Heritage* called and told me they have an opening for a reporter. The deadline is the first of September, and he encouraged me to apply for it."

"Isn't that where you did your internship?"

"It's where I ran errands and proofread everyone else's articles," Mac said ruefully. "My internship will help but the competition is pretty fierce. In order to get the job, I have to submit a sample of my work."

"You've been writing for the *Register* since you came home. It shouldn't be a problem."

"I've been covering meetings and community events. I need something that will grab their attention." Mac angled the camera toward the sky and snapped a photo of the eagle Ethan had seen the day before.

"Aren't you supposed to be taking photographs of the wedding venue?" he teased.

"That handsome guy is on the guest list."

Mac tucked the camera into her bag. "Did Hollis happen to mention a cake?"

"I'll add it to the list. Right after buying twinkly little lights but before the guy in the penguin suit."

Ethan's breath tangled in his lungs when Mac smiled. A real smile, as unexpected and enchanting as a shooting star.

It was the same one Ethan had seen on Mac's face in the video clip when he'd made the winning touchdown ten years ago.

The team had always looked at Mac like a kid sister, and that was what she'd been to Ethan. A kid. He'd never really looked at her at all.

He'd been an idiot.

It might have taken a decade, but never let it be said that Ethan Channing didn't learn from his mistakes.

CHAPTER EIGHT

Mac had forgotten how loud a van-load of teenage boys could be. Or how fragrant. She cracked the driver's side window of the van. The combination of testosterone and AXE cologne was a little overpowering.

Mac had stopped by the high school on her lunch break to drop a sandwich off for Coach — turkey on whole wheat — and found the entire team squirming on the bench.

School wasn't in session yet, but her dad was a stickler about the team getting into shape before the season started. Judging from the guilty looks on the boys' faces, they'd done something that hadn't been in the playbook.

"What do you think the consequences should be for having a shaving cream fight in the locker room, Mackenzie?" her dad had barked. "Crunches? Push-ups?"

It suddenly occurred to Mac that all that

restless energy could be put to good use outside the field as well. "I have a better idea."

She'd given Coach the sandwich and taken the keys to his van.

"Are we really going to meet Ethan Channing?" One of the boys leaned over Mac's shoulder. "My dad still talks about the play-off between the Lumberjacks and the Lions."

Was she the only person in Red Leaf who wanted to forget that game?

"I'm sure he'll be there." Mac felt another pinch of guilt for taking off and leaving him alone with his wedding checklist.

Not that Ethan had given her much of a choice.

So why did her brain tend to sift out the bad memories until all that remained was the look on Ethan's face when he'd said those four little words?

I need you, Mac.

Because she was a glutton for punishment.

There was no sign of Ethan when she pulled up to the house, but country music blasted from an old radio perched on a pyramid of paint cans.

Ethan emerged from the garage as Mac turned off the ignition. He stopped short when he saw the boys spilling out of the van, and his gaze cut to her, a question in his eyes. "What's going on?"

"You're looking at the starting lineup for the Red Leaf Lions."

"I usually perform physicals in an office," Ethan murmured.

"They aren't here to get a physical. What they need is a few hours of intense conditioning."

Ethan still looked so adorably confused that Mac couldn't help but shake her head. "I think you've forgotten what it's like to live in a small town, Dr. Channing."

Then why do you want to leave?

The words chased through Ethan's mind as Mac pivoted toward the van. Ethan caught hold of her hand, overwhelmed that she'd recruited an army of volunteers to battle the overgrown lawn. The boys had already opened the back doors on the van and were arming themselves with rakes.

"Thanks, Mackenzie. I wasn't expecting this." Or the current of electricity that rocketed up his arm when her fingers tangled with his.

"They should be thanking you." She slipped her hand free, but the color rising in her cheeks made Ethan wonder if she'd felt it too. "After a shaving cream fight in the locker room, trust me, they'd rather be here than on the field right now."

"I remember pulling stunts like that at the beginning of the season."

"Like drawing faces on the blocking sled that looked a lot like the cafeteria ladies?"

"A coincidence." Ethan grinned. "But how did you know that was me? I thought I covered my tracks pretty well."

"I was doing my homework in Coach's office when you snuck in and put the Sharpie back in his desk drawer."

"Really?"

"Really." Something flickered in Mac's eyes before she looked away. "You better tell the guys what you want done."

Watching her walk toward the van, Ethan knew exactly what he'd done.

He'd fumbled the ball.

But . . . Ethan smiled . . . the clock was still running.

A few hours later he dumped the last load of weeds from the wheelbarrow, a little amazed at how much they'd accomplished in an afternoon.

Mac had split up the team and assigned sections of the yard to each group. Together, the boys cleared most of the debris from the yard and raked the shoreline while Mac cleaned out the boathouse, scrubbing windows and removing the musty life jackets and boxes of fishing equipment that lined the walls.

Ethan had been sent to conquer the weed-choked flower beds on the opposite side of the yard.

A coincidence? He didn't think so.

It wasn't until the sun dropped behind the tops of the trees that Ethan realized it was getting close to suppertime.

Mac must have noticed, too, because she strode to the center of the yard and blew into the whistle hanging from a cord around her neck.

Not only had Mac borrowed Coach's team, she'd borrowed his whistle.

"Fifteen-minute warning, guys!" Mac pitched her voice above the radio.

Ethan peeled off his work gloves and tucked them into the back pocket of his jeans as he walked over to join her.

"Hydrate." Mac handed him a bottle of water.

Ethan took a swig, letting the cool liquid wash away the dust that coated his throat. "I had no idea a simple wedding could be so exhausting."

"Jesse Kent, my friend Annie's fiancé, said the same thing a few weeks ago when they

349

were making wedding favors."

"You didn't mention wedding favors." Who came up with all this stuff, anyway?

"A small gift for the guests . . . and chocolate is always acceptable."

Finally. Something that actually sounded simple. "Speaking of favors, is there something I can do for the team to thank them for helping me out?"

Mac tipped her head. "Now that you mention it, maybe there is."

"I can make a donation to the equipment fund or the booster club —"

"That isn't quite what I had in mind," Mac interrupted.

As if on cue, the players gathered around them.

"Guys, who would like Ethan Channing, the pride of the Red Leaf Lions, to throw a few passes for you?"

The deafening whoop that followed Mac's question told Ethan the vote was unanimous.

"Passes, huh." He held out his hands and pretended to consider the notion as Trevor tossed him the ball. "What do you say we have a little friendly scrimmage instead?"

The whoop turned into a roar.

"I'll be the official team photographer." Mac patted her camera case.

"You should play too." Ethan flipped the ball into the air and caught it again. Smiled at her. "This *was* your idea."

CHAPTER NINE

"I . . . no." Mac backed up. "Absolutely not."

"Come on, Miss D." Trevor grinned. "We need you to even up the teams."

Guys. They always stuck together.

"Great." Ethan took her silence for agreement. "First touchdown wins."

He divided the group into two teams, appointing himself and Mac as captains. The look of anticipation on the boys' faces, combined with the sunlight and pine-scented air, stripped away Mac's misgivings. She'd made a fool of herself in front of Ethan before and survived.

Ethan barked out a few rules — Mac suspected it was for her benefit more than the other players — and they met at an invisible line in the center of the yard.

The first few minutes, Mac tried to be an asset to her team by staying out of everyone's way.

"You're doin' great, Miss D." The running back cuffed her on the shoulder as they formed a huddle to plan their next strategy.

"I'm terrible and you know it." Mac swiped at the blades of grass stuck to her jeans.

"That's why no one will be expecting me to pass the ball to you," Trevor whispered.

A flea flicker. Coach's secret weapon.

"No!" Mac squeaked.

"All you have to do is catch the ball." Six teenage boys looked way more confident in her ability than Mac was.

She rolled her eyes. "If that's *all* I have to do . . ."

Sarcasm was obviously wasted on teenagers — or else they simply ignored it — because her entire team was grinning as they jogged back to the line.

Mac's eyes met Ethan's and he winked at her. The guy hadn't even broken a sweat while she felt damp and sticky and . . . green.

The play started and Mac broke to the right, following Trevor's lead. The football hurtled through the air and Mac was tempted to duck and let it sail over her head, but she *was* the coach's daughter. It wasn't only her reputation on the line.

To a girl who'd always stood safely on the

sidelines, she found a whole new perspective of the game when a group of teenage giants thundered toward her.

Fortunately, Mac had a head start. The rush of adrenaline coursing through her veins didn't hurt, either.

Halfway to the touchdown line, Mac made the mistake of glancing over her shoulder.

Ethan was right behind her.

"Oh no, you don't!" The football began to slip through Mac's hands and she tightened her hold. Glared at Ethan. "I'm not letting go."

"Have it your way." A strong arm snaked around her waist and a low laugh vibrated in Mac's ear as he lifted her off her feet.

"Put. Me. Down." Mac thumped her fist against Ethan's back as he slung her over his shoulder and loped toward the touchdown line.

No one from either team bothered to intervene. Even upside down, Mac could see the boys doubled over with laughter, cheering Ethan on.

Ethan scored the touchdown and set her back on her feet again — but he didn't let go. His arms tightened around her, and it didn't even cross Mac's mind to try and free herself this time. Ethan's gaze dropped to her lips and lingered there for a moment, and Mac felt the world tilt sideways.

Or maybe it was the blood rushing from her head.

That would explain why she was seeing things too. Like the woman standing in the shade of a birch tree.

"Ethan?"

Not a hallucination. Lilah Channing. In a rose-colored linen sheath dress and matching heels, Ethan's mother looked as stylish as Mac remembered. And her tight smile, the one that had always reminded Mac of the snap of a coin purse, hadn't changed, either.

"Mom." Ethan released Mac as Lilah glided toward them. "I didn't expect to see you until next week."

"I know." Ethan's mother regarded her son's clothing, rumpled and grimy from battling weeds all afternoon, and presented her cheek for him to kiss. "But your sister is getting married a week from tomorrow. There's so much to do before a wedding. I thought you could use some help."

"I have plenty of help." Ethan nodded at the football team, who'd taken one look at the visitor and slunk away in search of water.

Mac wished she could join them.

"So I see. And might I remind you that you're a doctor now," Lilah scolded him.

"You're supposed to be setting broken bones, not breaking some of your own."

"It was just a little scrimmage after we finished the yard work. No broken bones. No bruises."

"You're finished?" Lilah glanced at the boathouse Mac had spent the last three hours cleaning and shuddered. "I could have used my influence and booked the grand ballroom at Porter Lakeside. Why on earth did your sister insist on getting married here, of all places?"

"Because it's beautiful," Mac heard herself say.

Lilah turned to look at her.

"You remember Mackenzie Davis, don't you, Mom?"

"Of course." Lilah's gaze swept over Mac and lingered for a moment on the grass-stained knees of her jeans.

"Mrs. Channing." Mac resisted the urge to curtsy. "It's nice to see you again."

Lilah inclined her head. "I suppose your father is still working at the high school."

"Yes, he is." Mac's spine straightened a little. Only Lilah Channing could make teaching sound like a punishment instead of a rewarding career.

"Actually, Coach let me borrow his football team for the afternoon," Ethan interjected smoothly. "Mackenzie has been a big help."

"I'm sure. You were always quite the little tomboy, weren't you?" Lilah's tinkling laugh sent a chipmunk scampering for cover. "But I'm here now. I've hosted dozens of parties over the years, and I have a wedding consultant on speed dial."

Mac might not have been in Hollis's circle of friends, but she understood the meaning behind Lilah's bright smile.

Mac was clearly outside her element. An *outsider.*

Which meant it was time for her to leave.

Chapter Ten

"Is this seat taken?"

Ethan, who'd been skimming through the list of upcoming events in the church bulletin, glanced up at the whispered comment.

"Hollis." He rose and his sister threw her arms around his neck. The elderly couple seated across the aisle smiled indulgently at the exuberant greeting, and when Hollis finally released him, it was Connor's turn. His future brother-in-law shook Ethan's hand and added an affectionate cuff on the shoulder.

"What are you two doing here? You weren't supposed to be here until Wednesday."

"Connor's appointments went better than we expected, so we decided to come up a few days early."

Ethan's lips twisted. "There's been a lot of that going around."

"What do you mean?"

"Mom's here."

"I was afraid that would happen," Hollis groaned. "Mom thinks I'm going to be carrying a bouquet of dandelions and serving hot dogs cooked over an open fire at the reception. I shouldn't have left you to deal with everything, Ethan. You've probably had your hands full."

An image of Mac's expression when Ethan swept her off her feet flashed in his mind. He remembered her howl of mock outrage when he'd tossed her over his shoulder. And the way she'd felt in his arms . . .

"He's smiling." Hollis looked at her fiancé. "Why is he smiling?"

"You keep telling me that fresh air is good for people."

It was more than fresh air. It was Mackenzie. Ethan hadn't had that much fun in months. Years, even. Sure, he squeezed in time at the gym when he wasn't at the clinic, but his workout was disciplined. Designed to yield the maximum amount of benefit in the shortest amount of time.

Somehow Mac had known just what he'd needed. A football and a stretch of green grass.

And then his mother had shown up.

Five minutes later, Mac had herded the players into the van and driven away, taking some of the sunlight with her.

"Mornin', Ethan!"

"Hey, Coach." Ethan felt a stab of disappointment when he realized Mac wasn't with her father. "You remember my sister, Hollis, don't you? And this is Connor Blake, her fiancé. Connor, Ben Davis."

"It's nice to meet you, sir." Connor extended his hand.

"Call me Coach." Mac's dad chuckled. "I don't know how to answer to anything else." His gaze shifted to Hollis. "Mackenzie is volunteering in the nursery, but you should stop in and say hello after the service. I know she's looking forward to interviewing you for the *Register*."

"Mac?" Hollis turned to Ethan. "She's the one writing the story?"

"She's their reporter . . . and the photographer," Ethan said. "Didn't I mention that?"

"No." Hollis frowned. "As a matter of fact, you didn't."

Coach smiled. "Well, you both will have some catching up to do."

The pastor returned to the podium, and the buzz of conversation dropped to a whisper as everyone shuffled back to their seats.

"What's the matter?" Ethan asked as they

sat down again. "Mac grew up next door to us. You have to remember her."

"I remember her," Hollis murmured. "I'm just hoping she doesn't remember *me.*"

Ethan was a little puzzled by the cryptic statement, but he didn't have an opportunity to question her further because the worship team took their places at the front of the church.

The congregation joined in the opening song and Ethan struggled to remember the words. On the rare Sundays when he wasn't working in the ER, he'd tried to catch up on his sleep.

Ethan bowed his head and let the music flow over him.

He and God definitely had some catching up to do too.

CHAPTER ELEVEN

"They're getting married Saturday and they don't have a caterer?"

The stunned look on Annie Price's face told Mac that yes, this could present a problem.

"Not according to Ethan." Mac shook her head. "He claims that Hollis wants to keep things simple but when I was at the house on Wednesday, I kept waiting for a team of people to show up like they do on those makeover shows and build a ballroom over the outdoor patio. Maybe move the shoreline a little."

Annie chuckled. "I can't imagine changing a thing. I've seen Channing House when Jesse and I go kayaking. It's . . . big."

It was also the only house in town that actually had a name.

Mac adjusted the flannel bundle cradled in her arms. Once a month she volunteered for nursery duty during the morning worship service and she considered it divine intervention that she'd been paired up with Annie, who was only a month away from exchanging vows with Red Leaf's favorite county deputy. When they weren't rocking fussy babies, they'd been discussing Hollis's wedding plans. Or lack thereof.

"You look deep in thought." Annie, sitting cross-legged on the floor across from Mac, carefully extracted one of her platinum curls from Isabelle Gibson's chubby fist. "Is something else bothering you? Other than the fact Ethan bribed you into sharing your wedding expertise, of course."

"In my case, wedding expertise is an oxymoron." And Mac was sure Lilah Channing would agree with her.

"I don't know about that." Annie smiled. "From the way you described it, you seem to have a vision of the perfect outdoor wedding."

Mac felt a blush coming on and turned away, carefully transferring her sleeping charge into one of the cribs that lined the wall.

What she'd described — the floating lanterns, centerpieces made up of lacy-white hydrangeas, and twinkling lights — had been the wedding she'd spent hours dreaming about as a teenager. Only in those dreams Ethan had been the groom.

She checked on the rest of the babies before dropping down on the colorful square of carpet again. "Hollis will probably nix everything. I'm surprised she even wants an outdoor wedding."

In fact, when it came right down to it, everything about the Channing-Blake wedding was a surprise. Like the way Ethan had reacted when he'd found out his mother had contacted the newspaper. And Hollis returning to Red Leaf — the town she hadn't visited in years — to marry a celebrity.

An Internet search had sparked even more questions about Hollis's groom. Sure, *Dead in the Water* was the actor's first movie, but aside from the trailer and a few publicity shots taken with the other cast members, Connor Blake seemed to go out of his way to avoid the spotlight.

"You're doing it again!" A plastic doughnut sailed through the air and bounced off Mac's arm.

She blinked and Annie's face came back into focus. "Sorry. I just don't understand a bride who is too busy to oversee the details of her own wedding. The Hollis I knew in high school was a control freak with pompoms."

"You said you haven't seen her for ten years. People change."

"Their mother hasn't," Mac muttered. "You should have seen Lilah's face when she looked at the yard — and that was after we'd cleaned it up!"

"I think I might have seen Ethan when I picked up cinnamon rolls at the bakery yesterday," Annie mused. "What does he look like?"

"About six two. Broad shoulders." Really broad shoulders. "But he's not one of those muscle-bound guys with no neck," Mac added. "He has dark hair . . . and there's always one swatch that hangs in his eyes."

"Mmm. What color are they?"

"Light green. Like a willow leaf."

"A willow leaf." Annie grinned.

It occurred to Mac that she'd probably gone into more detail than what was required. "Is there something wrong with that?"

"You tell me. You're the one who's blushing."

"I'm not —" She was. Mac could feel her freckles beginning to glow. Which reminded her of the whisper-soft brush of Ethan's finger against her cheek. "You *asked* me for a description."

Annie leaned forward, careful not to

disturb Isabelle. "Ethan's an old flame, isn't he?"

"An old . . . no," Mac sputtered. "Ethan Channing was on the varsity team when he was a freshman. He was also the most popular guy in school. Dated the most popular girls."

"You weren't popular?" Annie looked so astonished that Mac burst out laughing. Sometimes she forgot her friend had moved from Madison to Red Leaf only a year ago.

"Not at all. Coach was allergic to stores that sold anything other than sports equipment, so I had no fashion sense. What made it even worse was that I didn't know I was supposed to care about stuff like that." Mac had had her own uniform in high school. Blue jeans and T-shirts. "I was either on the sidelines handing out water bottles or sitting on the bus next to Coach when we had an away game. The guys treated me like the team mascot instead of a potential girlfriend."

"And Ethan was one of those guys?"

"He didn't even notice me." Mac strove to keep her voice light. "It was high school. Crushes and broken hearts, they kind of go with the territory."

"Which one was Ethan Channing?"

"Both." Mac shrugged. "It's a long story."

"I manage a bookstore. I love stories." The flash of sympathy in her friend's eyes released an avalanche of memories. Mac had never told anyone what had happened after the homecoming game but suddenly, she was telling Annie everything.

The Red Leaf Lions had spent the days leading up to the game working on a strategy that would guarantee a victory, and Mac had been working on a plan of her own. She'd recently started her freshman year and it was time to break free from her cocoon. Show people she wasn't just the coach's daughter, content to remain on the sidelines. She was going to reveal a brand-new Mackenzie Davis.

She was going to reinvent herself.

She was going to wear a dress. Not just any dress. A sparkly here-I-am dress that would get everyone's attention.

And maybe . . . just maybe . . . it would get Ethan Channing's attention too.

Except the evening hadn't gone quite the way Mac had imagined. Beetle Jenkins had gotten sick and Coach had asked her to wear the mascot suit. Mac hadn't minded. There would be plenty of time between the game and the dance to get ready.

But after Ethan's winning touchdown, Chad Fletcher had gotten so excited he'd jumped up from the bench and landed hard on the ankle he'd injured during the first quarter of the game.

Two of Chad's teammates had helped him into Coach's office. Mac had administered the ice pack while Coach tried unsuccessfully to get in touch with Chad's mom, who worked at a resort a few miles from town.

The hospital was half an hour away, but Mac wasn't surprised when Coach announced he was going to drive Chad to the ER for X-rays.

Mac knew her dad felt personally responsible for every single player, but one look at the clock told her there was no way she was going to make it to the dance now. Cinderella had had a fairy godmother and a horse-drawn carriage. Mac was on her own. Coach wouldn't have time to drop her off at home on his way to the hospital, let alone wait until she changed clothes and did something with her hair.

She froze when Ethan wandered in, wearing a clean football jersey and a pair of jeans. He'd stopped for a minute to check on his injured teammate and then turned to her. "Ready?"

Mac opened her mouth but no sound came out.

"I asked Ethan to give you a ride home so you can get ready for the dance." Coach ruffled her already ruffled hair. "You don't mind, do you, Pumpkin?"

Mind? Mac had hoped Ethan would see her after the game. In her sparkly blue dress — his favorite color — not covered from chin to toes in faux lion fur. And smelling like stale popcorn.

As if by mutual agreement, neither of them said a word until Ethan pulled up in front of her house. Then he shocked Mac all the way down to her furry slippers when he offered to wait while she got ready for the dance.

All Mac wanted to do was forget the entire night.

"I'm not going." She bailed from the cab of his pickup and headed toward the front door.

Ethan caught up to her in two strides. "Why not?"

Why not? Because she would need at least an hour to get ready. Because she'd seen Hollis and Kristen walking into school and they looked dazzling and stylish, and why had Mac thought for even a minute that she would fit in?

She couldn't tell Ethan that, though, so she'd latched onto the first excuse that popped into her head. "I don't know how to dance."

"It's not hard."

Said the guy who was good at everything.

Mac kept walking. A little faster.

"You know how Mom sends me and Hollis

to Chicago every year over spring break, right?"

Mac managed a jerky nod. Everyone knew. When they returned, Hollis showed off her new wardrobe and boasted about the fancy restaurants and the concerts she and Ethan had went to with their grandparents.

"I'll let you in on a secret." Ethan bent down and his breath stirred a damp wisp of hair by Mac's ear. "Etiquette school. Chapter 8 was dancing lessons. This quarterback knows everything from the tango to the cha-cha."

All Mac could manage was a garbled sound when she found herself being nudged toward the center of the yard.

The moment Ethan took her hand and placed it on his shoulder, he'd captured her fifteen-year-old heart as well.

Fifteen minutes later, Mac's slippers were soaked with dew and the stitches holding her tail in place had started to unravel, but she didn't care.

One final twirl and Ethan ended the lesson with a courtly bow. "You're going to the dance, right?"

Mac nodded. Right now she would have agreed the happiest cows *were* from California.

"Good. I'll find you." He smiled down at her. "Save a dance for me."

Ethan wanted to dance. With her.

After his pickup disappeared from sight, Mac spun circles in the yard until she was dizzy.

Coach had gotten home as she finished getting ready and drove her back to school.

But Ethan never showed up.

Mrs. Hudson had needed help with refreshments so Mac tied an apron over her dress and spent the entire evening in the kitchen, cutting up bars and making punch. She did slow dance with Timmy Hudson, but he was nine months old and drooled on her shoulder so Mac decided it didn't really count.

She also decided that if she truly wanted to reinvent herself, she was going to have to leave her hometown to do it.

"Did you talk to Ethan and find out why?" Annie's question tugged Mac back to reality.

"And risk even more humiliation?"

"Maybe he had a good reason."

"He did. Kristen Ballard." Mac had heard her bragging about watching a movie at Ethan's house after the dance. "She was on the homecoming court four years in a row. I couldn't compete with her."

"Maybe you didn't have to," Annie said softly.

"Ethan was hoping to score some extra

points with Coach by being nice to his geeky daughter." And then he'd promptly forgotten about her. "I'm okay, Annie. It was a long time ago. *Ethan* was a long time ago."

"But he's here now," Annie pointed out. "In Red Leaf."

"And I'm leaving." Mac felt the need to point that out too.

"I don't know why." Her friend's face took on a look of dreamy contentment. "Red Leaf is perfect."

"You say that because you didn't grow up here. When I moved back home after Coach's heart attack, it was as if I'd never been away. It doesn't seem to matter that I graduated from college and lived in the city for a year.

"Every time I go into the bakery, Mrs. Sweet tells me that I'm too skinny and tries to force-feed me sprinkle doughnuts. When Vivienne Wallace sees me at church, she asks how my piano lessons are going."

"I didn't know you played the piano."

"I don't. Not since fourth grade anyway." Mac released a sigh. "If I stay, people are always going to see me as the geeky little girl with braids . . . Why are you smiling?"

"Because Ms. Viv *is* a bit eccentric . . . and because I can't wait until those kinds of things happen to me. I've lived in a lot of places but I never felt like I was part of them." Annie reached out and squeezed her hand. "You have roots here. A shared history. I don't think people look at you as the geeky girl with braids. They look at you with . . . love."

Mac didn't have time to process that because the door of the nursery suddenly swung open and a petite brunette charged in.

"Can I help — *Hollis*?"

"I talked to your dad," Hollis said without preamble. "He said you're the one who's going to write about my wedding."

Mac tried to come up with her qualifications but she really didn't have any. Or explain that her editor had given her the story based on the assumption they'd been close friends — but that would have sounded more like the punch line of a joke.

Leaving Mac with only one option. The truth.

"That's right."

Ethan's sister took two steps toward her, bringing them nose to perfect freckle-free nose. Then she threw her arms around Mac's neck. "Thank goodness."

Chapter Twelve

Ethan had wandered into his dad's office on Monday morning, cup of coffee and Bible in hand, not expecting he would find an answer to prayer when he was searching for a pen in his father's desk drawer.

But there it was. The most unusual collection of memorabilia Ethan had ever seen. Photographs of bald-headed babies and gap-toothed children. Stats cut from the sports page. Fishermen proudly holding up the catch of the day. Handwritten notes and a four-leaf clover preserved under a yellowed piece of Scotch tape.

As Ethan had slowly flipped through the pages, he realized these weren't random items. They were gifts from his dad's patients. Pieces of their lives.

Ethan closed the cover of the scrapbook, along with any remaining doubts he'd been having over his decision to stay in Red Leaf.

He'd been putting a fresh coat of paint on

the boathouse Sunday night when his mother had marched up to him.

"I just had an interesting conversation with Frank Heath in the frozen food aisle of the grocery store. He seemed surprised that I didn't know you're planning to take over his practice."

Mac was right. He had forgotten what it was like to live in a small town.

Ethan had tried to explain his reasons, but his mother looked more frustrated with him than she had when Hollis announced that Hank Ackerman had agreed to provide the music for the wedding reception.

"I don't understand you, Ethan. You have a *future* at Midland Medical. I can't believe you're willing to give up everything for a family practice in Red Leaf."

"It depends on your definition of everything," Ethan had said quietly.

Connor had shown up with a paintbrush and Ethan's mother had backed off, but he'd had a hunch the conversation wasn't over.

"Ethan?" His mother's voice floated down the hall.

And his hunch had been right. Ethan braced himself for round two.

His mother appeared in the doorway a moment later. "Have you seen your sister? I can't find her anywhere."

"No, but maybe she went into town. She wanted to talk to Mrs. Sweet about ordering cupcakes for the reception."

"Cupcakes." His mom's nose wrinkled with distaste. "I don't know why they're so popular. Cupcakes are for children's birthday parties, not weddings."

"It's what Hollis wants." A phrase Ethan had repeated at least a dozen times over the past twenty-four hours. "She and Connor want to keep things simple."

"Simple." She sniffed.

"That doesn't mean it won't be special. The two don't cancel each other out." Quoting Mac made Ethan think about Mac.

And thinking about Mac made him want to see her again.

When *was* he going to see her again?

On the way home from church yesterday, Hollis had told him that Mac wanted to interview her before the next issue came out, but she hadn't come over to the house.

Now that his mother had arrived, Mac probably assumed he didn't need her help with the wedding anymore. But he needed her honest opinion. Her spunk.

Her smile.

"I don't know what's gotten into your sister lately," his mother said. "She used to be so sensible."

No, Hollis used to do exactly what their mother wanted. She didn't know what to do with her offspring when they deviated from her perfect plan.

"Hollis is marrying a great guy, Mom, so I think you can trust her decisions." He pressed a kiss against her cheek. "Just enjoy the day."

"I'll do my best, but I still think they should have gotten married at Porter Lakeside —"

"I meant enjoy *this* one." Ethan didn't know whether to be amused or exasperated by his mother's tenacity. Considering it was a trait she had passed on to both her children, he should probably go with amused.

"I just took a batch of blueberry scones out of the oven." She pivoted toward the door. "I'll bring a plate out to the patio if you care to join me."

Ethan would rather have one of Mrs. Sweet's cinnamon rolls, but he nodded. "I'll be there in a minute."

He walked to the desk and slid the scrapbook back into the drawer.

"Thanks, Dad," Ethan whispered. "In a few weeks I'll be starting one of my own."

"Ethan!"

Ethan shook his head. The scones must

be getting cold.

"I'm right here —" He pushed open the French doors leading onto the patio, and the first thing he saw was an enormous black Lab camped underneath the table.

His mother stood a safe distance away, as if she wasn't sure whether the dog posed a threat to her or the scones. "I can't get it to leave! Do you have any idea who that animal belongs to?"

Ethan scraped a hand across his jaw to hide a smile. "As a matter of fact, I do." *Thank you, Snap.* "I'll make sure he gets home."

"I'm going inside." His mother closed her eyes. "I feel a headache coming on. If you see Hollis, please remind her that we have a list of things to accomplish today."

"I will." Ethan clapped. "Let's go, Snap."

The Lab zigzagged through the woods as Ethan made his way to Mac's house. The scent of bacon — so much better than scones — filtered through the screen in Coach's kitchen window as Ethan rapped on the back door.

A barefoot Mac appeared a moment later. She wore a T-shirt and denim shorts and the same guarded look Ethan had seen on her face when he'd stumbled upon her in the gazebo the day he arrived in Red Leaf.

"I think this belongs to you."

"Snap." Mac yanked the door open and the Lab shuffled past her. "He doesn't usually leave the yard when I let him out in the morning. He didn't get into any trouble, did he?"

"Are you kidding? He saved me from having to eat a blueberry scone. Now I can sneak into town and buy one of Mrs. Sweet's cinnamon rolls."

"Get one for me!" a voice sang out.

Ethan blinked. "Is that Hollis?"

"They came over a little while ago." Mac's reluctance was obvious as she ushered him down the hallway and into the kitchen, where his sister and her soon-to-be husband sat at a table in the breakfast nook.

"Well, this explains why Mom couldn't find you."

Hollis had the grace to look guilty. "I promised her that I would go through her wedding checklist this afternoon, but Connor and I made a list of our own."

Ethan glanced at the empty plates. "Starting with breakfast at the neighbor's?"

"That was an added bonus." Connor smiled at Mac.

"We want to take the canoe out to Granite Rock this morning, so I asked Mac if she minded interviewing me on the way there,"

Hollis explained.

Ethan's gaze shifted to Mac. "So you're working from a canoe this morning instead of your office?"

"A reporter has to be flexible." A smile chased through Mac's eyes and Ethan realized that was what he wanted to see.

Hmmm. Maybe *he'd* start a list too.

"Connor has never paddled a canoe," Hollis whispered, even though her fiancé was sitting right next to her. "He's a city boy."

"I've never climbed a tree, either, or caught crayfish under the dock," Connor confessed cheerfully.

"I haven't been in a canoe for years," Ethan murmured.

"You should come with us, then." Hollis rose. "Mac was just telling us that she would see you doing cannonballs off the side of Granite Rock."

Ethan looked at her with interest. "You did?"

"You can see it from the deck." Mac collected the empty coffee mugs from the table. She didn't look at him but Ethan felt a surge of satisfaction when her freckles turned pink.

Check.

CHAPTER THIRTEEN

"So." Hollis dipped her paddle into the water as Mac steered the canoe away from the dock. "What do you want to know first?"

Mac wanted to know what had happened to the Hollis Channing who'd dropped her wet towel on Mac's clothes in the locker room after PE, forcing her to go to history class looking like she'd taken a shower with her clothes on. The one who ran for class president just so she could lobby for full-length mirrors in the girls' bathroom.

When Ethan's sister had marched into the church nursery, Mac was sure she was about to be fired. Hollis's unexpected appearance had been as disconcerting as the hug that followed.

Over Hollis's shoulder, Annie had given Mac a see-I-told-you-people-can-change smile.

Mac wasn't sure about that. Until Hollis had shown up at Mac's door that morning, her ponytail threaded through the back of an old baseball cap and not a speck of makeup on, her celebrity fiancé in tow.

"Well," Mac said slowly, "when it comes to wedding stories, everyone wants to know how you met."

"At a hospital fund-raiser . . . What? You look surprised."

"I thought you were going to say you met at a club or a swanky party."

"No swanky parties for me." Hollis chuckled. "Running your own business doesn't give you much time to socialize. I'd been away on a business trip, previewing a new clothing line for Crush — that's the boutique I own — so I was late for the dinner.

"Ethan never mentioned he'd met Connor, let alone that they'd become friends. He squeezed in another chair at the table and Connor and I . . ." Hollis paused, searching for the right word.

"Clicked?"

"More like rubbed each other the wrong way. Connor was so standoffish. Whenever I tried to start up a conversation, he would get this strange look on his face."

"What kind of look?"

"The look a person would have if a window mannequin started talking," Hollis muttered.

Mac laughed and Hollis joined in.

"Poor Ethan." Hollis shook her head. "He couldn't understand why we weren't getting along."

"So you're saying it wasn't love at first sight."

"More like second sight. I decided to throw a party for Ethan when he finished his residency at Midland Medical, and he put Connor's name on the guest list.

"I'd spent weeks planning it, but the day of the party, everything went wrong. A freak storm buried the city in about a foot of snow. The caterer's delivery truck slid off the road on the way to my condo and ruined everything."

"No." Mac pulled in a breath, imagining Hollis's reaction.

"It gave a whole new meaning to the term *fusion cooking,* that's for sure. I thought I'd have to cancel the dinner, but at about two o'clock someone knocked on my door. It was Connor, looking like the abominable snowman.

"He'd raided his pantry and managed to convince a very reluctant taxi driver to drop him off a few blocks from my condo. We made spaghetti and canned green beans and garlic bread out of hot dog buns for the people who braved the weather. By the time

Connor served those little frosted animal cookies for dessert, I was already halfway in love with him."

Mac knew their subscribers would love that story. "How did he propose?"

To Mac's astonishment, Hollis blushed. "I . . . um . . . I kind of proposed to him."

"You proposed. To him."

"It was obvious Connor wasn't going to do it," Hollis said candidly. "So I decided the situation called for extreme measures."

"He didn't *want* to get married?"

"Of course he did. It just took a little time to get him to come around to my way of thinking." Hollis flashed her cheerleader smile. "When Connor finally said yes, I didn't want him to change his mind . . . hence the very short engagement."

"But . . ." Mac was still trying to wrap her mind around the fact that Hollis had proposed. "How? What did you say to him?"

"I'm afraid it wasn't the most romantic proposal," Hollis confessed. "I told Connor he was being an id— *stubborn* — and that I was afraid of the future, too, but as long as we were together, it would be perfect."

Perfect.

Mac had her perfect future in mind too.

Red Leaf would be a place to take a creative break from her career as an award-winning journalist, not her permanent home.

Her gaze strayed to Ethan, laughing with Connor as their canoe cut a straight line through the center of the lake. He'd made his mark on the football field in high school and now he'd returned to Red Leaf as a doctor. A doctor. While Mac was still writing about the secret life of tomatoes.

Hollis's cell phone chirped and her face lit up when she looked at the screen. "I've been tracking my wedding dress, and according to this message, it's scheduled to be delivered at ten o'clock. I want to surprise my mother, so I should be there to sign for it."

"That's all right." Mac felt a stab of disappointment. "We can finish the interview later. I should get back to work too."

"You are working! Ethan said something about your editor wanting all the pre-wedding details. I would think a sneak peek at the wedding dress would qualify." Hollis leaned forward and rested the canoe paddle across her knees. "Trust me. You're going to want to see Mom's reaction when I show her my wedding gown."

"Because it's . . . simple?" Mac guessed.

"Because it's the laciest, puffiest, *gaudiest* dress you've ever seen."

For all the changes she'd seen in Hollis Channing, the girl couldn't do gaudy. "And you . . . like . . . it?"

"Mom picked it out."

"But you just said it was going to be a surprise." Remembering details was part of Mac's job.

"Oh, it will be." Hollis giggled. "I sneaked it out of Mom's closet before we left."

"You're wearing your mother's wedding dress?"

"Sometimes" — Hollis's solemn tone was a counter-balance to the laughter in her eyes — "you do crazy things for the people you love."

Things like delivering food in a snow-storm.

Mac couldn't help but feel a pinch of envy.

"Change of plans, guys!" Hollis stood up and set the canoe rocking as she waved her arms to get their attention. "Time to go back!"

Connor and Ethan waved to acknowledge they'd gotten the message, but instead of heading to shore, they paddled in Hollis and Mac's direction.

Hollis sat down. "Do you mind switching places with Connor for the trip back?"

"Switch places?" Panic flared inside Mac. "Why?"

"There's something I have to talk to him about before we get to the house."

Mac flicked a glance at the canoe cutting toward them through the water. Connor Blake might have the sculpted perfection of a leading man with his tawny hair and sapphire-blue eyes, but Mac didn't experience even the tiniest blip in her heart rate when she looked at him.

But Ethan . . . well, she should carry one of those portable defibrillators in her pocket.

Which was why Mac had decided it would be better if she avoided him.

Unfortunately, avoiding Ethan didn't seem to prevent her from *thinking* about Ethan. And thinking about Ethan had stirred up memories.

Only this time they weren't painful high school memories.

They were memories of the way Ethan's arms had tightened around her after he'd carried her over the touchdown line. The flash of heat in his eyes that raised the temperature in the air around them.

Dangerous memories now that Mac was so close to achieving her goal of leaving Red Leaf.

Hollis must have sensed her reluctance because she tilted her head. "Is there a reason why you don't want to be in a canoe with my brother?"

"No." Not one she could admit to, anyway.

Hollis dropped her voice as Ethan's canoe drew closer. "I'm sorry, Mackenzie."

Mac smiled. "For wanting to spend more time with your fiancé? I think that kind of goes with the territory."

"For not being a very nice person in high school," Hollis said in a low voice. "To be honest, I don't think I was a very nice person until I met Connor. But love . . . it changes things."

Ethan reached out to steady Mac as she climbed into his canoe. He wasn't sure why Connor and Mac had switched places, but the situation couldn't have worked out better if he'd planned it.

Although the saucy wink Hollis gave him behind Mac's back when she and Connor's canoe glided away made him wonder if his little sister didn't have a plan of her own.

He steered closer to the shoreline and Mac frowned. "When you said detour, I didn't realize we were going to portage the canoe."

"We're not." Ethan peered over the side of the canoe. "Do you see that weed bed? Dad and I used to fish right here on Saturday mornings. We'd get up early and sneak out of the house before Mom and Hollis got up and —" Ethan's throat closed suddenly, unexpectedly, sealing off the rest of the words. "Sorry."

"Don't be," Mac said softly. "Is that why you didn't come back? Because there were too many memories?"

Ethan wished he could say yes, because that would mean he was a sensitive guy. The kind of guy who'd been guided by his heart instead of blind ambition.

The kind of guy a woman like Mac would respect. But she respected honesty, too, so Ethan told the truth.

"I didn't *want* to come back," Ethan finally said. "My plan was to graduate at the top of my class in medical school and get a spot on Dr. Langley's team at Midland Medical."

"What changed your mind?"

The only way Ethan could answer that question was by asking one of his own. "What do you remember about my dad?"

The tiny pucker between Mac's eyes deepened. "When I was in first grade, I fell off my bike and skinned my knee. I saw your dad in the checkout line at the hardware store and I ran up to him to show him what happened.

"There were people in line but he knelt

down right there and examined it, then he wrote something down on a piece of paper and handed it to me." A memory warmed her smile. "It was a prescription for a hot fudge sundae."

That sounded like his dad, all right.

"Dad finished his residency at Midland, too, but he didn't want to stay, let alone work in the trauma unit. Some doctors don't like the stress of never knowing what's coming through those doors, how you always have to be at the top of your game, but I thrived on the adrenaline rush.

"Last winter there was a three-car pileup on the interstate. We were told to prepare for multiple injuries, some of them life threatening." The night had become permanently etched in Ethan's mind. "I wanted to show off my stuff to Dr. Langley and prove that I could handle the situation, but first I had to examine a guy who came into the ER. He had a high fever and complained of fatigue.

"He said he'd gone through cancer treatments two years ago, and I could tell he was worried it had returned. But I blew it off. Told him he probably had the flu and handed him over to a nurse as fast as I could . . . and then I forgot about him."

"There were other people who needed

you." Mac waded into the silence.

Ethan's lips twisted. "We had enough help that night. I made a decision based on *my* best interests. Five or six hours went by before I even remembered to ask about my patient — and I couldn't even remember the guy's name. Bed Two. That's what I called him. The nurse told me he'd been admitted for further testing, and I couldn't shake the feeling that I should check on him.

"It was four in the morning but he wasn't asleep. He was sitting up in bed and he looked at me . . . and I could tell he'd been having a rough night. But you know what he did?" The memory roughened Ethan's voice. "He asked how *I* was doing. That was supposed to be my line. We ended up talking until the sun came up, and before I left, he asked if he could pray with me.

"For the first time in ten years, I actually took a day off to get my head on straight. I'd worked so hard to be like my dad — to honor his memory — but I forgot what it was that made him a great doctor. He always saw the whole person, not just a symptom or a disease."

Without closing his eyes, Ethan could see the waves on Lake Michigan reshaping the shoreline while something was at work on the inside, reshaping his priorities. "I asked

God what I was supposed to do, and a few days later I got a call from Dr. Heath. I knew what I wanted to do — but I had to decide who I wanted to *be*."

Mac was silent for so long, Ethan started to wonder if he shouldn't have been quite that honest. But when he dared a glance at her, she wasn't looking at him.

Mac's gaze remained fixed on the water, her slim shoulders set in a tense line. When she finally spoke, her voice barely broke above a whisper. "The patient in Bed Two. Did you ever see him again?"

Ethan smiled. "He's marrying my sister on Saturday."

CHAPTER FOURTEEN

"How are you doing on my front-page story, Mac?"

"Great." Mac closed her laptop so Grant wouldn't see that the only thing on the screen was the cursor, blinking out a measured SOS that couldn't quite keep up with the erratic beating of her heart.

It wasn't that she didn't have material for the second installment of the Channing-Blake wedding story. Mac had been trailing Hollis around Red Leaf for the past two days, checking things off the list. She took photographs of her and Connor sampling cupcakes at the bakery. Listened to Hollis and Amanda Greer, the owner of The Shy Violet, reminisce while she chose the flowers for her bridal bouquet.

It was the story behind the story that was giving Mac a serious case of writer's block.

The pieces had started to fall into place the moment Ethan had told her about Connor. The short engagement. The private ceremony with only family and a few close friends.

Hollis had said, "I told him that I was afraid of the future too."

Not afraid of commitment — afraid of the future.

Had Connor been reluctant to marry Hollis because he was afraid his cancer would return?

"Mac!" Grant snapped his fingers. "I need the story by two o'clock this afternoon."

"Okay." Mac knew the deadline.

But something was changing. The teenage Ethan of the charming smile and confident swagger, the Ethan who'd broken countless hearts and at least one promise, wasn't the one Mac saw when she looked at him. Now she saw a man with a charming smile who wanted to make sure his little sister's wedding day was everything she dreamed it would be.

A man who had chosen to return to his hometown to practice medicine because he hadn't liked the person he was becoming.

The man she was falling for all over again.

Mac's cell phone buzzed, letting her know she had a new text message from Hollis. She was almost afraid to look at it.

7 tonight. Don't be late. List almost complete.

Whatever was happening at Channing House that evening, Mac wouldn't be able to include it in this week's issue of the newspaper.

She considered her options. Ignore Hollis's text? Delete it? Pretend she hadn't received it?

Guilt nicked Mac's conscience. It occurred to her that Hollis, a girl Mac had once regarded as shallow, had more courage than she did.

The house was quiet when Mac unlocked the door. Snap didn't even twitch when Mac stepped over him to read the note that Coach had left on the coffee table, telling her his men's group had gone out for pizza.

Her last and best excuse — cooking dinner for her dad — disappeared as quickly as the miniature cherry pies that filled Mrs. Sweet's display case on Washington's Birthday.

Fine. She would go over to Channing House at 7 p.m. and be home by 7:15.

Mac changed into jeans and a sweatshirt and grabbed her camera. When she reached the Channing property, she followed a ribbon of smoke to the fire pit.

Hollis and Connor sat shoulder to shoulder on stumps from a dead tree Ethan had cut down, feeding pinecones and tiny sticks to the crackling fire.

Had she made a mistake? Wrong time? Wrong place? Mac was just about to pull out her phone and read the message again when Hollis spotted her.

"There you are!"

"Hey, Mackenzie." Connor waved her over. "Pull up a stump."

"Mom left for Chicago a few hours ago." Hollis rested her cheek against Connor's shoulder. "There were a few last-minute things she wanted to do before the wedding."

Mac was afraid to ask if Ethan had accompanied her.

"I got your text." She held up her camera. "What's left on the wedding checklist?"

"You thought . . ." Hollis chuckled. "Sorry. I guess I wasn't very clear. I wasn't talking about the wedding checklist. I was talking about ours. My fiancé is going to learn the art of roasting the perfect marshmallow tonight."

Connor looped his arm around Hollis's slim shoulders. "It's number nine."

The list. Mac had overheard Lilah complaining about Hollis and Connor spending more time "gallivanting around" than on the details of the wedding, but after Ethan's stunning disclosure, the couple's other list made sense too.

"But . . ." Mac didn't know another way to say it. "What do you need me for?"

"You've been working so hard, we thought you might like a break," Hollis said. "Have some fun. You can even take part in our marshmallow roasting competition."

Connor looked at Hollis in mock dismay. "You didn't say anything about a competition."

"You're marrying a Channing. It's kind of a given." A husky, masculine voice raised goose bumps on Mac's arms.

Without turning around, she knew which wedding guest hadn't left town.

CHAPTER FIFTEEN

"Now that we know who the champion marshmallow roaster is" — Hollis waved her marshmallow stick in the air and performed a little victory dance — "Connor and I are going for a walk."

Over the campfire, Ethan saw Mac's deer-in-the-headlights look as his sister dragged her fiancé to his feet.

"But —"

"You and Ethan can keep the fire going!"

Uh-huh. Ethan had suspected Hollis was up to something.

He'd mentioned earlier that he was going to drive into town and take a quick walk-through at the clinic, but Hollis had complained he would miss out on their last chance to have a campfire. She hadn't told him that Mac would be there too.

Not that *he* was complaining. With all the prewedding commotion, it had been impossible to get Mac alone over the past few days.

"Number ten." Connor slipped his arm around Hollis's waist. "Kissing the woman I love under a full moon."

Ethan looked up at the overcast sky. "You can't see the moon tonight."

"I'll settle for one out of two."

The look that passed between the couple could have roasted another marshmallow.

When they were out of sight, Ethan tossed another log on the fire, sending a shower of sparks into the air.

A warm breeze drifted across the lake, and Mac seemed pensive as she fanned out her fingers over the flames. "Connor . . . what kind of cancer was it?"

"Non-Hodgkin's lymphoma." The words unfurled with Ethan's sigh. "His last round of chemo was two years ago."

"You didn't recognize Connor when he came into the ER?"

"I'm not exactly up on that kind of stuff . . . and the trailers for his movie were just starting to come out. Hollis knew who Connor was when I introduced them at the hospital fund-raiser, but no one else did. I'd invited Connor as a friend, not a celebrity guest."

"Had the cancer returned?"

Ethan's hesitation sent a prickle of fear skating down Mac's spine. "No, it turned out to be a virus. But he's been feeling tired lately so his oncologist at Mayo scheduled some tests last week."

"That's why you offered to help with the wedding plans."

Ethan nodded. "Connor's numbers look good . . . but there's always a chance the cancer will come back. He tried to talk Hollis into waiting another year, until he was officially in remission, but she agreed to a compromise."

"What was that?"

"Two weeks."

"Hollis mentioned it was a short engagement."

"I think they might have set some kind of record." Ethan ground out a stray spark that landed in the grass.

"Are you . . . worried?"

"I'm envious," Ethan said. "And, to be honest, slightly nauseated."

Mac laughed. "I know what you mean. When they look at each other, it's like everything else disappears."

Caught up in the magic that was Mackenzie's laugh, Ethan met her eyes across the fire and everything . . . disappeared.

A log shifted, breaking the spell, and Mac

stumbled to her feet. "I should go home."

"I'll walk with you."

"I know the way."

"Coach would order a hundred crunches if he knew I let you walk home in the dark." Ethan ignored the exasperated look Mac cast in his direction and fell into step beside her.

"The yard is going to look beautiful on Saturday." Mac stopped along the path to admire one of the newly transplanted rose-bushes.

"Mom declared war against beetles in her garden. She's also pulling weeds before they come out of the ground."

"She did all this?"

"I think it was therapeutic. Beetles and weeds can't talk back."

"Your mom hasn't been too demanding." Mac nudged his ribs. "I think she's catching the vision of a rustic outdoor wedding."

"Because of you."

"Me?" Mac turned to stare at him.

"You can't deny it was pure genius," Ethan mused. "Using the words *rustic chic* to describe the decorations."

But the way Mac was staring at him — as if he'd lost his mind — told Ethan that she didn't realize what she'd done.

Nature, left alone, was unpredictable and

messy, but if it was incorporated into a theme, well, his mother could work with that. It had made the last few days go much more smoothly for Hollis and Connor.

"You're amazing, Mackenzie." And Ethan had a feeling that everyone knew it but her.

"I'm just . . . me."

The clouds suddenly parted, and Ethan laughed as a band of moonlight illuminated the gazebo on the hill. Mac was ten feet away before Ethan realized she'd thought the laughter was directed at her.

"Wait!" He caught up to Mac before she reached the trees. "Look up."

Mac tipped her face toward the sky and Ethan's eyes skimmed over the smooth contour of her brow, down her straight little nose with its dusting of freckles, and lingered on the plush curve of her lower lip.

"Connor and Hollis's full moon," she said, laughing.

"I'm sure we saw it first."

Mac's laughter died when Ethan drew her slowly into the circle of his arms.

"You're so beautiful," he murmured.

Looking into Mac's velvet-brown eyes, Ethan could see she didn't believe that, either.

He'd just have to show her.

■ ■ ■ ■

Ethan tugged her closer and Mac's breath rushed out, mingling with Ethan's as he captured her lips.

The night Ethan had taught her how to dance he'd kept a respectable distance between them. But now Mac could feel the rapid beat of his heart, the warmth of his hands on the small of her back.

The kisses Mac had dared to imagine when she was fifteen were nothing compared to the reality of being held in Ethan's arms.

Over the past few days, Mac had tried to convince herself that what she felt for Ethan was nothing more than nostalgia. The embers of a schoolgirl crush she'd had on the boy next door.

But as Ethan deepened the kiss, Mac wasn't thinking about the past. She wasn't thinking about dances and football games and all the times she'd been tongue-tied and blushing in Ethan's presence.

She was thinking this was a man she could spend the rest of her life with . . .

Lost in the kiss, Mac didn't hear Hollis calling Ethan's name until she stumbled out of the shadows. The panic in Hollis's voice split them apart.

Ethan was at her side in an instant. "What's wrong?"

"Brenda, Connor's agent, called a few minutes ago." Hollis sagged against him. "Someone from a newspaper contacted her and asked if she could confirm that the reason we decided to get married so quickly was because Connor . . . Connor isn't expected to live very long."

"What? How did that get out?"

"I don't know, but Brenda told Connor not to talk to the media until she figures out the best way to handle the situation."

"It'll be okay, Hollis."

"This is why Connor wants to keep his professional and personal lives separate. He knows the media is always looking for a story that will grab people's attention. They don't necessarily care if it's the truth."

Ethan was no longer looking at Hollis . . . He was looking at *her.*

He didn't think . . .

Mac instinctively took a step backward. "I should go." Her throat started to close. "So you can talk to Connor."

"Mac —"

Mac didn't wait to hear what Ethan had to say. Because his expression had said it all.

CHAPTER SIXTEEN

Mac caught a glimpse of her reflection in the mirror as she finished getting ready for work the next morning and winced. Now she understood why most women took the time to apply makeup. Right now she could have used something to hide the lavender shadows under her eyes.

She could call Grant and tell him that she was sick. Under the circumstances, it wouldn't be a lie . . .

"Sweetheart?" Coach's voice floated up the stairs. "You have company."

Mac's stomach turned a slow cartwheel. "I'll be right down."

She wove her hair into a loose braid and padded downstairs. Cast a longing look at the door before she followed her dad's cheerful baritone to the kitchen.

Hollis sat at the table, sipping hot chocolate from the lopsided cup Mac had made at summer camp when she was in fifth grade. Connor stood at her shoulder, the smile absent from his eyes.

The fact that Ethan wasn't with them added to the weight pressing down on Mac's chest.

"I'm going to take Snap for his morning walk." Coach set a cup of hot chocolate on the table across from Hollis before he left the room.

Mac didn't know whether to sit or stand. And for someone who made her living stringing words together, she had no idea what to say.

Connor's ragged sigh broke the silence as he pulled out a chair and sat down next to Hollis. "Ethan told you how we met —"

"Yes, but I wasn't the one who leaked the story," Mac interrupted. "I wouldn't do that."

"What . . . of course you wouldn't." Hollis looked stunned by the suggestion. "Why do you think I was so happy you were doing the interview? When you were on the high school newspaper, you had a reputation for being honest but fair" — she smiled — "even if you didn't particularly like the person you had to interview."

Mac managed to smile back.

"We came to ask for your help," Connor said.

"My help?"

"I told my agent about the cancer when I signed with her, but the opportunity to audition for the movie came up a few months after I'd finished treatment.

"Maybe it was pride, but I didn't want anyone to know about it because I was afraid it would become my identity. *That's Connor Blake. He's the actor who had cancer.* Brenda was more afraid that it might jeopardize future contracts. I could be considered a risk because I'm not technically in remission yet."

"The media has a way of twisting things, so we want to shut the rumors down as soon as possible," Hollis said. "And the only way to do that is to let people know the truth."

Mac realized they were both looking at her expectantly. "You want *me* to write the story?"

Connor flashed a smile that Mac knew would be on the cover of every entertainment magazine in a few months. "Mackenzie Davis is the only person I would consider sitting down with for an interview."

An exclusive.

Mac swallowed hard. "I'm honored —"

"Great." Connor folded his hands behind his head. "Then let's get started."

"You want me to interview you *now*?"

Forget the hot chocolate. Mac needed a cup of coffee.

"I've got other things on my mind. In two days we'll be getting married." Connor waggled his eyebrows at Hollis. "And leaving for our honeymoon."

"Men." Hollis rolled her eyes. "Where do we start, Mac?"

"We start by deciding what social media outlet you want to use."

"You decide." Connor shrugged. "Make it count, though. I only want to do this once."

"And I get to see the photographs first." Hollis lifted her chin. "Just to make sure you got my best side."

Mac could feel the tension slipping away. "I will."

"Speaking of best sides . . ." Hollis leaned forward. "You don't look so good. Your eyes are all red-rimmed and puffy."

"So are yours."

"Betty at the Clip and Curl can work miracles." Mischief lit Hollis's eyes. "She'll even do your nails."

"I'd rather eat a minnow."

They burst out laughing.

Connor's gaze bounced between them. "Should I even ask?"

Hollis rested her cheek against his shoulder. "Inside joke, honey."

"Got it." Connor smiled at Mac. "So . . . what's your first question?"

Mac asked the first one that popped into her head. "Does Ethan know you asked me to write the story?"

"Know?" Connor repeated. "It was his idea."

By Saturday morning, Hollis's wedding day, Ethan was convinced that suggesting Mac write Connor's story was the most idiotic idea he'd ever come up with.

"The media is always looking for a story that will grab people's attention," Hollis had said. "They don't necessarily care if it's the truth."

Ethan realized they could have both. Mac could help his sister and future brother-in-law — and have a shot at her dream job.

He'd had a long conversation with Connor and Hollis after Mac had disappeared, but it hadn't taken long for them to see the wisdom of choosing who would tell Connor's story. The fact they'd immediately agreed it should be Mac was a testimony to her character, not his powers of persuasion.

Because what Ethan really wanted to do was persuade Mac to stay in Red Leaf.

His mother breezed into the study, wearing the designer dress she'd purchased for the wedding. "The idea is to pin the bouton-niere to your lapel, not your thumb. Now give me that poor flower before you turn it into potpourri."

Ethan handed it over. "How's Hollis do-ing?"

"She's crying," she said matter-of-factly as she anchored the single red rosebud in place. "But that's normal for a bride on her wedding day."

"And the bride's mother?" Ethan saw the telltale sheen in his mother's eyes.

"The pollen is absolutely wretched this time of year." She stepped back to survey her handiwork. "You're as handsome as your father . . . and just as stubborn, I might add. I —"

"Mom." Ethan didn't want to revisit his decision to move to Red Leaf. Not on Hollis's wedding day. "Can we talk about this later?"

"Ethan Monroe Channing, please don't interrupt me when I'm speaking."

"Sorry," Ethan muttered.

"I was going to say it was one of the things I loved about your father," his mom said softly. "When he accepted the job in Red Leaf after medical school, I thought it would be temporary, just a few years until he got some experience. But your father loved Red

Leaf. He loved the people and the slower pace of life in a small town. I think he even liked the snow. To ask him to give it up . . . it would have been like asking him to cut off a limb."

"But you weren't happy here."

"I was happy with him." Their eyes met in the mirror and she smiled. "Your father was home to me . . . everything else was just geography. I don't think I told him that often enough.

"After he died, I couldn't face the memories. The whole town was grieving and I didn't feel strong enough to carry their burden and the weight of my own grief. Besides that, Chicago was my home too. Your grandparents were there. Friends I'd known since high school. I knew your father would understand why I couldn't stay."

"If you never planned to come back, why didn't you sell the house?"

"Because" — his mom reached out and straightened his tie — "even though I wanted my son to have a prestigious, fulfilling career in Chicago, I had a feeling that someday he would need a place to live."

Ethan wasn't sure he'd heard her correctly. "You *knew* I'd want to come back?"

"Ethan. Please. I'm your mother. I know everything. I also know you're going to be a

411

brilliant doctor and this little town won't even realize how blessed they are to have you."

Ethan finally found his voice. "I'm the one who's blessed."

"Your father would have said that too."

Ethan wrapped her in a hug and breathed in the familiar scents of hair spray and White Diamonds. "Thanks, Mom."

"Not so tight, dear. Satin wrinkles." But she clung to him a moment longer. "I'm proud of you, Ethan," she whispered. "I haven't told you that often enough, either."

"I suppose I better get ready to walk my baby sister down the aisle." Before Ethan started blubbering like a baby and was forced to turn in his man card.

"It gives me peace, knowing my child found someone who will love them as much as your father and I loved each other."

"Connor and Hollis will have a great life together."

His mother tucked her arm through his. "Who said I was talking about them?"

CHAPTER SEVENTEEN

"You did a great job on the interview."

Mac lifted her head at the sound of Grant's voice. She hadn't expected him to stop by the office on a Saturday. "Do you really think so?"

"Don't you?" her editor countered.

The words on Mac's computer monitor blurred. "It's hard to be objective about your own work."

"Fishing for compliments?"

Mac shook her head. "Just the truth."

"Well, then, here it is." Grant gripped the edge of her desk and hunkered down until they were almost nose to nose. "You're a gifted writer, Mackenzie."

Mac stared at him in disbelief. "Then why won't you give me a real story? You want me to cover garden club meetings and fashion shows and community fund-raisers. It's like you don't trust me."

"Not trust you?" Grant sputtered. "You're

the only one I do trust . . . because people trust you."

"Because I'm Coach's daughter."

"Because you're . . . *you.* You don't just ask questions; you listen. Remember when I sent you over to Lakeland Terrace to take a picture of Sylvia Morris because she was about to celebrate her one hundredth birthday?"

"Of course I do."

"You didn't just take a picture of her, did you? You interviewed her for almost two hours."

Mac wasn't sure where Grant was going with this. She'd noticed a wicker basket filled with crocheted baby blankets in Sylvia's room and found out the woman sent them to an orphanage in Uganda where her granddaughter served as a missionary.

On the way back to the newspaper, Mac had decided a photograph of Sylvia wasn't enough.

"Sylvia's an amazing woman, but she didn't see herself that way."

"That's what I'm talking about, Mac. The stories you write . . . they're like a mirror. People see themselves and realize they matter."

Mac jumped when Grant pounded his fist on the desk like a gavel.

"If that editor at the *Heritage* isn't smart enough to hire you when he reads that interview with Blake, then I will. As my assistant editor. Now I have a wedding to attend."

"*You're* going to Hollis's wedding?"

"Beverly bought a new dress. She can't believe she's actually going to one of Lilah Channing's fancy shindigs." Grant slid a business card across Mac's desk. "And you have an interview with Senator Tipley in an hour."

"But —"

"What?" Grant tossed the word over his shoulder as he stomped toward the door. "I'm still your boss and I promised you this story. This was what you wanted."

Yes, it was.

So why wasn't she jumping up and down at the chance to meet with the senator?

And why hadn't she already hit Send?

The door snapped shut behind Grant and Mac closed her eyes.

What should I do?

As soon as the prayer slipped out, Mac realized it was the first time she'd asked God for direction. Asked him to direct her steps, the way Ethan had, instead of forging ahead on her own.

Mac had told Grant she wanted to write

real stories. She hadn't considered that was what she'd been doing all along. Writing real stories about real people.

People who'd known her for years. People who were frustrating and quirky and fascinating and amazing.

People she loved.

People who loved *her.*

Hollis was right. It did change things.

What do you want me to do, Lord? I promise I'll listen this time.

Coach always said God had a sense of humor, but Mac still laughed when her cell phone rang.

"Where are you?" Hollis demanded.

"I'm at my desk."

"I figured that out, but why aren't you *here?*"

For some reason the imperious tone made Mac smile. "Because you're getting married in . . ." She glanced at the clock on the wall and choked. "An hour."

"I know what time the ceremony is. I'm the bride," Hollis said. "I thought you were supposed to be covering the wedding for the *Register.*"

"You hired a photographer. And I can get the rest of the details from your mother." The excuse sounded weak even to Mac's ears. She was hiding, plain and simple.

In fact, she'd been hiding for the past few days.

From Ethan. From herself. From the future.

Hollis's very unladylike snort told her that she knew it too.

"I'm not technically on the guest list."

"You're my friend."

The Channing siblings didn't fight fair. "All right."

"I'll see you in five minutes," Hollis said.

Panic squeezed Mac's chest, but it wasn't because she was imagining what the ramifications would be if she postponed the interview with Senator Tipley. She'd just taken a silent inventory of her closet. "Fifteen."

"Ten." Hollis hung up.

CHAPTER EIGHTEEN

He'd lost her.

One moment Ethan had been watching Mac teach his grandfather — a man Ethan was convinced had been born wearing a three-piece suit — how to polka, and the next she was . . . gone.

"I heard you're moving back to Red Leaf." Grant Buchanan, Mac's editor, blocked Ethan's path as he reached for a cupcake on the buffet table. "Would you be willing to sit down for an interview?"

"Sure." Ethan discreetly scanned the yard. Where was Mac? He hadn't been able to talk to her since she'd arrived for the ceremony. Their eyes had met briefly when Hollis and Connor were exchanging vows, but Ethan had been busy making sure the day went smoothly.

Now it was time to start thinking about the future . . .

"I'll call you Monday and set up a time,"

Grant said.

"A time?"

"For the interview. Unless you want to talk to Mac about it now." Grant's face was the picture of innocence. "I saw her walking up the hill a few minutes ago."

"Thanks," Ethan said over his shoulder as he strode toward the path leading through the rose garden.

Mac wouldn't be going home already. Not without saying good night. Would she?

His steps slowed when he spotted a flash of yellow inside the gazebo. Mac sat on the bench, stunning in the strapless yellow dress she'd worn to the wedding.

He couldn't repress a grin when he noticed she'd kicked off her strappy high heels.

"Hey."

Mac's head jerked up. "What are you doing here? You're supposed to be at the reception."

"I know. I came up here to get some fresh air."

"It's an outdoor wedding, Ethan."

"Truth? I wanted to ask you to dance." Ethan held out his hand.

She stared at him. "Here?"

"Why not?"

"There's no room to polka . . ."

Ethan ignored Mac as he drew her to her feet.

As if on cue, Hank Ackerman began to play a love song on his fiddle. The music provided the perfect accompaniment to the lap of waves against the shoreline, the spray of stars above Ethan's head, and the woman in his arms.

Mac didn't seem to know what to do. Her hands moved from his arms to his shoulders and back again.

"Did you forget everything I taught you?" Ethan chided.

Mac's lips parted, and it took every ounce of his self-control not to kiss her.

"You remember?"

"Of course I remember." Ethan spun her around and Mac's fingers tightened on his shoulder. "It *was* pretty embarrassing."

Color flooded her cheeks. "Tell me about it."

"I have to admit it was the first and only time I've been stood up."

"I stood *you* up?"

"I asked you to save me a dance, but when I got to the gym, you weren't there."

"I was in the kitchen. I thought . . ." Mac looked away. "It doesn't matter."

Ethan could tell it did. "One of the guys on the team called me when I was on my way back to the school. His car had broken down so I gave him a ride home first. I got to the dance a little late and looked for you, but I figured you'd changed your mind."

"And I thought you felt sorry for me."

"Why would I feel sorry for you?"

"Because I was awkward and . . . freckled. And I was dressed like a lion."

"I remember that too." Actually, Ethan remembered she looked kind of cute.

"I would never want to relive my high school years." Mac shook her head. "I'm glad all that is in the past."

The past. Right.

"Connor said the interview went really well," he said slowly, unable to read Mac's expression in the shadows. "You were worried you wouldn't have a great story to submit with your résumé, but an exclusive with Connor Blake will get the editor's attention. It looks like you'll make your deadline for the *Heritage* and have your dream job."

But what if her dream had changed?

Over Ethan's shoulder, Mac watched Hollis and Connor dancing near the water.

The wedding gown was everything Hollis had claimed it was. Lacy and puffy and gaudy . . . and she looked absolutely stunning. And totally content in her husband's arms even though she had no idea what the future held.

Maybe it was time for her to show a little courage too.

"No," Mac said softly, "I won't get the job."

"You have to believe in yourself, Mac." Ethan frowned at her. "You're a great writer."

"I won't get the job at the *Heritage* because I e-mailed it to Grant. It's going to be on the front page of the *Register* next week."

"Why would you do that?"

"My boss made me an offer I can't refuse . . . although he probably didn't realize it at the time."

"What kind of offer?"

"Assistant editor if Connor's interview didn't get me the job at the *Heritage*." Mac peeked up at Ethan through her lashes. "But Grant didn't stipulate that I had to apply for it."

"You're *staying* in Red Leaf?"

"It looks that way. Why would I leave a place I love, people I-I . . . love, when I'm already doing *what* I love?"

"I think I actually understand that." Ethan released a slow smile. "But changing your plan . . . now I'll have to change mine."

"What do you mean?"

"I had it all figured out. I was going to make dinner reservations at Salvatore's in Milwaukee. Woo you with chocolate and flowers and convince you that we could make a long-distance relationship work."

"You were?" she squeaked.

"In case you haven't noticed, I'm pretty crazy about you, Mackenzie Davis, and I really hope you feel the same way."

A good reporter always told the truth . . .

"I'm actually pretty crazy about you too," she whispered.

Ethan's hands tightened around Mac's waist. "Then I suggest we come up with a new plan."

"What kind of new plan?"

"A burger at the Korner Kettle tomorrow night. After that, we'll take a walk around the lake and look for a full moon. How does that sound?" As Ethan drew her closer, Mac saw the promise in his eyes.

The promise of a future together.

"It sounds" — Mac smiled as Ethan bent his head to kiss her — "absolutely perfect."

ACKNOWLEDGMENTS

A heartfelt THANK YOU to Daisy Hutton and the amazing team at HarperCollins Christian Publishing for giving me another opportunity to use all the wedding intel I gathered two summers ago when our children (all THREE of them!) got married.

Editor Becky Monds, Lorie Jones, Karli Jackson, Elizabeth Hudson, and Katie Bond — you all make this so easy (and so much fun!).

And to Pete, for providing Friday night pizza, melt-me hugs, and the occasional emergency cupcake when I'm having a bad day. But especially because you still look at me the way you did when we were married twenty-seven years ago . . . even though I no longer look like I did twenty-seven years ago!

And to the Creator for writing the very first romance and showing me what true love is all about.

DISCUSSION QUESTIONS

1. Ethan made a radical decision when he realized he'd lost sight of what was really important. Describe a time when you had to make a life-changing decision. What were the circumstances? The outcome?
2. Painful memories from Mackenzie's past made it difficult for her to see herself the way others did. What characters in the book were instrumental in changing her perspective?
3. What was the most embarrassing thing that happened to you in high school? If you could go back in time and change one thing, what would it be?
4. Hollis tells Mackenzie that "sometimes you do crazy things for the people you love." Give an example of that from your own life.
5. What was your favorite scene in the book? Why?
6. Why do you think Mac decides to stay in

427

Red Leaf? If you were in her situation, what would you have done?

ABOUT THE AUTHOR

Kathryn Springer is a *USA Today* bestselling author. She grew up in northern Wisconsin, where her parents published a weekly newspaper. As a child she spent many hours sitting at her mother's typewriter, plunking out stories, and credits her parents for instilling in her a love of books — which eventually turned into a desire to tell stories of her own. Kathryn has written nineteen books with close to two million copies sold. Kathryn lives and writes in her country home in northern Wisconsin.

VISIT HER ON FACEBOOK:
KATHRYNSPRINGERAUTHOR

The employees of Thorndike Press hope you have enjoyed this Large Print book. All our Thorndike, Wheeler, and Kennebec Large Print titles are designed for easy reading, and all our books are made to last. Other Thorndike Press Large Print books are available at your library, through selected bookstores, or directly from us.

For information about titles, please call:
  (800) 223-1244

or visit our Web site at:
  http://gale.cengage.com/thorndike

To share your comments, please write:
  Publisher
  Thorndike Press
  10 Water St., Suite 310
  Waterville, ME 04901